LONE SURVIVOR

Stormrider blitzed straight into the dusty-green bush, a sound like drawn-out prairie thunder rising about him: the blatting of scores of big outlaw bikes revving up for fight or flight. Right now it was Option One. A burly nomad was bearing down on him on a rangy scooter, raising the cat's-head standard. Stormrider fired two semi-auto from one knee. Two fist-sized splotches of red appeared on the rider's grimy T-shirt . . .

Stormrider watched his boys blasting away on full rock 'n' roll, chasing the outlaws over hills and down arroyos with their bullet-streams. The rider he'd downed was lying nearby. "You—" the Cathead croaked. "You ain't no Citizen."

"No. I'm not."

"What . . . are you?"

"I'm the last of the Hardriders."

The man's eyes bulged. "The Hardriders are dead!" Blood gushed from his mouth. His head fell back against the hard-packed caliche.

"Not yet, they're not," Stormrider quietly said.

STORM RIDER

ROBERT BARON

JOVE BOOKS, NEW YORK

STORMRIDER

A Jove Book / published by arrangement with
the author

PRINTING HISTORY
Jove edition / June 1992

ISBN: 0-515-10828-6

Jove Books are published by The Berkley Publishing Group,
200 Madison Avenue, New York, New York 10016.
The name "JOVE" and the "J" logo
are trademarks belonging to Jove Publications, Inc.

PRINTED IN THE UNITED STATES OF AMERICA

10 9 8 7 6 5 4 3 2 1

For Scott "Scooter Trash" Phillips
May your Road be long and smooth, bro

PROLOGUE

The clouds were white wisps, like the heads of wild wheat against the sun-bleached blue of the sky where Plains met Rockies, the day the Hardriders died.

They made their final stand on a low hill by the side of the road—not a Hard Road, just a dirt track through tan summer grassland, eroded into parallel gullies by the rains since the legendary StarFall. On the track the convoy they had captured the day before burned, raising a black pillar against the white-streaked blue. The drivers—older men, and youths not quite old enough to be fledged as warriors—had torched the captured vehicles as a last gesture of defiance before withdrawing up the hill.

The smoke would be their sole memorial, unless their clan allies made up fanciful songs of their end, based on the City's dry yet boastful broadcasts of the fight. No one doubted that after seeing the dust plumes feathering out from beneath the tires of the cavalry company's light combat cars sweeping out east and west of them: the jaws of a trap already drawing shut. The heavy-laden cargo trucks had slowed the drivers to a pace hardly greater than a walking horse's, enabling the pursuers to half surround them before even the 'Riders' keen eyes could spot them.

Only true catastrophe could compel Wyatt Hardrider, *the* Hardrider of the Hardriders—the baddest, boldest biker on the

1

Plains, who could outrace the prairie wind and strike like a thunderhead's lightning tongue—to accept a static defensive fight.

Mortar rounds were beginning to burst among the huddle of colorful ramshackle trucks and vans on the hilltops as the last 'Rider laid his bike down in the defensive circle around the hill's broad belly. The nomads' vehicles were spaced far enough apart that the low-powered, relatively cool explosions of their ethanol tanks wouldn't start a chain reaction.

The 'Riders began to return fire, with rifles and a few light machine guns. A recoilless rifle thumped three times from the rear of a pickup decorated all over with bits of bright plastic trash scavenged from ruins. An armored car blew apart in a yellow flare of diesel and sparkle of exploding ammunition. A burst from the quick-firing cannon in the turret of another found the recoilless gun, and the nomads had no more weapons that could both reach and breach the armored vehicles that now completely hemmed them in. A few teenagers huddled behind the perimeter, clutching buzz-bomb launchers that could crack heavier armor than any the City troops had brought. But these possessed short range, and would only serve when the enemy made his final assault.

But the cavalry captain was a man without honor. He had his men safe behind mobile walls of alloy plate. He had his mortars and his quick-firing cannon and the strange, terrible weapons the nomads called river guns, which poured out bullets in a torrent like the Platte in flood, so fast they made a whining noise instead of a crackle like honest gunfire.

He had all the ammo and all the time in Brother Wind's wide world. And he preferred spending them to spending the lives of his men. He stood back and poured fire onto the hilltop until it looked like the gape of a newborn volcano.

Through it all he stood at the roll-bar–mounted gun of his own unarmored light-assault car and watched, a small, erect figure in a coal-scuttle helmet and spotless camo battle dress, his eyes invisible behind mirror shades glinting in the sun that looked down without favor or mercy.

When the bombardment had gone on an excruciatingly long time—when some of the green troops in the combat cars were beginning to be fearful of the protracted rippling thunder of their own guns, and their stomachs had rebelled against the smell of spent powder and explosives and hot lubricants and the sick, thick smell of human meat roasting in the alcohol-fueled flames that crowned the hilltop—his troop commanders started to clamor in his headset for advance.

"Nothing could survive that bombardment," they said. "It's time to move."

He gave no order to move. The shelling continued. He was a young man, but the lines were deep at the corners of his mouth.

Finally from the hill came a snarl of engine, a whine thinly audible above the crackling and booming shells. A lone rider appeared from the smoke. He was a big man, made bulkier by a silver wolfskin vest. He had sweeping mustachioes and black hair tied in braids that flapped behind him like pennons. A single eagle feather bobbed at the nape of his neck. Tendrils of smoke streamed from his hair and shaggy vest.

Every weapon in sight of him opened up on him. He seemed to sense each bead as it was drawn. He whipped his gaunt chopped cycle this way and that, veering to avoid a line of shell-bursts from an auto-cannon, pivoting on a leather-clad leg around the dust-cloud of a mortar bomb, bounding his machine like a pronghorn over arroyos and hummocks.

The men of the City had never seen riding like that—not even among their own cycle scouts, their vaunted *corps d'élite*. They cried out in admiration even as they tried their damnedest to cut the wild rider down.

From a scabbard behind the low-slung seat the Hardrider whipped a box-fed light machine gun. He slapped it down between the upswept handlebars and triggered a burst. A light-assault car gunner down the line from the captain screamed and clutched at himself as the bullets clawed open his chest. Another burst and a vehicle commander slipped, noiselessly and bonelessly, down into the cupola of his armored car.

The firing redoubled as gunners single-mindedly hauled back on triggers or mashed firing studs. Already the Hardrider was too close for the mortars to be used. Automatic weapons began to fall silent as their barrels overheated or their feed-belts tangled.

A line of explosions from an automatic grenade launcher ripped open the tawny earth right in front of the bike's front wheel. The City soldiers held their breaths. Now the madman *had* to fall.

The bike emerged from the smoke, airborne and mostly upright. It struck with a pelvis-crushing shock. A booted leg went down, steadied it, and it came on—the rider always firing, and always making for the erect captain in his car.

The captain spoke into the microphone that curved like an insect leg in front of his mouth: "Cease firing."

The command made no sense to the City officers and men. But they obeyed at once. Silence hit the prairie like a thunderclap.

In the sudden stillness the motorcycle's roar seemed harder to hear than in the midst of bombardment. The wild rider caught his machine gun under his right arm, punched the button to discharge a spent magazine, pulled a last mag from a pouch, and slammed it home in the well. Then he grasped the pistol-grip again, and uttering a hate-scream of fury fired the weapon at the command car, now less than a hundred yards away.

Moving without apparent haste the captain took hold of the pistol-grip of his own mounted machine gun and swung its barrel down to bear. His driver grunted softly and slumped behind the wheel as a pair of bullets struck him in the sternum with small slaps and puffs of dust.

The captain fired. The rider went over to his right, then down, into a rolling tumbling dust-spewing tangle. When momentum tore man and machine apart and sent them hurtling in diverging directions, it was as if one single body had been ripped in two.

The captain dismounted. Slowly he walked forward. The gray-brown dust matted out the mirror polish of his boots.

The rider lay on the ground thirty yards in front of the car. He had miraculously held onto his machine gun until the very end; now it lay ten feet away, and he was trying to drag himself to it, leaving a trail of brownish blood-mud behind him.

The captain stepped between him and the fallen weapon. Painfully the Hardrider raised his head to look at him. His mustache was soaked in blood, and blood poured in a constant stream down his chin. His right eye had either been shot out or swollen shut. His face was such a mask of blood and grime and soot that it was impossible to tell. The remaining eye was blue, and burned with hate like a laser beam.

The nomad's left hand whipped to his belt, at the small of his back. As he yanked out a knife with a foot of gleaming saw-backed blade, the captain drew his sidearm from his shoulder holster and shot Wyatt Hardrider above his glaring blue eye.

The officer stood for a moment, gazing down at the body of his opponent. Then he holstered his handgun, ordered medics to tend to his driver, and ordered up another car so that he could lead the advance up the hill.

The hilltop was silent now, but for the sizzle of almost-invisible alcohol flames and the endless sighing of the Great Plains wind. The captain ordered his new driver to stop at the nomads' defensive perimeter. He ordered the infantry in the armored carriers to dismount and secure the hilltop on foot. Then he stepped to the ground next to the body of a blond-bearded giant who lay sprawled on his belly behind his bike, a lever-action rifle in his hands, his eyes staring at a neat blue hole in the center of his forehead. Bare-handed, the officer began to walk forward.

Behind him his aides rapped hasty orders. A squad of troopies with assault rifles double-timed up to escort him. He didn't acknowledge their presence.

He walked among the burning vehicles, ignoring the pale flames that reached for him and the stinking smoke of burning bodies. Once he paused, gazing down at a little blond girl in a dirty linen smock. Her left arm had been blown off. She had bled to death into the thirsty dust. Her remaining arm clutched a crude doll, a rag with a knot for a head and drawn-on eyes and idiot smile.

A muscle worked at the corner of the captain's jaw. He walked on, his escort discreetly behind.

A standard had been raised at the crest of a hill, a gleaming pair of handlebars swept like a wild bull's horns, fastened to the top of a metal pole along with a spray of hawk feathers and animal tails. A mortar burst had knocked it askew, but it still stood. A couple of the troopers snickered and spat about the absurdity of savage superstition.

At the base of the standard a woman lay. She was tall and rangy, and her unmarked face was beautiful, in a hard, drawn way. Her red-auburn hair was roached up in front in a defiant crest. Her right hand still clutched the grip of an unfired buzz bomb. A steel splinter from a mortar-casing stuck out of her neck, right behind an ear pierced with seven silver rings.

The captain stopped. From behind the dead woman a boy of ten or eleven rose to a crouch. He wore buckskin pants stained with grease and blood, and his bare chest was a washboard beneath a tattered denim vest. An arrowhead chipped from obsidian hung from his neck by a rawhide thong. His hair was jet black and hung down his back in braids. His eyes were pale blue, and as wild and devoid of intelligence as the eyes of an animal in the jaws of a steel trap.

A soldier raised his assault rifle. The captain knocked the barrel up, and it stammered into the sky.

"What the hell do you think you're doing?" the officer demanded.

The trooper looked hurt. "But Captain Masefield, sir—nits make lice."

"No one is to fire without my command. *No one.* Is that understood?"

Reluctantly, his escort nodded. The acknowledgments of his squad leaders chorused in his lightweight headset.

He turned back to the boy. The child rocked back on his heels and brought up his hands. They held an enormous single-action pistol. He aimed it at the center of the captain's chest and pulled the trigger.

The hammer snapped on a spent cartridge. It was the most forlorn sound in the world.

The boy stared at the weapon. It was as long as his skinny arm. He hauled back the hammer, pointed it, pulled the trigger again. Nothing.

Slowly the captain lowered the arm he had held up to prevent his men from firing. The boy snapped the hammer fruitlessly on every chamber, then started around the cylinder again. The officer reached forward, took the pistol by the barrel, and gently pulled it from his fingers.

The boy collapsed across the woman's body and clung, sobbing so violently it seemed his bones, connected by such little flesh, would shake themselves apart.

"Police up the weapons and blow them," the captain said. "Finish any wounded. We pull out in fifteen minutes."

He knelt and pulled the boy to his feet. "Come on, son. This is your past. The City's your future now."

PART ONE

TRISTAN

1

By the time the light scout car had reached its destination the day had turned savage, with the suddenness that marked this place where the long cast of the Plains crashed against the foot of the Rockies. The sky was full of clouds, black, seething like the filth in a DemonCaller's cauldron. The wind whistled and moaned around the slanted cement walls of Sedgwick Youth Hospice like the souls of prairie dead, denied entrance to Hell and Heroes' Holm alike for some unimaginable transgression. Flecks of fine volcanic grit carried aloft on high winds and dumped on the Front Range blew on that wind, along with drops of rain like tears.

Alerted by radiotelephone, the staff was waiting when the two cavalry troopers came through the glass doors that were sheltered by overhang, being set back within the wall. The taller of the two stopped beside the solid oak reception desk and swung the bundle he carried beneath his arm like a roll of carpet down, setting it on its doeskin moccasins on the rubber floor runner.

The smaller trooper adjusted his dark sunglasses on a frequently broken nose, settled his weight back on his heels, and hooked his thumbs in his gunbelt. "Had to truss him up some," he said in that studied slow cavalry drawl. "Mind your fingers there, ma'am. He's a biter, this 'un."

A nurse, pretty and crisp in her whites and little cap, knelt beside the boy. He was swaddled from hip to shoulder in rough army blankets, cinched by web belts. His head hung to the weight of total exhaustion. She brushed back a strand of the tangled black hair that obscured his face.

He raised his head then, finding the wherewithal inside to glare at her with eyes blue as cutting-torch flame.

She wiped a powder-smoke smudge from his cheek. "But he's beautiful!" she exclaimed.

The taller trooper, who had the name DAVIS stenciled in black on his camouflaged blouse, had taken something from his pocket and was examining it through his sunglasses by the nervous fluorescent light: an arrowhead exquisitely chipped from black volcanic glass, knotted in a thong. When the nurse turned from the boy he tucked it away again quickly. These therapeutic types had no concept of the right of conquest. They'd probably think the arrowhead belonged in some museum and snitch on him.

He exchanged green-glass glances with his more abbreviated partner, Munn. "Up to us, we'da left him out on the Plains for the vultures with the rest of the biker trash," the banty-cock Munn said. "But Black Jack insisted. Got some soft spots in him."

"You'd be hard-up to put your finger on 'em, most of the time," his partner said laconically. "We'll leave this 'un in your capable hands now, ma'am."

At the beginning of that day, the reports had come filtering back by radio crackling with atmospherics. The City soldiers had surrounded the Hardriders with their river guns, their thunderthrowers, and their cages of iron.

Jen Morningstar, Tristan's mother, heard the news with her lovely features set. She checked the loads in her short Absaroka lever-action carbine, then turned away to prepare the setting out of the clan's emergency medical supplies.

Wyatt Hardrider stared off into the spoiled-milk line of dawn drawn across the Plains horizon, out where invisible enemies awaited the signal to move. Then he sighed, and lifted the thunderbolt amulet from around his muscular neck.

"Here, son," he said to Tristan, who stood nearby trying to keep from fidgeting with excitement. Shaken awake by his father's best friend Quicksilver Messenger, he had come up too late to hear most of the static-scratchy reports. He did not yet understand the depth of their predicament. "This has been passed down by your ancestors from long before we held the name of Hardriders. Guard it well. No enemy may do you harm while you wear it."

He settled it around the boy's neck. The thunderbolt stone fell inside the front of the wolfskin jacket he was wearing. The obsidian seemed to burn against his skin as if it had come fresh from the FlameLands lava.

He clutched it with his hand. Black Jammer, the Electric Skald of the Plains, stood nearby. Though his eyes as always were hidden by his wraparound mirror shades, Tristan felt them upon him now. He sensed that this moment would be long remembered on the Plains. He feared to know why.

"But Father—"

"The time has come for it to be passed along, boy, as it always has." He lifted his head and looked off west to the distant rampart of the Rockies. Their peaks were beginning to take on a cherry tinge, like iron in a forge. "I think today's a good day to die."

When Trooper Davis relieved him of the thunderbolt, en route to Sedgwick, Tristan had snapped at his hand like a wolf-cub. It brought him a buffet on the side of his head that made his stomach roll and sparks fly around behind his eyes.

He said nothing, then or later. A Hardrider asked his enemies for nothing, save the chance for a clean fighting death. Young as he was, Tristan knew for sick certainty he was going to be denied that mercy. City folk were harsh that way.

The kind and gentle City called Homeland took an active interest in parenting affairs. Parents who didn't measure up to the City's exacting standards were common, especially in the Blocks. Sedgwick did a brisk business in troubled youngsters.

The new arrival was taken back to an examination room by the pretty black-haired nurse and a couple of burly matrons in lime-green smocks. When they started to lead him deeper into the building he came alive suddenly, kicking, thrashing his head, screaming.

With a practiced heave, the matrons hoisted him into the air. He was skinny and slight, but surprisingly strong. But they had a whole lot of weight on him, and they knew what they were about. He managed only to agitate air.

"Poor dear," the pretty black-haired nurse said. "He's scared half to death."

One matron tossed the other a look behind the nurse's shoulder. Her partner nodded, making a quick evil-averting gesture with her thumb. The principal religion within these stressed-cement walls was Psychiatry, but the matrons were closer to the streets. They knew that these Plains scum were all devil-worshipers; be a surprise if the brat *didn't* have a demon. But you couldn't tell these therapeutic types that.

In the exam room they sat him on a stainless-steel table. The matrons held the boy still as the nurse checked him, shining lights into his eyes and ears. He made a couple of feeble attempts to bite, but she stroked his hair and crooned to him, gentling him like a horse. The matrons rolled their eyes, but the boy calmed.

"There, sweetheart, that's better," the nurse said, shining her light up his nose. "What's your name."

He glared at her. "It's all right. You can tell me. I won't put a curse on you."

"Trrtn."

"Pardon? I didn't catch that, dear."

"Tristan."

"Tristan," she repeated. Her smile was blinding in the fluorescent shimmer. "What a beautiful name. You're going to be a very handsome young man, once we get you cleaned up."

With her gentle touch on his shoulder, he held still as the matrons unwrapped his restraints and piled them to one side. She shook her head and clucked sympathetically at the way the cool air raised goose bumps on the boy's skinny chest. Visibly, he was starting to trust her despite himself.

Then she brought out a gun. He stiffened, eyes snapping left and right. *No escape.* He was not the first of the Hardriders to fall to the wiles of a pretty woman, though it looked as if he probably would be the last. He held his chin defiantly up.

The nurse held the gun to his arm, pulled the trigger. He made no sound as pain lanced through his arm—well, you couldn't count the involuntary mouse-squeak; his lips stayed shut tight.

"There," she said, withdrawing the silvery device, "you were very brave. That was a broad-spectrum antibiotic. No telling what you might have picked up out there on the Plains."

He glared at her, belatedly realizing that he had not been shot. It felt like it, though. He rubbed his aching arm.

"I'm leaving you now, sweetheart," the nurse announced brightly. "Matrons Matlock and Hollins will take care of you now. I'll try to look in on you, though."

She bent, kissed him on the forehead, and went out.

He looked up at the matrons. They looked at him. They looked at each other.

One of them lashed out with a backhand, laying him on his back on the steel tabletop.

"Now," she said, as he picked himself up to the sitting position. He had trouble hearing her over the ringing in his ears. "We understand each other."

He darted for the door through which the pretty nurse had exited. A meaty hand snagged his elbow, slammed him up against a counter. Open-hand blows rocked his head back and forth until his knees sagged.

"There," the matron who had done all the hitting said with a huff of satisfied exertion. The name MATLOCK was embroidered on her vast right breast.

It took Tristan a moment to puzzle it out. He was one of the few Hardriders who would have known how; his mother and Quicksilver Messenger, his father's best friend, had worked together to teach him to read, though normally they had little use for each other.

He would remember the name. There was so much he had to remember. . . .

Groggy and sick from the beating, he was docile when they clipped the gleaming raven's-wing hair from his head with a device that buzzed like a tiny motor scooter. He refused to take off his buckskin pants when they told him to. There was no shame in nudity among the Hardriders, and among most of the High Free Folk, but young as he was he understood the vulnerability and submission involved in being compelled to stand naked before an enemy. Matlock, the burlier of the two, pinned his arms from behind while the other snipped away the trousers with a gleaming pair of broken-nosed scissors.

"Go ahead," she said when he struggled, "kick all you want. You'll lose more than just the pants that way."

"Be best for all concerned to make sure you don't pass on your wicked tainted blood," Matlock said. "And that's a fact."

They dragged the naked boy on deeper into the strange cavelike building. Tristan had never before been in a hardtop, not even when he had accompanied his father to the Taos Rendezvous last year to trade goods and lies with the other clans, the bros, and traders and even sodbusters.

He didn't like it. A bro's place was in the wind, under the clouds and stars. There was more than the sense of freedom involved. The stars and clouds never fell on your head, no matter how hard the earth shook.

They brought him to a room of tile, all bluish-white, with the floors slanting down to pierced metal disks and things like steel flowers sprouting from the walls. "You know how to bathe yourself, Plains trash?"

Belatedly, Tristan recognized the steel flowers as shower heads. The High Free Folk used them, set up with water tanks on platforms or truck beds so that gravity could make them flow. He had never seen them sprout from cold ceramic walls before.

Matron Matlock turned on the shower with a vindictive twist, bringing the water on hot. Tristan danced back, skin reddening. The matrons laughed at his antics, but finally relented and adjusted the flow to a cooler temperature. They didn't want to scald themselves holding him in the shower.

He bathed in some stinking soap the matrons squirted on their palms from wall dispensers and smeared on his pallid skin with quick disgusted dabs. It made what hair they had left him feel sticky and stiff. He dried himself with rough white towels that left him feeling as if he'd gone over the high side on the little Green River bike his father had given him his last birthday.

They tossed a blue denim shirt and pants at him. Feeling numb, he just caught them in time to keep them from falling on the damp floor. He dressed mechanically and let them drive him onward, deeper, like a herd beast to the knife.

They came to a door. The matrons thrust him inside. He had a moment to take stock: a tiny room, no more than ten feet by eight, with some kind of wan illumination from above like flamelight with no soul, and a cot with a rough blanket.

The door slammed.

Tristan screamed. He was numbed by what he had lived through that day, logy from the beating, and though he didn't realize it, showing some reaction from the vaccination the black-haired nurse had given him. The pain of loss had retreated within him to a dull throb. The unease of being confined by a roof and walls of cement had receded.

Now he was trapped. Confined for the first time in his life. His internal defenses ruptured, and panic burst out of his scrawny young body like a pyroclastic flow.

He screamed again, flung himself at the door, hammering with his hands. The door was metal, cold and unyielding as a Citizen's heart. His eyes were blind from tears, spittle flew from his mouth, and he had soiled his new denim pants.

He clawed until his nails broke. He threw his shoulder against the door repeatedly until it felt as if a lance was being thrust through his chest. He screamed as if to turn himself inside out.

There was no response. The walls of Sedgwick were proof against small boys and their screams.

There came a time when he hit the door and could move no more, could not even hold himself up. He slid to a heap at the foot of the door. And now the loss of his father, his mother, his friends, and his world rushed upon him like a buffalo stampede. His losing of the thunderbolt, entrusted to him by his father, filled him with shame. Though he should have been empty of wind and water and emotion, he began to cry, loud and hard.

Through it all, a part of him remained detached, calm almost. That was the worst of all. Because as he lay there collapsed with his grief racking his body like the aftershocks of a mighty quake, he knew that the death of the Hardriders was his fault and his alone.

2

He was sitting with his fingers on the keyboard on his lap when he felt the day change.

He looked up. He knew what he would see. He had heard the key-change in the camp-buzz around him, and he had felt it, that sudden dead leaden stillness. And even if he hadn't, you could see it in the light.

The sky had been overcast, slate-gray clouds hanging so low above the hills along the Horse River you could touch them, or ought to be able to. Nothing unusual about that. Earlier raindrops had brushed his face like the fingertips of a playmate applying camouflage paint for games of war. But the squalls had passed, and at Golden Marcia's urging he had gotten out the keyboard. It wasn't turned on; she was leading him through fingering practice.

That was forgotten now, in the yellow light that drooled through clouds gone black as the soul of a City judge. On the Plains, light like that meant one thing.

"Oh, dear," Golden Marcia said in her beautiful voice.

"Wolf-bitch tits," murmured a Hardrider with goggles pushed up on top of his head who had stood up from tinkering with his sled. The clouds had begun to resemble the swollen mammaries of a pregnant she-wolf. The biker bit the tip of his thumb and spat to avert evil.

"Get the vehicles ready to roll," a calm, penetrating voice

said. The fear quivering in Tristan's belly and the insides of his thighs steadied. That was the voice of his mother, Jen Morningstar—and no other woman of the Hardriders spoke with such command.

The 'Riders, young and old, began to move, purposefully, not hurrying but not dawdling either as they doused fires, knocked down tents and drying racks, bundled belongings into trucks, rolled surplus bikes up ramps into trailers and chained them down. Drill and regimentation were alien to the High Free Folk, but these moves they had practiced, over and over again. Over the generations they had learned: There was no other way to survive.

Tristan's mother stood at the crest of the hill, head back, back slightly arched, fists held out from her hips on rigid arms. People gave her wide berth. Her birth clan was the Smoking Mirrors, and they sacrificed men and women to ancient gods of the South every bit as horrible as the DemonCallers' devils. She worshipped no Monster Gods herself; she had acted as willing accomplice when Wyatt Octane, not yet Hardrider of the Hardriders, had kidnaped her from her folk. Most of the Hardriders thought she was a bit on the eerie side still—the Smoking Mirrors had a powerful reputation—and called her Afrit Jenny. But she was reputed to have Power over the Stalking Wind, the most feared killer of the Plains, and so at times like this they were glad enough of her presence.

Tristan moved among the children of the Hardriders, making himself walk deliberately though his heart hammered as if he'd trapped a quail in his rib cage. His place was not to order the others around—the Hardriders didn't respond well to *commands*. Until he could earn a place in council on his own merits, as his father had, and Anse Hardrider the One-Eyed before him, his place was to set the best example he could. He took the duty seriously; it helped to steady him.

He saw Jamie, his best friend, who was a year older than he, helping to herd some of the younger children back to the arms of mothers trying desperately to contain their incipient panic. Jamie's father was an independent, a moondog one-percenter who often rode with the Hardriders because he and Wyatt went back a ways. As frequently happened, Jamie felt the pressure of

Tristan's gaze, looked up, gave him a flashing smile and a thumbs-up.

In moments camp was struck. Where hemispherical tents had sprouted like brightly colored mushrooms there was only a hilltop, the grass flattened, the earth tracked by boot heels and tires. A week of wind and rain and it would be as if the Hardriders had never passed this way. That was the way of the High Free Folk, the Stormriders of the Plains.

Jen Morningstar mounted her bike and led off deliberately to the north. The four-wheeled vehicles on which the Hardriders had loaded their possessions followed, as did most of the bike-mounted 'Riders.

Tristan watched the cages go with a pang of guilt, knowing his mother would miss him and be worried when she had attention to spare from trying to attune herself to the coming Stalking Winds and keep her clan out of their path. In the past his place in such emergencies had been riding in the four-wheeled cages, though he had a small scrambler bike of his own, assembled from trade parts for him by Nick Blackhands. In his own estimation he was a skillful rider, and he routinely outrode his age-mates and all the clan's children up to two years older, except maybe Jamie. He did not want to ride with the kids and baggage today. This was his eleventh summer. He was too old for that.

Now a handful of riders sat their machines just below the crest of the hill, watching the black and yellow sky with tense anticipation. Off to the east, a black tentacle seemed to reach down from the clouds toward the dun prairie. Seemingly coy, it extended and retracted several times before touching the earth.

A joint sound came from the watchers, half cry, half sigh.

Quicksilver Messenger, best friend and chief advisor to Wyatt Hardrider, leaned on arms crossed over the handlebars of his bike. He was a small man, wiry and fox-faced, clean-shaven, with pale hair and eyes like polished steel. He wore a breechcloth and buckskin leggings, and his skinny chest, scarred from the Sun Dance, was bare beneath a vest gaudy with Absaroka beadwork.

Every chromed surface of his stripped-down scrambler bike—handlebars, forks, frame, exhaust pipes—was engraved with dense, intricate patterns. Despite his legendary impatience, he had done the engraving himself. The Messenger could ride that bike cross-country faster than any man or woman on the Plains. The name *Silver Arrow* and a sunburst were painted on the gas tank, silver on blue. It was a classic, made by the Carondelet Machine Works on the Big River, closed for a generation by earthquakes.

"So the dance begins," he said. "Been a while since we Danced with."

Wyatt Hardrider nodded his long chin. He was a tall man, with heavy shoulders and a big chest with a big gut beginning to develop below it. As usual he wore a loose shirt of unbleached muslin, bloused around the wrists, blue jeans with leather chaps, and black boots with his trademark Mexican silver chain around each heel. He stood with long legs astride his own more utilitarian Osage scrambler. In legendary times past, back before StarFall, a bro and his bike had been one. Wyatt was bent on writing some legends of his own, and had made a fair start, but he would not have tried to lead the life of a warrior and leader of the High Free Folk with only a single bike to his string, even his beloved cruiser, Warrior.

"What do you got in mind?" he asked. The first tornado-tentacle had retracted into the wolf-teat clouds, but three more danced on the horizon. They seemed to be drawing closer.

"Are we Stormriders or Citizens?" the Messenger asked, and gunned his engine.

Wyatt Hardrider's lips pressed to a line beneath his ferocious handlebar mustache. The Messenger was the most quick-witted of the clan, except for Afrit Jenny. But he was prone to slashing changes of mood, from exaltation to black depression. It was never easy to read him.

"You're lookin' to go Dancin' with Mr. D?" Hardrider asked.

A fat raindrop struck Tristan on the cheek. More raindrops slanted in, not many, but big and hard, striking the prairie like spent bullets.

"We can play it safe," the Messenger said, his voice taunting now. "We can Ride the Storm way out in front, chase each other between the raindrops, and tell ourselves we've got big balls brave when lightning strikes half a mile away. Or . . ." He nodded at the dancing twisters.

The Hardrider scratched his chin. "Been a while."

Stony Bill, the 'Rider who'd been working on his scooter

when the weather broke, had hung back with the others. "I'm up for it," he said now, dropping his goggles in front of his eyes.

Wyatt Hardrider nodded abruptly. *Putting the hammer down*, they called it on the Plains when he sealed a judgment with a stroke of that famous chin. Nothing known could sway him from a decision thus finalized.

He looked around then, saw Tristan hanging back. "Cuss me for a Kiowa. The boy."

"What about him?" Quicksilver asked.

Hardrider skinned his lips back from his teeth. They were large powerful teeth, like a horse's. His wife made him keep them clean. "Got to take him back to the caravan. Jen'll be all over me like flies on buffalo shit."

"No!" somebody blurted out. Everybody turned and stared at Tristan. He looked around wildly and realized he was the only likely somebody. Children among the High Free Folk were indulged, but there were limits to their license, and these kicked in when serious talk among bros was involved.

But Tristan figured he was kinda stuck in it now anyway. "Please don't send me back!" he blurted out. "Let me go Stormriding with you. I'm old enough. Please?"

Then he got a grip and braked himself quick, because you didn't wheedle Wyatt Hardrider. With an engine snarl Quicksilver darted his bike forward and slewed it sideways to a stop right in front of Tristan, who didn't flinch, even though dirt washed over the legs of his buckskin pants.

Quicksilver stared hard in the boy's eyes. "We're not just talking *Stormriding* here, boy. We're talking Dancing with Mr. D. Do you know what that means?"

Tristan nodded.

"You still want to go with us?"

"Yes!"

The Messenger stared into his eyes a moment more. A rushing roar rose about them. A wild light blazed up in his eyes. He threw back his head and laughed at the boiling skies.

"Yes! That's it!" he shouted. "Act without thinking! Never hesitate! That's the Stormrider way." He gunned his engine, hauled his big-cleated front tire up into the air, and accelerated away down the flank of the hill.

Wyatt Hardrider laughed too. He slapped the passenger seat. "Jump on, son. Time's getting short."

Heart drumming eagerness, Tristan clambered onto the bike behind his father. Wyatt Hardrider gunned his own bike toward the twisters.

They seemed to be trending north-northeast, directly away from where Jen had led the caravan. Tristan felt fiercely proud of her and her Power, which had preserved the clan again.

The sound was getting louder. There was a whistling scream threaded through it now, like a teapot boiling on a buffalo-chip fire. The funnel clouds were growing close, swaying and flickering like black inverted flames. Tristan watched them past his father's hulking back, and though he couldn't admit it to himself, began to question the wisdom of his decision. There was no menace more feared on the Plains than the Stalking Wind, not wildfire, not lightning, not flash floods, not the choking ashfalls from the FlameLands nor the skull-crushing Plains hail. Here were three twisters in full throat, beginning to make the transition of perspective from *lying before* to *towering above*, so near he could see the clouds of dust and dried vegetation with which the funnel clouds cloaked their business ends.

The 'Riders rode in ragged line abreast, Wyatt in the center, Quicksilver Messenger to his right. To Wyatt's left Stony Bill rode his own Osage. As he glanced that way, Tristan saw Bill gesture with a gauntleted hand.

Tristan twisted. A fourth rider came close behind Wyatt Hardrider. Tristan gasped as he recognized Jamie hunkered over the bars of her little Diablo, unbound auburn hair blowing in the wind, her single long braid trailing like a pennon.

He clutched his father's sleeve, and pointed backward when Wyatt glanced over his shoulder. Hardrider turned in the saddle to look. Tristan felt him grunt. Jamie was nearing womanhood; if she chose to go for blooding right here and now, that was *her* lookout, and if her father Gap didn't like it, that was between the two of them.

Tristan kept glancing back at her. He was agitated now, his insides watery. This wasn't right. She shouldn't be out here risking the wrath of the Stalking Wind—the thought terrified him more than any danger to himself. Of course it was her right; Hardrider women honored their men but spoke their minds, at least since Jen Morningstar had joined the clan. But Tristan could hardly stand it.

He was distracted as they rode through a zone of silence, in which even the whine of the engines was muted and distant. And then a horrific howling passed right overhead, seeming so close he almost ducked through the fender, and a shower of dust and pebbles enveloped them.

Tristan felt a wild war-cry explode from his father's chest. And he saw the black lance-tip of a tornado thrust into the earth *behind* Jamie's bike.

She wobbled, recovered even as Tristan thought his heart was going to pop out of his mouth. For the first time she acknowledged her friend. She grinned and held up one thumb.

Coughing on the dust and the tiny chunks of dried vegetation that swarmed about him like gnats, Tristan snapped his head forward. The other two funnels loomed to either side like the pine trees of the mountains around Taos but immeasurably larger, as if they were tall as the Rockies themselves and about to fall on him. He wanted to bury his face in his father's great back and sob. Instead he made himself sit upright, head back, eyes open. He was a Hardrider.

They passed between the wavering columns, and Tristan realized the funnels were a good mile to either side. Quicksilver Messenger broke right, through one-eight, and sprinted back in pursuit of the funnel that had skipped over them. Wyatt Hardrider turned after him. Stony Bill strung behind. Jamie put down a foot in a high-topped Apache moccasin and spun her bike to follow.

Tristan felt his father leaning into the bike, cutting wind-drag, practically willing it forward faster. The boy realized they were in a race with Quicksilver, a race to be first to slow-dance Death. The fear came back, splashing scalding across his mind like boiling water from the pot he'd brushed at play when he was seven.

He made himself concentrate on the moment and the movement, the short grass blurring by to either side in the piss-colored light, the snarl of the engine cutting across the monster bellow of the wind, the smell of rain-spattered prairie and exhaust. He tried to anticipate the way his father leaned left or right to veer around clumps, and push upwards on the rear pegs when his father pulled the bike up into a jump.

For all his father's skill he could not catch Quicksilver Messenger—quite. Had the Stalking Wind moved straight along none of them could probably have caught it, for the funnels moved fearful-fast. But the tornado was in a playful mood. It began to swing left and right across their path, a dark gray tube appended to the sky, seeming to wait for them.

The tip was narrow where it touched the earth, the vortex proper not fifty yards across. Tristan remembered his campfire lore. These twisters were the most dangerous, for it was said they moved more quickly and unpredictably than the tornadoes five hundred yards or a mile across that stalked their stately way east across the Plains.

The noise was mind-crushing. Yet somehow Tristan was sure he could hear Quicksilver Messenger's mad laughter as he steered Silver Arrow toward the heart of the vortex. Wyatt Hardrider followed as fast as mortal man could ride. Tristan clung until he wondered that his father's ribs didn't crack.

It was as if Quicksilver played chicken with the tornado, and the Stalking Wind gave way. It darted left. The Messenger vanished into the attendant cloud, as if daring the vortex to suck him up. He reappeared a heartbeat later, just as Wyatt Hardrider plunged into the cloud.

Darkness. Flying dust raked Tristan's cheeks. The circular wind of the vortex had tumbled into turbulence here, but it was violent enough to tear the breath from Tristan's lungs. Somehow his father kept them upright, kept them from straying into the lethal maw of the funnel itself.

They were out again, clear. Thoughts of his own survival no longer overriding everything else, Tristan twisted in the saddle to look back in apprehension. Surely, Jamie was too slight to have withstood the battering wind. . . .

But here she came, clinging grimly to her little Diablo. A moment later Stony Bill burst from the roiling brown mass, hunched forward and looking grim because he couldn't keep up with a thirteen-year-old girl.

And so they danced, their paths and the paths of the monster storm weaving an intricate braid north and east along the broad Horse basin. On the fourth recrossing Hardrider and Jamie followed Quicksilver Messenger right, while Stony Bill's inspiration steered him left. His Power was bad that day. Tristan saw him and his orange-trimmed Osage plucked up off the ground by a casual veer of the funnel, saw man and bike fall away upwards, separating each from the other, gone. He watched, in fascination, until there was no more to be seen.

The funnels dissipated shortly thereafter. Stalking Wind did his destruction and left; long farewells were not his way.

They rode together in silent glowing-cheeked camaraderie, the three remaining bikes and four remaining riders, at once too exalted and too subdued for speech, as the day opened up around them and the sun fell across the Plains like the touch of a god's hand.

They found Stony Bill's bike, bent into a U, a mile and a half from where he'd been taken. The Stalking Wind had kept Stony Bill a while longer. He was found beside a creek almost two miles further on. He was bruised, but no more so than from a medium-good stomping by someone who meant to make an impression but not kill him. A froth of blood had dried on his lips and nostrils. Tristan's mother and Black Jammer, the Electric Skald, who was traveling for a time with the Hardriders and who had picked up more than a little healing lore on his journeys among the High Free Folk, agreed his lungs had burst. But all that came later.

Jen Morningstar was waiting for the Stormriders when they rejoined the caravan fifteen miles away. She was unhappy that her husband had gone Dancing with Mr. D, but as a bro in good standing—not to mention the chief—of the Hardriders clan, that was his prerogative; to complain would have been tantamount to asking him to divorce her.

But taking their eleven-year-old son along to play tag with tornadoes . . . that was a different thing. The more so since the sport had caused one 'Rider's death. It could easily have cost more.

Jen and Wyatt had the worst fight then that Tristan could ever remember seeing them have. Or anyone else in the clan, as it turned out. Wyatt was irresponsible almost to the point of killing their son; Jen was In His Face and On His Case. That Tristan had met and passed the test of manhood was no help. As Jen contemptuously pointed out, he had not faced the Stalking Wind by himself, in control of his own bike and his own fate. It didn't even count.

They were passionate folk, and had learned to be flexible with each other as a willow learns not to fight the wind. But this time each said things that even time and cooler blood could scarcely ease the sting of. Things that left open wounds in pride.

So that ten days later they were still keeping each other at the end of invisible porcupine quills, and moving stiffly, as though through the World-Behind-the-World. And so, when the allies who had come together for the successful convoy raid—the Caballeros and Sand Kings and the independent riders, including Jamie's father—had taken their loot and gotten out while the getting was good, Wyatt, with his prickly pride, had kept the Hardriders back, awaiting more spoils. And Jen Morningstar, with her prickly pride, had declined to raise a dissenting voice in council.

So died the Hardriders.

And it was all Tristan's fault. If he hadn't stayed behind that day, if he hadn't insisted on Stormriding with his father, he would still have a father and a mother and a clan, his friends, his freedom, his life.

3

That first night of captivity Tristan wept until he passed out from exhaustion on the alien floor that was not stone, nor wood, nor earth, not knowing whether he'd ever again feel the wind in his hair or the rain on his cheek.

But in the world of dreams, the World-Behind-the-World which many Plains people found more real than the waking world, his parents were waiting for him. They were strong and safe, and best of all, they were together again.

His father spoke first. "You must be strong, my son," he said, at once stern and gentle, as he often was in life. "But now, to be strong means to survive. You will not avenge your clan, your mother, or me by permitting the Citizens to crush you with their laws and walls of stone. *Live*."

"Live," his mother echoed, her beautiful face both radiant and sad. "We both love you, dear, now and always. We want you to be happy and free. And you will again, if you don't despair. *We love you*."

"Remember," his father said. "The man who killed us lives in this City. You must grow up strong and wise and brave. And you must kill him."

They faded. In his sleep Tristan knew the vision was true, and his sleeping young face smiled, and he rolled to his side and cradled his cheek with his hand.

But the dreamworld wasn't through with him. It seemed to

28

him that he stood on a vast wasteland of black rock, jumbled and sharp-edged, stretching to where its juncture with a cloud-filled sky was hidden by dark smoke. It seemed dusk, or just before dawn. Away in the distance, near where the horizon ought to be, he saw a tiny point of glow, like a campfire seen across a valley. No more.

But a chill passed through him. He recalled how in his dream something had crossed his mother's face like cloud-shadow over prairie. Did she know of the glow? It filled him with a sense of urgency and power. He feared it, yet he ached to look upon it and to know.

He could not. The dream faded, and if he dreamed more he never remembered it.

When he awoke his first reaction was panic. He was caught, constricted; the walls and ceiling, gleaming hideous unnatural white, pressed inexorably in upon him. He cried out and hid his face in his hands.

It came to him that he wasn't making a very good showing as Hardrider of the Hardriders. From the other world he heard his mother's voice saying, *There, my darling, be calm. They're only walls. If you wait, they will be gone. All it takes is patience.*

For the son of Wyatt Hardrider, *patience* was a lot to ask. But it came to Tristan that he didn't have much choice.

Once he got the panic under control, life in Sedgwick wasn't too bad. He missed the sky and his freedom, he missed his friends—Quicksilver Messenger and Golden Marcia and Nick Blackhands, the wrench, and Jamie—and most of all he missed his parents. Watching his clan and family die had been like an amputation, and as often happened trauma had an anesthetizing effect. After his explosion of grief and panic in his cell, he was a bit stunned.

He was old for Sedgwick. The Powers of the institution didn't know what to do with him. Part of the reason he was there was to quarantine him in case he happened to be carrier for any of the awful, unnameable, and untreatable plagues that the Citizens knew swept the Plains as incessantly as the wind. Besides, who knew what the young barbarian would do? The administrators and therapists all believed in the efficacy of modern mental care, but it took time, and meanwhile they were scared green of him. All things considered, they thought it best to keep him away from the other inmates, lest he intimidate or taint the younger children.

He missed the bustle and noise and constant companionship of camp life along with everything else, and that lack was sharpened by the lack of company. But the people of the Plains knew the value of solitude, and were raised not just to accept it but seek it out; visions and Power were seldom to be had in crowds. He really didn't have much use for a pack of stuck-up City brats. Besides, the policy kept him from having much contact with the matrons.

On the other hand, the pretty black-haired nurse paid a lot of attention to him. She was studying him, and at the same time monitoring his health, both mental and physical. When he explained—very grown-up, as he thought—that the best way to insure that his mind was healthy would be to set him free, she shook her head and smiled sadly.

"I wish it were that simple, Tristan. But freedom . . . freedom's a dangerous thing. It's something to be respected, maybe even feared. Being free means you have the freedom to make wrong choices, to hurt yourself and others. Are you sure that's what you want, dear?"

He didn't hold it against her. He'd never expected it to work; Quicksilver Messenger had taught him always to *try*. "Ask," the Messenger would say. "They might say no, and then what have you lost? Then again"—that flashing grin—"they might say yes. The first rule of life is *you never know*."

The days passed, he felt sure. He didn't know; there was never day or night inside Sedgwick. There was only the constant fluorescent shine that managed both to be weak and to hurt Tristan's eyes, falling like light rain from the overheads, and the cycle of meals slipped through a slot in his door. The only things that kept Tristan from a madness of despair was the resilience of childhood, his dreams, and his friend, the black-haired nurse.

She gave him a battery of tests, some of which he found entertaining, some pointless and dull. She was quite surprised to find that he knew how to read.

When he let the fact slip, he regretted it instantly. Maybe if he'd pretended he *didn't* know how to read, she would have spent still more time with him, teaching him. He liked the black-haired nurse a lot. He knew she liked him too.

His emotion must have shown in his face. She laughed, instantly making him defensive and aware that he was letting his guard dangerously low.

"It's all right, Tristan, dear. I know you enjoy the fact that I'm spending so much time with you. I enjoy it too. You're a very intelligent young man."

She leaned down to kiss his cheek. "Don't worry. I plan to watch your development here very closely. Now, run along so Matron can take you back to your room, and I'll see you tomorrow."

She'd lied, but she didn't know it. The next day he was transferred to McGrory Dorms, and he never saw her again.

McGrory was a facility for adolescents. In Sedgwick he had been a big kid indeed. In the Dorms he found himself at the opposite end of the spectrum. He was one of the youngest inmates, and small for his age by City standards.

The City in its wisdom believed it knew better how to manage its Citizens' lives than they or their families did. In its wisdom it dropped a small fish into a pool of large and hungry ones.

In contrast to the cell in Sedgwick, claustrophobic and antiseptic, the dormitories of McGrory were spacious, grubby barracks filled with row on row of bunk beds. When he was led in they were echoingly empty, the occupants elsewhere. The smell was rank and musty and made Tristan's face wrinkle.

The monitor was a heavyset man of medium height whose slab face was so devoid of expression that Tristan had the sensation you could stick pins in it without drawing a response. He led Tristan to a bunk in the middle of the big room, uncomfortably far from the fly-specked windows.

"This one's unoccupied. Kid got released on indenture. Yours now. Those all the things you got?" His blunt fingers gestured at the bundle of bedding clutched under Tristan's arm and the toothbrush in his hand. Along with a new set of flimsy denim clothes, this time a lifeless green, they had been issued to him on admission. He nodded; with his own miniature Osage scrambler wrecked by a mortar round, his fine Black Mountain knife lost Brother Wind knew where, and his thunderbolt amulet stolen, they were all the property he could claim.

The monitor left him there. He glanced around the room. There were no obvious places to hide, and no unobvious ones either; the bunks had been built low to the wood floor to prevent youths from hiding under them.

With no City eyes on him he might slip out and try to get out of McGrory. But he had seen the ten-foot fences with the three-foot inward-slanting courses of knife-wire at the tops of them, and the guard towers and the gates. He trusted the Citizens to know how to build a cage.

His ten days of captivity had already taught him something about futility. His nurse friend had taught him to sleep on a bed. He lay on the bunk and stared up at the rope supports of the mattress above.

After a while—he didn't have much sense of time units shorter than a day and a night, since the High Free Folk made few appointments by hour and minute—the other occupants came roughhousing back into the barracks. He felt a tension in his stomach, but didn't move.

"Hey, look at this," a voice said. "There's a new fish."

A knot of youths stood around the bunk, staring at him. They were all bigger than he was. "Who told you you could bunk here, fish?" one of them asked.

"The monitor," Tristan said.

When they heard his accent they elbowed each other and giggled. The one who had asked who told him to bunk there pointed to the top bunk. "You're up there now, fish. Understand?"

Tristan sat up and looked at him. He was a rangy boy, with brown hair growing unevenly out of a burr cut and hazel eyes. "Why?" Tristan asked.

"Because I said so."

Tristan was on everybody else's turf here, and knew it too well. That imposed restraints on his behavior; a bro did not show class by abusing hospitality. He stood up, scooped up his blanket and liner, tossed them onto the upper bunk, and climbed up after them.

A little while later an area supervisor with a squint and a clipboard came through. When he came to Tristan he spent a while looking from him to the clipboard and back. Tristan had the uneasy impression that clipboard knew something about him.

"Your task will be housekeeping for now," the area supervisor finally said. "The other boys will show you where the appropriate implements are before they go to lunch. *You* will not be going to lunch; this place is a disgrace. See that it's cleaned of dirt and ash and you may acquire some privileges."

Tristan's stomach panged. He was always hungry. But he was also used to it. He had been fed more in the days since his capture than he ever had before in his life. He figured he'd survive.

At one end of the barracks was a closet with buckets, brushes, mops, and brooms. The other residents dutifully showed them to him before spilling out into the cloud-filtered noonlight.

When the youths came back from lunch they found Tristan on his knees, holding the yellow straw head of a broom in his hands, dabbing a tiny pile of grit across the floor with it.

They started to laugh uproariously. "Is that stupid or what?" asked a wiry black-haired boy not much larger than Tristan, looking all around to see if his remark brought approval.

"What more do you could expect from no-good Plains nomad trash," said a stocky redheaded kid a good six inches taller. "They ain't human anyhow."

By the time a half-dozen other youths pulled Tristan away from him, Tristan had already made some appreciable dents in the wooden frame of a bunk with the back of the boy's head.

Assistant Administrator Hanrick was very understanding when Tristan explained, grudgingly, that he had never seen a broom before and had no idea how to use one.

"We'll certainly see to it that you receive proper instruction in the requisite skills," the Assistant Administrator said. Tristan wasn't really sure what he looked like, other than that he was balding on top and had prominent ears. The whole length of the wall behind him was venetian blinds, and with the clouds breaking up, the afternoon sunlight shining through them dazzled Tristan.

Hanrick twisted long fingers together on the baize blotter on his desk. "We are certainly not accustomed to tailoring our program to individuals, young man. But we do understand that allowances must be made for your . . . unusual background, certainly."

Tristan thought Hanrick was like a kitten with a shiny new ball-bell toy, the way he batted that word *certainly* around.

"We realize that this afternoon's incident arose from an unfortunate misunderstanding," the Assistant Administrator said. "All the same, we do have rules to regulate behavior, and we have them for a reason. Our whole work here is to prepare our young men for return to society . . . I suppose that isn't entirely appropriate in your case. Still, I am going to have to impose some punishment on you for your outburst. You can understand that, certainly?"

What Tristan understood—certainly—was that the Man had him down, and would do with him as he pleased. He had heard enough campfire tales from formerly downed bros to have that straight already.

His punishment was to be temporarily forbidden to go with the others in the evenings to watch movies. He didn't miss that much. He hadn't *seen* many movies; the Hardriders had been too poor to have any vidplayers or TVs. Also, Jen Morningstar, for all that she rejected much of her own upbringing, still partly shared her birth-people's instinct to mistrust any tech that wasn't concerned with the vital functions of transport or killing; even Golden Marcia's keyboards and Jammer's electric guitar made her uneasy.

She could not prohibit such things to the Hardriders, and did not wish to; the clans of the Plains were ruled by frequently complex customs, traditions, taboos, and the personalities of their leaders, but the High Free Folk were generally hostile to attempts to regulate their personal lives. Membership in a Motorcycle Clan, like rank, was a matter of mutual consent. The Hardriders respected Jen's feelings in the matter because they respected her, and because they feared her black Smoking Mirror Powers, which she did not claim but which most of them suspected she possessed anyway.

Tristan had seen movies at Rendezvous, of course, and at shivarees with friendly clans who had TVs and players. He loved them, but they weren't an important part of his life. All that was *really* important was surviving until he could somehow regain his freedom.

That night he dreamed again of his mother and father. Jen Morningstar reassured him that he was loved and that he would one day be free. His father urged him to remember his duty to avenge the clan.

The glow seemed brighter, off across the fanged lava rock. Seeing it, he stirred and whimpered in his sleep.

4

Routine did not come easily to the proud ones who called themselves Stormriders or High Free Folk. The songs their bards sang incessantly reminded them that their ancestors had embraced the rigors of life on the Plains in order to avoid having their lives cramped into routines.

In dreams Tristan's father told him he had to survive, for the good of the clan and the honor of the Hardrider name. Stiffnecked Wyatt Hardrider had never bowed to any man, and his son assumed his father's spirit knew what it asked of him. So Tristan did his best to learn to endure the McGrory routine.

There were some things he could not endure. He hoped his father understood.

His first few weeks in the Dorms went about as well as they could, considering. The shoes they made him wear hurt his feet. The food wasn't plentiful, and didn't taste like much of anything.

The other kids gave him plenty of wheel-room. Though he often saw them hanging out in clumps, looking at him and laughing as they talked among themselves, they were careful to say whatever they had to say out of his earshot. That was righteous as far as he was concerned. As long as nothing was said to his face that honor had to avenge, he didn't give a polecat's ass what the City scum said.

He had no friends, of course. He assured himself it didn't matter.

It would be too much to say he mastered the intricacies of cleaning the barracks. He did learn how to handle the various tools without tripping over them or otherwise embarrassing himself. The place did start to smell better, and there were at least spells when you could walk across the floor without gritty ash, from eruptions as far away as the FlameLands, which were northwest beyond the Rockies, crunching beneath your feet.

He still felt there was no damn point in living indoors. Outside you didn't have to always be sweeping the Plains. Brother Wind did that for you.

If he was still not in the wind—and he would not be in it for as long as any vision or Power he had could show him—at least he got to feel it on his cheeks regularly, and see the clouds blowing free above. Every morning the inmates of the Dorms were herded out into the yard for calisthenics before going to their work details. After he got the initial soreness caused by unfamiliar moves worked out of his limbs, he had no trouble with the exercises at all. Even a Plains kid with his first bike spent much of his time running loose like an antelope; only when he was a full-fledged bro would he disdain to walk farther than from his tent to his scooter.

In that way, at least, McGrory was superior to Sedgwick. The living death of being constantly indoors, shut off from Mother Sky and Mother Earth, would have driven Tristan crazy despite the friendly attention of the black-haired nurse.

He thought about her often. For some reason he missed her almost as keenly as he missed his family and friends. He kept hoping to hear from her, but he never did. He tried to make an appointment with Administrator Hanrick to send a message to her, but the Administrator's receptionist sent him packing.

Sometimes, in the pit of the night, when the others had finally left off snickering at one another's dirty stories and drifted into silence, he lay on his back on the bunk, small body quivering and rigid, hands fisted, joints and teeth locked, trying to hold the sobs inside. Though sometimes his body jerked as though to the shocks of a giant earthquake, no sound escaped his jaws to shame him. Silent, his tears turned his mushy institutional pillow to a morass.

In sleep there was respite, though. He dreamed of running laughing through the sudden chill and exhilarating violence of a prairie thunderstorm, too young to fear the lightning, rejoicing at the smell of wet earth and wildflowers and ozone, laughing at the crack of thunder with Jamie racing by his side. And the thunder of a run, half a hundred big bikes growling their song of power, winding it out down the Hard Road, heat-shimmering in the sun. And late nights, with the lonely half-guilty pleasure of being last awake in his tent, his father's snoring cut off when his mother prodded him in the ribs, neither waking; and Trickster Charlie and his silver-furred bros yipping on the next hill over, singing a love song to horny Sister Moon, who was all knocked up again. . . .

Sometimes they appeared to him, his mother and father, with their words of strength and reassurance. Not always, only when he really needed it.

But at least once each night he found himself on that barren field of lava rock, straining into the haze at the faraway glow. Each night it appeared a little brighter. Each night his heart beat a little faster with fear and anticipation, as if the glow presaged a thing both terrible and wonderful.

After he had been in the Dorms for forty days several boys in his barracks left. Three had their seventeenth birthdays within a few days of each other—sixteen was the maximum age for McGrory—and were shipped out, two to service in the Homeland Defense Force, the third to Coleman Unit, a labor farm run by the City penal system. Two other boys, both twelve, were adopted. With birth-limits strictly enforced in Homeland as in most Cities—among most Plains folk too, for that matter, since the legends taught overpopulation had caused the Great Shakedown—couples were frequently denied the right to bear children. Some were desperate enough to have children to take almost anything they could get, even adolescents. To sweeten the pot, youngsters adopted past the age of ten were law-bound to the service of their new parents for five years or until their seventeenth birthday, whichever fell later.

The remaining boys engaged in a brief but fierce struggle over who got possession of the coveted lower bunks the three older boys had vacated. Tristan did not join in. If he wasn't sleeping on the hard, clean earth of freedom, he barely cared where he slept.

Then five new residents were transferred in, big, boisterous youths in their mid-teens who promptly evicted the occupants of five lower bunks, including two who'd just won the scramble for them.

The leader of the group was a strapping boy almost six feet tall, with light brown hair cut to a plush. "Listen up, everybody," he announced to the barracks at large, while his four pals stood around him with arms folded and tried real hard to look fierce. "I'm Billy Walsh. I'm your new Dorm Warden. It looks like things have been real slack around here, but that's about to change. From here on, everybody in this Dorm is gonna be a model Citizen. And that means *everybody*."

Tristan was lying on his bunk staring up into the rafters. He saw no reason to pay attention to the newcomers' antics. He had a vague sense that a warden was appointed out of the population of each barracks to be responsible for the behavior of the rest. The last one in this dorm had been one of the boys who went to HDF. He had been very low-key about the whole thing. Tristan had only become aware of his position when he broke up a fight between two boys, one of them armed with a sharpened screwdriver. He had slapped them both comprehensively around, with help from some of the other Dormies. "You assholes puncture each other," he said, "and I'm doing time in the Hole with you, along with everybody they think even watched. You got any more problems like this, you come to me, or I'll show you what problems *are*."

The only reason Tristan had been hauled off to the Administrator for jumping the boy who taunted him, he gathered, was that the warden at the time had not been around, but a monitor had.

He was thinking about that, remembering that the bros who had been down said you never went to the Man for *anything,* when a hand caught him by the ankle and spun his legs off the bed.

"Yo! Butthole! You pay attention when Billy's talkin'." It was one of the new boys, a blond with a mean fist face and a broken nose.

Tristan's eyes blazed, but he sat up and did nothing more.

Like the other boys who weren't working details away from McGrory, he spent his mornings in other barracks being lectured at by an assortment of old farts about hygiene and duty and discipline and the Road alone knew what. He could fake listening with the best of them.

Burly Billy ranted for a while, then left to go to the rec room to watch *Outrider,* a locally produced television show. There was no other kind of television show. TV broadcasting was pretty much a line-of-sight operation, and the violent endless winds weren't kind to repeater stations. They weren't kind to broadcast or reception antennas either. You only received if you lived near the station. That was another reason the Hardriders didn't bother with TV much. To them it smacked of the sedentary life of the Citizens, or worse yet, the Diggers.

After lock-down and lights-out Tristan lay awake for a long time with his fingers laced behind his head, wondering if he had been a coward for not going for Billy's henchman who'd grabbed him by the ankle. Laying hands on a bro was a serious matter.

When he finally slipped into sleep his father was there. "You know that, pound for pound, the weasel's the meanest critter on the Plains, son," Wyatt Hardrider said. "Meaner than a Comanche who ain't been laid in two full moons. Brother Weasel never backs down from a fight, not with coyote, cat, or bear. But he don't go *lookin'* for fights he just can't win. Remember Brother Weasel, son."

After that he slept soundly. If he dreamed of the glow, he didn't remember it later.

"Hey! You there, blue eyes!"

Coming off the breakfast line with a plastic tray full of pallid steaming stuff that smelled like boiled laundry, Tristan turned his head to look. Billy and the boys were making their swaggering way across the cafeteria, right for him. He set the tray down on a table of which he was suddenly the sole occupant, and stood facing them.

"Yeah, *you,*" Billy said. He didn't seem able to communicate at less than a bellow. "I'm talkin' to *you.*"

"That's right," said the small black-haired boy who practically skipped at his side. Tristan recognized the kid who had started the taunting of him for his lack of domestic skills. "He's talkin' to you."

Tristan said nothing. A closed mouth gathered no flies, as the Mexican bros said.

Billy stopped with his bullies behind him and the kid with black hair dancing around the perimeter like a little yap-dog. "Mikey here says you're an anti," he said, folding thick arms across his chest.

Tristan didn't reply. He had no idea what Billy was taking about.

Billy's face clouded. "Well? What's the story? You coppin' an attitude on me?"

"What?" Tristan said.

"Billy's asking the questions," the fist-faced one said.

"You don't like me," Billy said. "You're not with the program."

"I don't know what you're talking about."

Billy looked from side to side, inviting comments from his lieutenants.

" 'I don't know what you're talking about,' " mimicked a brown-haired boy in a mincing tone. "Jeez, they're sure making the biker trash dumb these days."

Skinny Mikey hooted laughter. Tristan looked at the brown-haired henchman and remembered his father's advice from the dream.

"Why we botherin' with this one, Billy?" asked a bulky kid with his nose mashed practically flat. "He's too little to mess with."

"I don't know," Billy said, drawing it out. "I think he's kinda cute."

The boys loved that one. Brown Hair reached out to stroke Tristan's cheek with the back of his hand. Tristan snapped his head back and glared at him.

The bully-boy pulled his hand away and looked at his pals with exaggerated concern. "He's reacting hostile to an affectionate gesture," Brown Hair said. "Uh-uh, can't have that. The boy needs *treatment*."

"You got that right," said the fourth goon, who had short stiff light-brown hair and not much by way of chin. "And we know just the treatment."

"Yeah," said Fist Face. "I'd say he's just about cute enough to fuck."

Billy caught Tristan by the chin. He was quicker than he looked. "We all been in this hellhole a long time," he said, "and you are kinda pretty. I think we'll make you our sweetheart. What about that? Will you be our little girl?"

"No," Tristan said. He pulled away.

"What? What's that?" Billy turned his head and cupped a hand beside his ear. "I don't think I heard you right, Blue Eyes."

A monitor stood by the serving-line, a rumpled big-bellied man with bushy eyebrows and a port-wine birthmark smeared across one side of his face. Everybody called him Blind Burt, though as far as Tristan could tell there wasn't one damned thing wrong with his vision. He'd tried holding up his hand in front of the officer's face, and the man had almost bitten him in two. Tristan didn't look at him now.

"If we can't get along," Tristan said, quoting a favored saying of his father's, "let's get it on."

Billy laughed hugely. "Ho. That's good. That's really good." He shook his head as if trying to clear his eyes of tears of mirth. "All right. That's about enough. Wacker, Pollard, lay some arm on our new little friend here. He's manifesting antisocial behavior. It's time for a good dose of discipline."

"Yeah," Mikey hissed, spraying spittle with his urgency. "Teach the dirty nomad a lesson. Teach him *good*."

Chinless and Brown Hair advanced on Tristan, confident in their age and size. Tristan evaded the beefy brown-haired youth with a sidestep and then doubled Chinless with the toe of his hard uncomfortable Dorm-issue shoe in the balls.

He remembered Bro Weasel then, just as his father advised.

Billy really was fast. He managed to turn his face aside in time to save his nose. Instead Tristan fastened his sharp white teeth in the bigger youth's cheek, and hung on.

5

It was no great mystery why they called it the Hole.

Tristan tried to tell himself that the utter blackness of the solitary cell was no worse than the blinding-white and lifeless room he'd occupied in Sedgwick. He was a Plains nomad, accustomed to bright colors and fast motion and the play of sunlight and cloud-shadow across the endless grasslands. Blank whiteness was just as bad as the dark.

It was bullshit. He had been able to look around his Sedgwick room, to see the walls, uniform as they were, the rough blanket on his cot, the stout metal grille that covered the always-burning fluorescent light overhead. The Hole lay underground, in a tornado shelter overbuilt to survive the frequent earthquakes that rattled the Front Range. It wasn't just dark, it was utterly devoid of light; no matter how accustomed his eyes grew to the blackness, there was nothing to see.

For a child of the Plains it was torture.

It wasn't just being deprived of the feel and taste of the wind; that had happened at Sedgwick. Nor was it the deprivation of sight or sound—unless he made his own sound—or of any smell except dungeon damp and his own unwashed body. It wasn't even the awful sensation of being confined on all sides by solid walls, neither longer nor wider than his outstretched arms.

The worst thing was that he was trapped *underground*. In a

hole in the ground where a good tremor could seal him in forever and ever, no matter how well built it was. If nothing had
been learned in StarFall and since, it was that man could build
nothing at all that Nature couldn't knock down.

When he was first sealed into blackness he simply started
screaming. That continued until his voice wore out. Then he lay
huddled in a ball, knees to chin, arms over head, and his
thoughts were all bright lights and noise.

At some point he passed from near-madness into dream. His
mother waited, soothing him with loving words. Perhaps they
helped.

Then he dreamed of the lava waste. The glow now shone like
a tiny sun; he could scarcely bear to look at it.

He awakened screaming almost soundlessly.

In his mind he played as much as he could remember of all
the movies he had seen. He retold himself all the high and wide
Plains tales he knew, of Mavis Mankiller and the Scooter of
Gold, Snuffy Sublette at the Satan's Throat fight, how Electric
Bill won the One-Eyed Giant's daughter.

He called back the glories of his own lineage. How his grandfather, Anse the One-Eyed, had been sent by his clan-chief,
Nasty John of the Prairie Hawks, to the Heaving Lands to steal
WildFyre—the very last Carondelet bike, hand-built by Black
Bill Landrum, the greatest wrench of all time—from the Ko-
bold King. How he succeeded in his quest, only to receive a radio distress call, fortuitously skipped slantwise across the entire
Plains, that the Blackfeet had his clan surrounded on the Powder River.

It was fifteen hundred mostly roadless miles. Anse made it in
three days, earning his name Hardrider. When the surrounding
forces saw him appear in their rear, mounted on his legendary
prize, they took it as a sign. The Blackfeet's allies, the Cathead
MC, pulled back in consternation, leaving the disgruntled Siksika no choice but to let the Prairie Hawks go. And when the
well-named Nasty John finally made one mistake too many and
got himself and most of the Hawks massacred, the survivors decided to form a new clan with the hero Anse as head. Thus were
born the Hardriders.

Tristan remembered too the tale of how his own father, then
Wyatt Octane, had gone to the great Taos Rendezvous: a bold

young buck, son of a bro whose exploits were sung from the Missus Hip River to Medicine Hat, who had to get cracking and distinguish himself if he wanted to succeed his father as chief of the Hardriders. How he met there a sad and beautiful princess of the Smoking Mirror clan.

The Smoking Mirrors were universally feared, outlaws even by the freewheeling standards of the Plains, where plunder and violence were everyday occupations—heart-cutters, man-eaters, human sacrificers whose shamans danced in their victims' dripping skins. Monsters though they were, they enjoyed the absolute armistice of the Rendezvous, enforced on pain of torture and death by the Jicarillas and Dog Soldiers appointed by the attending clans.

But Rendezvous didn't last forever. On the trail back to their hideout in Chihuahua, the Smoking Mirrors camped three days south of Taos, below where the Rio Grande had turned into the River of Fire through the BlackLands. After dinner—beans and tortillas only; other clans made sure they left Rendezvous well ahead of the Mirrors, and headed in different directions—the maiden named Morning Star stepped away from the fire and her *dueña* to relieve her bladder. Instead she slipped over the hip of a hill, and in front of the sissy-bar of Wyatt Octane's cruiser Warrior.

The way in which Jen's cunning and Wyatt's skill at riding and fighting enabled them to escape the furious Smoking Mirrors—cross-country, where their scramblers were much faster than Warrior—had become an epic only slightly less popular than Anse's Hard Ride. . . .

Tristan quit thinking about the legends of his own clan then, even though there were many more. He knew the final story all too well.

Telling stories to himself got him through two bowls of gruel pushed through a panel in the base of his cell door. He knew they didn't give you three a day in the Hole, but whether they gave you two or only one, he didn't know. Whoever brought the slop was quiet as a coyote's shadow and knew the way by touch, because never a flicker of light showed.

He slept again. In his dream his father seemed pleased that he had fought well—and necessarily, this time, however hopeless it was—and also that Tristan was remembering the old tribal epics.

"You're still in the fight, boy," he said. "Remember that. When the Man has you down, you're on the front line."

"The City folk aren't intentionally being cruel," was Jen's word to her son. "They don't know any better. They don't realize how it wounds your spirit to trap you between walls like this. You mustn't let the weight of earth and concrete crush you, dear. You have the strength inside you to break forth and fly free like your brother the red-tailed hawk."

He had been in the City's lockups too long already, had picked up a taint of the Citizen's slick cynicism, because his mother's loving words rang, just faintly, of facile bullshit. But they must have helped, because he was able to face the far-off glow with only a thready pulse of fear in his chest. It seemed nearer, again. He tried walking toward it, across lava that cut at the feet of his moccasins like knives, but he could approach it no closer no matter how far he went.

He woke when another bowl of food, if you could call it that, came through the panel. He launched himself in a dive, but the panel slid soundlessly shut before he could reach it and he jammed his fingers for his pains.

His voice had come back, so he sang all the songs he could remember, the songs Jammer and Golden Marcia and the other bards had made, and also the ancient songs, handed down from generation to generation, that still stirred the soul though the meaning of half the words were strange: "Ach, Johnny I Hardly Knew Ye," "Born to Be Wild," "The Last Mile," "Copperhead Road."

When he was out of songs and his voice was sounding like sand in the gearbox again, Tristan tried building a bike in his head. Unfortunately, he was the second generation of Hardrider to bring despair to the clan's master wrench, Nick Blackhands. His father had learned enough to keep his sled functional, and handle very basic repairs. But to design and build a bike from the ground up was beyond him, and it was beyond his son as well.

Then he just sat, and the blackness and the loneliness pressed down on him as if he had Pike's Peak stacked on top of his damned tiny cell. He felt his mind beginning to fracture under all that weight.

He willed himself away. He didn't know where: just *away*. And suddenly he was.

He was lying by a gentle-voiced creek, with the earth warm on his back, the sun on his face, and the wind in his hair. One leg was drawn up: a long leg, the leg of a tall adult, encased in dust-colored trousers and knee-high tan boot.

He looked around. He could not move more than his eyes, or maybe he was afraid to try. He could see that he was wearing a faded olive-drab vest or T-shirt. A harness of some sort constricted his left side; he smelled leather and lubricants, and saw the butt of an unfamiliar kind of pistol jutting from his left armpit. Almost around the corner of his vision he saw a bike propped against the same slope he was lying on. The butt of a scabbarded carbine protruded above the far side of the seat.

He sighed. He was safe. He was free.

He tipped his head back. The sun was almost overhead. Almost between him and it a black shape wheeled, round-tipped wings and short broad tail outspread. A hawk. Red-tail.

Tristan laughed. His voice was deep, a stranger's voice, yet totally familiar. Maybe his mother's dream-saying wasn't all bullshit after all.

His body was still in the lightless pit beneath McGrory. His spirit was out here on the Plains, free, at peace. He knew that his spirit could find this place again anytime it needed respite. Just as he knew one day his body would find this place, the bank, the stream, the sun, and the hawk.

When they led him out of the Hole it took a monitor on either side to keep him on his feet. He had to keep his eyelids screwed tight shut. Though the day was black-overcast, the light stabbed his eyes like daggers.

One of the monitors told him he'd been down a week. *Kind of a long spell, boy, but just between you and me and these here walls, think they kind of wanted to make an impression.*

He knew they lied. They said a week. He knew it had been a lifetime.

6

Two nights after the summer solstice, when Tristan reckoned he'd been down two moons, he was jarred awake by the sound of an explosion.

He was down off the top bunk in a flash, the plank floor cold beneath his feet. He'd been transferred after he got out of the Hole; his new Dorm echoed with the frightened or curious cries of the other occupants. Some of them flocked to the windows, trying to crank the steel hail-shutters open farther so they could get a better look in case of fireworks. Others started pounding on the locked door, screaming to be let out before the Dorm caved in on them.

Normally Tristan would have been right there pounding with the best of them—his consistent nightmare since imprisonment was of being caught indoors in an earthquake. Instead he dropped to his belly and tried to wriggle under the bunk. This was the one time in the whole wide world when it made *sense* to be inside and under cover. He knew that sound too well—he thought.

He was wrong. He wasn't the only one to make that mistake. Later on he heard a rumor that Chief Administrator Dowell, a medicine-ball shaped man, had bowled over Assistant Administrator Hanrick during the stampede for the underground shelter—in the same place where they kept the Hole—and cracked his head wide open on the cement steps. The Administrators in their wisdom had figured they were under mortar attack by nomads, or maybe even a commando squad from Dallas. The Texans had been making threatening noises again.

The dorm was not locked until two hours after the normal time, at which point the occupants were in quite a state, most of them speculating as fast as their adolescent jaws would work, some of them just crying. A significant exception was Tristan, who after a tense period had decided that whatever the blast had been there weren't going to be any more, and had climbed back on his bunk to get some sleep. He had slept at shivarees and Rendezvous; *this* was nothing.

Before breakfast was even served they were herded off to the gym for Assembly. There a sheep-faced Sub-Administrator named Robertson revealed that the mystery blast last night had not been a terrorist attack on the Dorms, nor on the City. It had been the sound of a volcano blowing its top in the Cascades, in the Western FlameLands, a thousand miles away.

At least that was what the City's scientists had calculated, from what their seismographs told them. Nobody actually *lived* in the FlameLands. Nobody who would relay information to Homeland anyway.

So much his words said. His *tone* said nobody Homeland would want to hear from, and he paled visibly as he spoke. For once, Tristan sympathized with a Citizen.

The Eastern FlameLands weren't so bad—lava vents and geysers scattered around a godalmighty huge hole in the ground, fifty miles across, some said. Tristan's father had been in the fringes of that country, and Anse the One-Eyed had hidden there from another angry Blackfoot patrol, in the days before he stole WildFyre and won his name.

But further west—there were things living there it was worth a man's soul to see. You caught a glimpse of one, and it would haunt you to the last of your days, the old bros said. And maybe even after.

The next morning it looked as if snow had fallen in June. That wasn't really unlikely, but this snow was gray. It wasn't cold, and it wasn't wet. It looked and felt like cement.

What it was was ash from the volcanic explosion. Everybody

knew that, Tristan included; everybody west of the Mississippi
had seen plenty of the stuff. People east of the Great River were
only excluded because damn few travelers ever got back alive
to tell what people over there *had* seen.

His push broom across his shoulder, Tristan paused to stare at
the poster of a man's florid face and balding head, plastered on
a grimy alley wall. "John Amos Schenk for Mayor," he read
aloud, just for the practice.

"Hey there!" a monitor called from down the alley. "Move
along there. No dawdling."

Tristan laughed. After a week on ash detail, he knew Monitor
Steubens wasn't a genuine hardass, in spite of the long-barreled
Cherokee Pump 12-gauge he carried, ostensibly in case one of
the Dormies made a break for it. The second day out he had
confided in a low voice to Tristan that the thing wasn't even
loaded, as far as he knew. *He* didn't know how to load it anyway.

"Not that I'd need it to catch you and break that skinny neck
of yours if you try to run on me, you little bike tramp," he'd
added in a growl. Tristan had laughed then too.

Monitor Steuben came slogging up, wheezing, arms pump-
ing, the shotgun clutched in one fist like a rolled-up newspaper.
The ash had drifted to six inches in places in the alley, and it had
rained the last two nights, turning the stuff into muck.

He gouged the big poster with the muzzle of his shotgun.
"John Amos Schenk. *Fagh*." He spat, narrowly missing the
steel-reinforced toe of his work-boot. "What a weenie. John
Anus *Stink*, I call him."

"What's the matter with him, Steubie?" Tristan asked.

"He's a bleeding-heart limp dick, that's what's wrong with
him! Reconciliationist, he calls it. He wants us all to make nice
with every sag-nuts barbarian on the Plains. He has his way,
Homeland'll be over*run* with heathen biker rubbish just like
you. Now, haul butt, you miserable little polecat; we're already
way behind schedule."

He made as if to swat Tristan in the fanny with the butt of his
pump gun. Tristan dodged easily and ran off down the alley to
where the other boys in the work-gang were disappearing into

the back of a building, under the watchful eye of another monitor.

Maybe it wasn't pretty, but Tristan had evolved a push-broom technique that suited him. He wrapped one or both fists over the very tip of the handle, then rested it against his breastbone and just walked, using his mass to push the broom forward, driving a bow-wave of gray dust forward to join the mound being built up against the low fire rampart that ran around the roof.

The other kids bitched endlessly about ash detail. Tristan liked it fine. He was *out*, out in the air and rain and sometimes sun, out from between the walls of McGrory. So far he and the rest had all been watched too closely to bolt. But as Quicksilver Messenger had told him, *you never know*.

The ash gang also kept him from having to go to his daily sessions with the McGrory staff psychiatrist, Dr. Parkinson, who wanted to know the source of his hostility. Parkinson felt the deep Plains aversion to authority was rooted in fears of inadequacy. He had a severe tic that at intervals convulsed the right side of his face like a wildcat tremor. He was writing a monograph.

"Why the hell can't we just shovel this shit off the roof?" asked a kid leaning on his shovel to wipe sweat from his eyes. His hand left a track of gray mud across his forehead. "Why in hell we got to put it in *sacks*, for Christ's sake?"

"Because we've been instructed to, and good Citizens always follow instructions," said the tall, beak-nosed blond youth who had charge of the detail on this rooftop. "And I'll thank you to please watch your mouth. I'd hate to have to report you for cursing and blasphemy, not to mention questioning authority."

"Give it a rest, Lindemuth," another kid said. "No way you're gonna get adopted out by a deacon. You're way too old, and anyway they only go for girls. *Young* girls."

"Naw," the boy with the shovel said. "Lots of 'em like boys just fine. Trouble with Lindemuth is, he's too damned ugly."

Lindemuth went the color of liver. "That's it! That's it! What are your names? I'm going to report you both." He whipped a pencil and notebook from the breast pocket of his green Dorm shirt.

"Abbott," the shovel-handler said.

"Costello," said the other. Lindemuth scribbled furiously.

Tristan crunched back across the roof for a fresh broom-load. A boy fell into step beside him. To Tristan's surprise he was even shorter than Tristan.

"You think they gave him their real names?" the newcomer asked.

Tristan stopped, dropped his broom-head to the rooftop, and rested his palm atop the handle while he studied the boy. The kid had long hair for a Dormie, otter-brown, almost hanging in eyes of some color Tristan couldn't quite put a name to.

"Are you kidding? How long have you been down?"

"Down?" The boy frowned and shook his head.

"Inside."

"Longer than you," the boy said. "I'm Ferret."

"Tristan."

Ferret nodded his sharp face. "Yeah. You're the biker kid."

Tristan felt blood reach his face.

"Take it easy. We heard how you took down that blown-up dickwad Billy and pulled Hole time. It was pretty cool."

For some reason Tristan felt like looking at the toes of his shoes, which were naturally caked with gray crud. "Thanks."

"Yeah. Now listen. You're interested, we got something going."

"What?"

"Something."

"Oh."

"C Dorm, an hour after the chow line closes. Be there or be square."

7

Tristan did not need a Citizen to tell him whether he was or was not square. Still, he turned up at the time and place Ferret had said. Dorm C had a sinister reputation at McGrory. That right there was enough to recommend it to him.

At his knock a voice called, "Who is it?" through the closed door.

It was not a very welcoming voice, and suddenly Tristan felt foolish and unsure, as if he should know a secret password or something. "It's Tristan. Ah, Ferret said . . . he told me to come—"

The door opened just wide enough to admit him.

Inside was murky, half-lit. The lights in the Dorms were controlled from the Admin building, and there was no way at all to turn off part of the lights. Apparently some kid had scrambled up among the rafters and undone about three-quarters of the fluorescent bulbs, leaving them in place but dark. Tristan took two steps into the room and stopped.

The bunks had been pushed toward the walls to clear a space in the center of the barracks. That was startling enough; rearranging the furniture in the Dorms was strictly antisocial activity, and the Dormies he'd bunked with so far had never had the nuts to even think of such a thing, as far as he could tell.

"Yeah," said Ferret's soft voice behind him. "Terrible, isn't it? We're breaking *regulations*. Now watch this."

Two kids, both bigger than Tristan and bare from the waist up, were circling each other in the middle of the cleared space. The terrible intensity on their young faces told him they weren't just dancing.

Each was in a crouch, his left arm extended, right held close to his ribs. Each held something in his right hand, but whatever it was was small, and between the gloom and constant motion even Tristan's prairie-keen vision couldn't make it out.

They circled warily to the right. The dark boy's right hand darted forward. The blond boy caught the wrist with his left hand; his own right snaked out. The dark one whipped his left side back, opening with his left shoulder. By chance the corner of Tristan's vision, naturally following the attacking hand and the move to evade it, saw the dark boy's trapped hand twist in his opponent's grip.

A red line appeared down the inside of the blond boy's forearm. He let the other go, jerked his hand back. The dark boy came on, warding a panic-slash with his upraised forearm and earning his own red line. His right hand slashed across. A red line appeared across the blond boy's bare chest, above the nipples. It began to drip as he stepped away, lowering his head and clenching his fists with defeat.

The onlookers murmured approval. It came to Tristan that they had made virtually no noise during the bout. He had never seen a fight in which the spectators didn't hoot and holler and cheer their champions on, and often as not wind up trading blows or cuts themselves.

"This is practice," Ferret said. "We have matches weekly to see who's best."

"What do they fight with? I don't see any knives." The Dorms were frequently inspected by the monitors, and of course the Administration had snitches everywhere, and not just the officially recognized Dorm Wardens.

Ferret gestured. A spectator came over and held out his palm. Resting on it was a simple metal spoon from the cafeteria. A quarter inch or so of the tip had been sharpened into a point. The handle had been cut off and smoothed down so that when it was grasped, the whole spoon vanished in the fist except for the mirror-bright point.

"It's just a play knife," Tristan exclaimed. "It's not real."

Ferret and the others passed a knowing look around. "We're all buddies here. This is just practice. We're not looking to lay serious hurt on anybody."

Tristan grunted. He was disappointed. He had expected something mysterious and nefarious—the kind of thing that would appeal to *any* self-respecting eleven-year-old, not just one Plains-born. Instead he found more Citizen bullshit and games.

"What does your Dorm Warden say about this stuff?" he asked.

That got a good laugh. "He's right there," Ferret said, flipping a thumb at a tall jet-haired youth who had a moon face set atop a rail-thin body. The Warden nodded and grinned. "He's in it too—he's pretty slow, but that reach makes him tough."

"What happens when you get a Warden who ain't in on it?"

Ferret showed sharp teeth. "Usually he asks for a transfer pretty quick. Life isn't very *comfortable* for him."

Tristan watched two more bouts. Part of him was excited—this was a lot more lively than sweeping tons of ash off rooftops—but the bro in him remained studiously unimpressed. Yeah, it was quick and flashy. So what? It was all just kids' stuff. *City* kids' stuff.

When the second match was done Ferret turned to Tristan. "Okay. Want to try it with me?"

Tristan stared. This was insane. He was a warrior off the Plains; a knife was as natural to him as his scooter. His father was—had been—a stone artist with the blade. Tristan had seen him at work, and Wyatt Hardrider had taught his son a lot before he died.

He was being called out by a kid smaller than he was. A *City* kid. What could a Citizen brat know about iron? No Citizen was worth a damn in a fight unless he was inside a full-armored cage with a river gun hung off the front of it.

"It's okay," Ferret said, black eyes holding Tristan's like teeth. "You can't get hurt bad."

That did it. Next thing Tristan knew he was out in the middle of that floor, barefoot and bare-chested, with his silly-ass spoon in his hand.

"Okay, fish," the Dorm Warden said, "here's the rules. No going for the face or below the belt. No punching, kicking, tripping, gouging, or hair-pulling. This is *friendly*, just keep that in mind."

"No biting either," Ferret said easily. "I'm not Billy."

Everybody laughed. "No biting either. You got that, fish?"

"I got it." It was a lot of rules, but not excessive. Practice sessions among the Hardriders had similar restrictions. You couldn't have people getting seriously racked up in fighting practice, or you'd have no warriors functioning when the Catheads came shrieking out of the dawn.

Ferret hit a crouch, a similar fighting posture to what the others had used: knife back, free hand extended. *This is gonna be like riding down Diggers far gone on corn beer,* Tristan thought.

He took his own stance, right foot and right hand forward, feeling a little silly with no more sticking out of his fist than a quarter inch of sharp spoon. He looked at Ferret's eyes. The smaller boy stared fixedly at a point around Tristan's belly button. He was obviously awaiting his move.

Might as well get this over with, Tristan thought. He lunged forward on his right foot, striking for the chest.

Ferret's right hand flashed across his body. Pain blazed on the inside of Tristan's knife-arm as the spoon slashed him just above the wrist.

Plains pride and discipline kept him from crying out at the pain, though it stung like hell. He had been cut before. He knew no real damage had been done—these silly toy spoons *couldn't* hurt you bad, unless you caught one in the eye, and that was why there were rules against going for the face.

He expected Ferret to taunt him or at least give him a grin, but the smaller boy had just settled back into his crouch, weight forward on the balls of his feet, staring at the middle of Tristan.

Tristan ignored the blood welling on his right arm. *Time to try something different.* He bent low, holding his "blade" almost by his ankles, the way he'd seen fighters from the East do.

He expected Ferret to match him, protecting himself from a low-line attack. Instead Ferret lashed out for Tristan's collarbone. Reflexively Tristan whipped up his knife-hand. It had a long way to go, and when it reached his upper chest, Ferret's weapon wasn't there; the attack was a feint. Momentum carried Tristan's arm way up over his head.

Ferret stepped in and cut him diagonally across the chest.

This time Tristan had to bite down hard to hold back an exclamation of pain and frustration. "Game over," the Dorm Warden said.

Tristan skinned his lips back from his teeth. "Again."

The warden looked at Ferret. "It's cool," the small boy said.

They assumed their fighting positions once again. Tristan began to circle to his own right, to put pressure on Ferret's free hand. Ferret circled right along. Tristan kept his spoon to waist level this time.

The runt was devilish quick, Tristan had to admit. He could try to charge in on Ferret and power him back, but he knew if he did he'd get cut to ribbons. The thing to do was see if he could take out his knife-hand.

He tried a few phantom cuts with his spoon, not even serious feints, to see if Ferret was so wound he'd respond. The smaller boy never twitched.

So he can read me. Belatedly it was occurring to him that no matter how fake this spoon-play was, you could learn some real lessons from it if you worked it long enough. The body-language signals for an attack or a feint would be the same whether the blade in your hand was a quarter-inch long or a whole foot.

Righteous. He slashed high at Ferret's chest. Ferret started to hack for his arm. Tristan changed directions and slashed at the knife-hand.

Quick as thought Ferret's weapon hand flashed back away from danger. The motion opened him slightly, but his left hand came in to cover. Tristan didn't notice whatever opening was there; he was going to have that *hand*, dammit. He slashed furiously for it. Missed.

Ferret lunged at him. Tristan launched a wild defensive cut. Ferret took it across his left forearm. Tristan felt his tiny blade bite. His triumph was short-lived, because then Ferret slashed his belly, deep, from side to side.

It hurt like a stone mother. Tristan lost it. He just jumped on top of Ferret, knocked him to the floor, and started pounding on him.

Through the puffy slits of his eyelids Tristan could just barely make out the form of Assistant Administrator Hanrick, lost in the dazzle pouring in through his blinds. From his time outside the walls on ash detail he had become a bit more hip to details of civilized life such as buildings and windows, and he wondered at the extravagance of exposing such an expanse of glass to the mercy of the frequent savage hailstorms.

"Now, son," the Assistant Administrator said, steepling his fingers, "I'm going to ask you one more time. Who did this to you?"

Tristan shook his head. Doing that didn't make him want to throw up anymore. The boys of Dorm C had done a righteous job of dancing on him, but stomp survival was something a bro learned at an early age. He tucked into a ball and kept his head and nuts and fingers out of harm's way. Of course, by the time they got tired and dumped him in the Yard he wasn't in really *great* shape, but it could have been a semi-trailer-load worse.

"I don't think you understand, young man," Assistant Administrator Hanrick said. Usually Administrators addressed the inmates as *Mister So-and-so*—as opposed to the monitors, who usually just said, "Hey, minge-face." But Tristan was forbidden to call himself Hardrider anymore, and so had no official last name. "When you refuse to name the perpetrators of an antisocial act, you become an accomplice to that act. That's the law of civilized society. You may think these ruffians attacked *you*, but that's wrong, wrong, wrong. They attacked *society*. If you shield them by your silence, you are as guilty as they. So come on, do yourself a favor, and do your duty. *Tell* me."

He sat back. Tristan sensed the man's expectancy, and knew he was smiling encouragingly.

The Assistant Administrator clearly deserved a straight answer. "Up *yours*," Tristan said, as clearly as he could.

Being in the Hole wasn't quite so bad this time around. As soon as the door slammed on him he put his head back against the condensation-slimy wall, closed his eyes, and tried to summon up his sunlit creek.

And *bang*, he was there, with his bike parked beside him and the hawk wheeling in Father Sun's hot all-seeing eye.

When he slept his mother commiserated and his father praised his courage. "You can't let these City slimeballs show you up," he said.

For the first time Tristan found voice to answer back. "What about Bro Weasel?" he asked.

His father looked surprised, and for a moment Tristan thought the spirit was going to get pissed. Instead Wyatt nodded. "That's a fair question, son. Bro Weasel stays out of trouble when he can. But he's got his honor, he's got his pride, he's got his bros; he's got to show class. It's like with that big minge Billy—"

"Wyatt!" Jen Morningstar said sharply. She hated that word.

"That butt-stuffer Billy. Sometimes even Bro Weasel just has to do his best and take his stomping if that's what the Wind blows him."

That made sense, sort of.

Once again he tried trudging toward the glow, though even in dreams his body ached all over. It did no good, but he kept on until the vision vanished.

Awake again, he found himself with tears in his eyes because, of all things under Mother Sky, he missed his best friend Jamie. It wasn't that she was a *girl*. She wasn't one. Okay, she was, but she didn't *act* any different than a boy, and she didn't *look* any different, so what was the difference?

The point was, she was his *friend*. Somebody he could talk to and run with and just be Tristan with. He didn't have that now, inside the Hole or out.

He wished he could dream of her. And then he stopped himself, horrified. He dreamed only of the dead. But he'd wished to dream of Jamie. Did that mean he'd wished *her* dead? On the Plains they knew that wishes, like dreams, had Power. Wishes often came true.

He squeezed himself into a ball, though it made his cuts and bruises start throbbing all over. *Nononono!* he thought, in case any Powers or spirits were listening in. *I don't mean it! Don't make Jamie die, don't make me make her die!*

It was just perfect. He'd had the crap kicked out of him. He was buried in a black pit underground. And now he couldn't so much as *think* of his best friend, for fear of killing her.

His karma clearly sucked.

They kept him down only two days this time. Refusing to take a snitch jacket was, after all, a less heinous crime than biting a chunk out of a duly constituted Dorm Warden.

It had hailed while he was in the Hole, a real head-banger. While he was being supported out of the shelter he saw men working, fitting a new sheet of glass to the Assistant Administrator's office, and there were still drifts of fist-sized hailstones piled up against the walls, melting slowly together. Sometimes a bad volcanic eruption just made the weather crazy all over the Plains, as if Mother Sky was cranked at getting thrown up on. Then again, the line where the Plains fetched up against the Rockies got bad storms all the time without any help from the fire-spewers.

There was still ash waiting to be removed—it would take at least a moon to get rid of it all—but today the McGrory boys were pressed into the more urgent job of policing up the shattered glass that lay in glittering patches all over town.

He was plying his broom in front of a clothing store down on Civic Duty Drive—nothing in there *he'd* wear to see dogs fight, and that was a fact—when he felt someone sidle up beside him.

"You didn't snitch."

He glanced over. Ferret was sweeping away, right at his side. "We kicked your ass pretty good," the smaller boy said.

"Reckon you did."

"You did time in the Hole. Why didn't you turn us over?"

He felt like just blowing him off. Actually, he felt like cracking him a good one over the head with his broom, but he had a feeling Bro Weasel wouldn't go for that. Not much class shown in beating up smaller boys with brooms anyway.

"A bro never tells the Man nothin'," he said from the corner of his mouth.

Ferret grinned. "Right answer. Now, do you have any idea why we stomped you?"

Tristan sighed. "Because I jumped your shit. I broke the rules." He spat. "I don't like fuckin' *rules*."

"Hey, these aren't the Man's regs we're talking about. You agreed to our rules up front. Didn't you have rules in your bike gang?"

"Well . . . yeah."

"And people had to agree to abide by the rules if they wanted to join?"

Tristan nodded. His thighs and butt and what he could see of his back still looked like a bad potato. He was starting to ache all over again.

"So what happened if people broke your rules?"

"We kicked 'em out. Sometimes we kicked their butts first."

"So we kicked yours. But you took the Hole instead of ratting us off. That's cool. We took a vote and decided to ask you in. You can run with us . . . *if* you stick to our rules."

Tristan stopped and looked at him. Emotions fought furiously inside him. He wanted to say something that would show this slimy City tadpole just what he thought of him and his Dorm gang.

Also he wanted to run with them. So badly it almost choked him.

"Why should I wanna run with you?" he finally made himself ask.

Ferret grinned. "Maybe you could learn a thing or two," he said.

8

When he was fourteen Tristan was adopted out of McGrory Center.

In the intervening years he'd done a mess of growing, as the saying went. From the smallest boy in McGrory, except for his friend Ferret, he had shot up to be the tallest kid in Dorm C. Somebody else was the Dorm Warden—the rules said Dorm Wardens had to be sixteen—but by the time he left, Tristan was the dominant figure in the Dorm's nameless underground.

For a time it had been Ferret. Despite his size Ferret was two years older than Tristan, and his wits were quick as his hands. Still, after the turn of Tristan's third year of captivity the news came that Ferret was being adopted.

"Well, good for you, hoss," Tristan said as they sat on his bunk—a lower bunk—in the deserted Dorm that afternoon. Tristan was doing his best to hide his confused hurt. Ferret had become his best friend—his only real friend, though the others in Dorm C were comrades, and even the fish—the newbies— knew how he'd gone in the Hole rather than rat on them. But that was different, though Tristan couldn't articulate exactly how, even to himself.

Now he was losing Ferret. It seemed that everyone he loved, he lost. "At least you're out of this shithole early," he said in a clotted voice.

Ferret's dark face twisted savagely. "Bullshit."

"What do you mean? Ain't you happy? You'll be *free*."
When he said the word it was like tasting chocolate after you
hadn't had any for years.

"Free? *Free?* What the fuck do you know?"

His fury stunned Tristan. "But I thought—"

"You *thought*. We all know what good it does when a bike
tramp tries to *think*."

Tristan bit down hard on the inside of his cheek. Ferret was
his blood brother. To strike him would be about the lowest thing
a man could do. No matter what he'd said.

"I don't understand," he said in as neutral a tone as he could
muster. "What's wrong with getting out of here?"

Ferret sighed. "It's the same old scam. Adoption terms are,
you're bound till you're seventeen or for five years, *whichever's
longer*. By waiting until I turned sixteen, they got themselves a
near-adult worker, and they get my ass until I'm twenty-one."

Ferret jumped off the bunk. "Listen to me, nomad," he said,
keeping his pointy dark face averted. "You've learned to act
real civilized since you came here. But let me tell you something. *Never trust the City.* You might find a man you can trust,
maybe even a woman if you're the luckiest man on legs. That's
fine. But whatever happens, don't trust the City. *Ever.*"

He ran out then, without a backward look or a good-bye. Because inmates didn't have property inside McGrory he had no
things to come back for. Tristan didn't see him again.

His last memory of Ferret made Tristan feel real good when,
just over two moons later, he got called in after a full day of
helping install boilers for a new fuel-alcohol distillation plant to
hear old Hanrick, now Deputy Chief Administrator, say his own
adoption had gone through.

His adoptive parents were the Tomlinsons, Bruce and Eileen. If
he had ever had nightmares about what it would be like to be
adopted by Citizens, the couple would have starred in them.

The living room was a horror of chintz curtains and matching
sofa, and chairs with reddish-pink floral patterns on them and
scrolled wooden legs, and delicate tables with little lacy covers
on them, and samplers saying HOME SWEET HOME and
OUR LOVE NEST on the walls beside amateurish paintings of
streams and mountains and the Plains under snow. By one of the

chairs sat a wicker basket, piled with balls of yarn and knitting needles, and on the table next to it was a little stuffed dog with a red and white checked body used for a pincushion and a thimble cradled between its forepaws. Flanking the fireplace were shelves, on which were pictures of the Tomlinsons in their younger days—Eileen, apple-cheeked even then, beside a toothily smiling Bruce, skinny and skinny-headed in his white-sidewall haircut and Homeland Defense Force tunic and garrison cap—and little silver statues each showing a manlike figure holding a long thin club with a knobbed end cocked over one shoulder, and painted ceramic birds.

And in the midst of everything stood the Tomlinsons, stocky starchy gray people, beaming at Tristan as if he'd descended from the heavens on a ramp of gold.

Bubbling up inside him was the urge to *smash*. To sweep the cloying alien clutter off the shelves and walls with the wicked-looking black poker on its rack on the hearth. To mash those round glowing faces. These were Citizens, the ancient enemy, and their smug snug constricted lives were the antithesis of everything the High Free Folk lived for and by.

But he could not carry out his impulse. Two burly City cops stood flanking him, keeping a firm grip on his arms and flicking knowing glances at him behind their green sunglasses.

Mrs. Tomlinson wrung her plump hands. White hands, soft hands, the hands of a woman who never scraped a hide or set a broken leg. "Oh, *Tristan*," she cooed. "I can't *tell* you how wonderful it is that you've come to live with us. And what a *lovely* name."

The cop on Tristan's left dug his steely fingertips into the muscle just above the elbow, momentarily immobilizing him with pain. Tristan swallowed and set his jaw. Mr. Tomlinson smiled vaguely past his wife and nodded.

"Why don't I leave you menfolk to handle the final details while I take Tristan up to see his room?" Mrs. Tomlinson asked, wiping her hands on her apron.

The troopers frowned. One of them started to speak. Mrs. Tomlinson broke in. "Oh, tush! We'll be fine. I'm his new mother."

As he followed her up the stairs he kept his eyes focused on the knot of her apron, in the small of her broad back. *My mother*

STORMRIDER 65

isn't a waddling tub of suet, he thought savagely. *My mother is tall and slender as a willow, beautiful as sunset on the Musselshell.*

He should probably break her neck. He could do it easily enough. After he'd started to get his growth McGrory began farming him out on hard-labor jobs, construction crews, heavy-machinery maintenance, road gangs. He was still adolescent-coltish, his muscles wiry rather than bulky, but his wrists were as thick as his forearms.

He should do it, but he didn't.

Up the stairs and down a short, indecently cheery hallway. Mrs. Tomlinson stood by a door and, smiling in triumph, swung it open. Unable to help himself, Tristan looked inside.

The Tomlinsons hadn't had much advance warning as to the exact age of the child they were being assigned for adoption. The City did not believe in coddling Clients. After months of form-fillings, hearings, and endless waiting, they had only been informed yesterday that their request to adopt a City ward was approved. They'd first known what they were getting when they saw Tristan, standing on their doorstep with his wrists and ankles sticking out of the too-short civilian clothes they had thrown at him in McGrory after a hurried shower.

Also, the Tomlinsons had no prior experience of child-rearing. They were making things up as they went along.

A wood-and-paper model airplane hung from the ceiling, not of one of the squatty, timid modern craft that made rare dashes from point to point during lulls in the killer winds, but an ancient machine, streamlined, elegant, fast, and feral-looking from the pointed spinner of its propeller to the rounded tail. On shelves were primers and picture books, on the floor toy trucks, and sitting on the big plump pillow by the carved wood headboard was a compact stuffed bear. The Tomlinsons were trying to cover all the bases.

Moving slowly, as in a dream, Tristan walked to the bed. He stood looking down for a moment, then picked up the bear. It was a small grizzly in a standing position, its black button eyes almost lost in short, soft, brown fur.

He felt an urge to twist the thing's head off. Instead he held it up.

"Huh—" His first attempt at speech sounded like a wheel with a bad bearing. He cleared his throat. "What is this?"

"Why, that's yours. I thought it was simply adorable, and Bruce approved it as sufficiently masculine. Don't you like it? I was afraid it might not be old enough for you, but we didn't know for sure."

He said nothing. He just walked past her out of the room.

The two policemen seemed reluctant to leave the Tomlinsons to the tender mercies of their new "son." But Mr. Tomlinson assured them again and again that everything would be fine. Eventually the cops shrugged; they'd done their job. If the Clients wanted to do crazy stuff . . . well, that was why the City needed a strong government. To pick up the pieces when Citizens made a mess of their own lives. The officers said their good-byes and left.

Mrs. Tomlinson glanced out the window. Sickly sunlight was slanting in almost horizontally beneath steel-colored clouds. "Oh, my," she said. "It looks as if it's time for dinner."

The timing, she thought, was very fortunate indeed. There was nothing like a good old-fashioned home-cooked meal to break the ice, she fervently believed.

Dinner started with a salad of lettuce mixed with green onions, fine-chopped cauliflower, rich red tomatoes the Tomlinsons were proud to have grown themselves, and radishes, dressed with vinegar and oil. Then Mrs. Tomlinson served pork chops and mashed potatoes under gravy, green peas, corn on the cob, and fragrant rolls, light as cottonwood cotton, that steamed when you broke them open. To drink there was lemonade, fresh-squeezed by Mr. Tomlinson's own hands in an odd metal contraption with a long lever arm. Even Tristan knew that was a considerable luxury; lemons came from the holdings of the City of Dallas, and Dallas was on no good terms with Homeland. The goods that passed between them, legally and otherwise, cost dearly, and not just because of the depredations of the High Free Folk.

Tristan hesitated when Mrs. Tomlinson first ladled his plate full. He had eaten most of the proffered foods before, but never in this combination, or prepared this way. It was all alien. He was sure he wouldn't like it.

And then the smell penetrated his belly by way of his nostrils.

And his belly realized that it hadn't felt truly full in three years, and what it had gotten hadn't been very good.

The capable if soft hands of Mrs. Tomlinson had set out enough food to feed a mechanized cavalry squad. By the time Tristan came up for air, she and her husband had finished a modest plate apiece, and all the food was gone.

"I hope you left room for dessert, son," Mr. Tomlinson said with a wink. "The Missus makes a mean pumpkin pie."

To his surprise, Tristan, who'd thought the only thing he could do was waddle off in the bushes and stick his finger down his throat the way the bros sometimes did at Rendezvous, did have room left. He ate two pieces of the pie.

When the meal was done the day was too. The stars were shining for once as Mrs. Tomlinson cleared the dishes. She hummed cheerful tunes as she washed them in the sink. Her husband sat in the dining room with Tristan, smiling. He didn't look at Tristan overmuch, and he didn't speak to him. Just sat and let him be.

When Mrs. Tomlinson was finished in the kitchen she came bustling back in smelling of soapy water. "You must be exhausted, dear. Why don't you go on up to your room now and go to bed?"

He stood up, suddenly feeling uncertain and acutely self-conscious. He had eaten bread and salt with these people. A Plains nomad took hospitality as seriously as he took his bike and his honor. He was bound not to harm them unless they treacherously tried to do him harm, and to defend them from harm should it be offered. That didn't leave him clear as to what he *should* do.

Mrs. Tomlinson came bustling round the table then, threw her arms around him, and hugged him tight. "Tristan, dear, it's so wonderful to have you here. Isn't that so, Father?"

Mr. Tomlinson nodded.

"It means so much to us to have you here. You make us very happy." She looked up at him with tears in her blue eyes. "We'll do everything we can to try and make you happy." She stood on tiptoe to kiss his cheek.

He had grown up with plenty of physical affection. The High Free Folk were highly demonstrative, as they were highly emotional—among their own kind. But Tristan had not been hugged since his mother had laid aside her Absaroka carbine briefly to embrace him on the hilltop that morning three years ago. He had never even hugged Ferret; kids that age were very touchy about appearances, especially in the Dorms.

He turned and ran, up the stairs and into his room.

Mr. and Mrs. Tomlinson came up to look in on him later. When Mrs. Tomlinson threw a spare comforter over the boy to keep him warm against the chill of a spring night, he was curled up asleep with the little grizzly in his arms, its artificial fur damp with tears.

9

No chains bound him to the Tomlinsons' house, pleasant and white and two stories high as though the winds and earthquakes never happened. He had a lock on the door of his upstairs room, but it worked from the inside.

Accustomed to the Dorms' ironclad schedule he rose early. The Tomlinsons were up before him, Mr. Tomlinson reading the morning newspaper and preparing to go to work at some job Tristan could not really comprehend, his wife fixing breakfast in a cheery bustle. After a glance into the kitchen Tristan slipped unnoticed out the front door.

The sky was beige and pink, shading to slate overhead. The pitched roofs of the houses on the tree-lined block kept him from seeing the Plains stretching away to the rising sun.

That didn't have to be a problem. He could walk where he pleased. He could walk to the end of the block and look. He could walk east, to meet the sun. Maybe he wouldn't get picked up, maybe he could slip somehow through the wire-tangle perimeter hung like a necklace around Homeland. Maybe he would find friends out there, bros scoping the City defenses, someone who remembered the Hardriders, if any still did. *Maybe* . . .

"Tristan!" he heard Mrs. Tomlinson's voice call from within the white house. "Tristan, honey, breakfast's ready."

He turned and went inside.

• • •

Tristan began attending Roosevelt Middle School. It was an easy enough transition. School meant regimentation, and his Plains spirit rebelled against that, but he had long ago learned to keep that rebellion inside. Compared to the Dorms, school was a breeze.

In City terms he was ignorant. On the Plains he had learned to read and write, to play music and sing the songs of the bards. But beyond that his education had run to the skills of road and field, riding, wrenching, shooting, hunting, tending the herds, repairing tents and clothing, learning the ways of Wind and Sky and Earth. His math skills were rudimentary, and the closest he came to science was Plains magic and Plains mechanics. While he knew many of the songs and sagas of the High Free Folk, he knew little of what the City thought of as history.

He was placed in a special education class, along with two dozen other students who could not quite keep up with their fellows physically or mentally—blind children, children slow of speech and thought, children who could not walk but had to push themselves around on little carts, all called "special" and tossed in a bin together.

It made him feel a little eerie at first. He had never seen severely impaired children before. They did not survive long on the Plains.

He did sense that the other children at his school thought he was one of them, himself *impaired* in some sense. Contrary devil that he was, his reflex therefore was to identify with his classmates, an outcast among outcasts. The other kids quickly learned not to play too rough with the children in the "special" classes.

Tristan went through a growing spurt that year, so that he was soon the tallest boy in his grade, rangy and quick as a whip. And while the rules frowned on fighting among pupils, and punished self-defense as vigorously as aggression, if not more so, those in charge of enforcing them—the teachers—were mainly gentle, Health-minded types, not Strength supporters who prided themselves on their hard-nosed ways. They felt a strong sympathy for their "special" students. On the few occasions Tristan had to manhandle someone for abusing those students, the relevant paperwork—which might have seen him shipped back to the Dorms or worse—somehow never got filed.

Once Tristan's mates in the "special" class realized that this half-wild outsider with the dark hair and meltwater-pale eyes was not going to be another tormentor, but indeed a friend and protector, they opened to him. Not all of them were slow learners; the most intelligent child in school, at least in the teachers' opinion, was one of his classmates, an overweight pasty-skinned blond girl who could not walk without metal crutches. Like Tristan, Doreen had been lumped with the "special" class by virtue of being different. With her and others to help him along, Tristan quickly learned the things he was supposed to know—so quickly that he wondered why it was students had to go to school for nine years to learn it.

He didn't ask. Some instructors permitted students to ask questions about the subjects, instead of insisting that they should obtain all that they were supposed to know from the rigidly scheduled program of instruction. But asking questions about the system was never encouraged. You were even supposed to tell on your classmates if they did it—or on yourself, at the weekly self-criticism sessions.

In the Dorms Tristan had learned very early indeed that the best way to deal with the Man's system was to stay out of its way—not to be seen by it at all. It surprised him how few of his classmates had absorbed that lesson—and not just in the "special" section.

Tristan encountered several boys he knew from the Dorms who like him had been let out for adoption. They acknowledged each other with nods and secret glances; Dorm life did not produce much in the way of lasting friendships, nor a tendency to physical demonstrativeness. It did produce a bond, though. In very special circumstances, Tristan understood, he could rely on his former comrades. And they on him.

There was one exception to the lack of lasting friendships. Tristan began searching for Ferret as soon as he got adopted out.

He didn't know who had picked up his friend's option. Worse, he had never learned Ferret's real name. And the Man's system, needless to say, did not keep track of its Clients by their underground nicknames. He kept trying, but it was useless. Not even the network of former Dorm rats could turn up the one true friend he'd known since the death of his clan.

The year rolled around to fall. Time came for Tristan to advance a grade. And suddenly the rules changed again.

"What do we have here?" the wiry youth with the close-cropped brown hair said.

"Looks like Plains trash pretending to be a Client," his big blond companion answered.

The study hall was a large room whose cement walls and low fluorescent-paneled ceilings gave Tristan the claustrophobic impression of being buried underground, even though the room was on the second floor. The gray walls, which still had on them the marks of the forms into which they had been poured, were covered with posters shouting YOU ARE THE CITY'S EYES AND EARS! and LIVE RESPONSIBLY! Others showed clean-cut children with their backs pressed to walls, peering around the corner at dark figures transacting illicit business, which could be anything from trading marbles—any kind of trading was forbidden to juveniles—to vending outlawed drugs like chocolate and tobacco, to selling City secrets to Dallas spies. WHAT YOU SEE, TELL! these said. Others bore the slogan of the liberal Health Party: SHARING, SAFETY, SECURITY.

Long tables surrounded by chairs lay in precise rows under the nervous glare of the lights and the informing poster kids. The tables had begun emptying rapidly with the sound of the bell. Near Tristan they had achieved a near-vacuum with the appearance of the trio of older youths in red, white, and black letter jackets in a semicircle around him.

The third youth, who was stocky and dark, held his nose. "Trash actin' like trash."

The blond boy, whose hair was shaved to a silvery plush, and whose muscular chest was stuffed into a white T-shirt bearing the conservative Strength Party slogan, SECURITY, SAFETY, SHARING, slapped the third boy's thick shoulder. "Don't go getting above yourself now, Halt. You're a Client too, remember."

Halt glanced around, a lock of black hair hanging down his

forehead, grinning a loose you-guys're-kidding-me grin. He was shy a front tooth.

"Hey, we're almost Admin," he said defensively. "My dad's a big contractor. He does a lot of business with the Council. He could be a Councillor too, if he wanted."

"Sure, Halt, sure," the wiry boy who had opened the conversation said. "Brace, lighten up. We're discussing what we almost stepped in here, remember?"

Tristan continued gathering his books and papers together, ignoring the three. He felt a dark knot in the pit of his belly, acid and cold. At the front of the room he could see the study period monitor, Mr. Higgs, craning in his direction, his face, looking like a white balloon with a little mustache inked on, bobbing anxiously above his collar and tie. Tristan expected no help from that direction; a teacher got down-rated if he reported disturbances in his classes or study periods.

"So, bug-teeth, what do you think you're doing, smelling up the place where real civilized people are supposed to be studying?" the brown-haired youth demanded.

Tristan started to walk right past him. He moved quickly, and so purposefully that he was between the ringleader and the blond henchman on his right before either could react.

A hand caught his shoulder and spun him. He resisted the urge to bat it away. "Hey, bike trash, I'm talking to you," the brown-haired youth said. "Don't you know who I am? I'm Dirk Posten. My dad's Bob Posten. He's on the City Council. He'll be Mayor someday. Don't you watch TV? I can make big trouble for you."

"Naw, Dirk," Halt said. "He don't watch TV. Scooter trash ain't bright enough."

Without replying Tristan turned to leave again. He walked into the broad chest of Brace. *Important lesson*, he thought. *Never lose track of your opponents.*

Brace turned him around to face Dirk, who was right up in front of him. "You think you're as good as the rest of us, don't you?" He poked Tristan painfully in the shoulder with stiffened fingers. *"Don't you?"*

Right and wrong were different in the City than on the Plains. Outside, a man—or woman—could defend himself against aggressors, and people would not just accept but approve. A

Stormrider was *expected* to hold his ground or hers, except in the face of overwhelming odds, when retreat was a legitimate ruse of war.

Like now, Tristan reminded himself, swallowing rage. And fear. Fear not of what these three might do to him, but of what would happen if they pushed him so hard he couldn't contain his fury any longer.

Because in the City's skewed, harsh logic, self-defense was a worse crime than aggression. As their Civic Studies lessons repeated over and over, the individual had no rights against the *community*, the City. To defend yourself was to assert yourself, to claim that which the law denied you.

Remember the Dorms, son, he heard his father's voice say. *Remember Trickster Charlie.* Except it might not be to the Dorms this time; Tristan was older now, and getting big, and if he were judged incorrigible enough he could be sent to the living death of the Black Gang. Or he might face Rehabilitation. Horror stories whispered in Dorm and schoolyard, reinforced by watching slack-jawed Rehab subjects in grimy pastel jumpsuits shuffling about their menial tasks, reacting with empty-eyed confusion to the taunts of packs of children, made Tristan wonder if Rehabilitation wasn't even worse than grubbing in the mines beneath Hellville, waiting for a quake to shake a mountain down on top of you. He kept his hands carefully by his sides.

Realizing his victim wasn't going to fight, Dirk smiled and raised his hand again. "Don't you boys have classes you have to get to?" Mr. Higgs's voice inquired from over his shoulder, with barely a quaver.

Dirk turned away with a snarl. Higgs fell back a step, belly jiggling. He raised a soft white hand.

"You don't want to get in trouble for reporting in tardy, Dirk," he said. "Please."

Tristan took the break in focus as an opportunity to firm his grip on his schoolbooks and scoot between his tormentors. He broke into a run, eyes filling with hot tears of rage and humiliation.

Behind him he heard Dirk's sotto voce grumble, "Biker lover." But he heard no pursuit. He was getting clean away.

This time.

10

"These are the stacks," the voice said. It rang like an axe-handle off a stone.

Hunched over an outspread City newspaper with photographs as large-pored as a day-laborer's nose, Tristan jumped, spattering drops of rain from his still-soaked hair. He was mightily uncomfortable to begin with. The Public Library was a huge brick building north of the center of town. It made Tristan's skin crawl to go inside it. Even with all the time he'd spent among walls, he could not feel comfortable having all that weight surrounding him. If an epic thunderstorm hadn't been breaking against the Front Range he might not have been able to make himself enter.

"The stacks are for adults," the voice said. "You aren't an adult, are you?"

That struck Tristan as a purely dumb thing to say. Before he could react, there was this *hand* groping all along the side of his face. He felt shock—*what's going on here?*—and turned in his uncomfortable wooden chair, ready to snap, *What are you, blind?*

The man was, clearly. He was a tall, gaunt old man with a bowtie and a brown suit that looked as if he'd wadded it in his hands before putting it on. His skin was a yellowish brown, and where it stretched taut across his forehead and his cheeks it shone like a polished cypress knee. His hair was a short black brush that came down in a suggestion of a widow's peak. The eyes were pale amber, and stared off past the top of Tristan's head in a way that said they saw nothing.

Tristan scrambled to his feet, his smartass remark sticking sideways in his throat. On the Plains blind people were thought to be under the personal protection of Sister Moon. To mess with them invited heavy shit.

"No, sir," the boy said. "I'm studying."

The man stared past him, off between the dusty-musty shelves of books. Tristan found it unnerving. "Do you have a pass?" the man asked.

"Uh—yes, sir." He had long ago learned to use the honorific without thinking. Long before his captivity began, the campfire tales had taught him that the wise bro didn't piss off the Man injudiciously. He didn't say *sir* to this man just for that reason, nor because deep down he couldn't squash the silly superstitious fear that a goddess of the Plains would yank a knot in his wing-wang if he didn't show proper respect. He wasn't entirely sure why he used the word.

He held up the Library pass Mr. Higgs had given him. "Here, sir."

His reflex was still to run. The shelves were cliffs faced in dusty bindings, hemming him in, but he could scale them easily, his natural agility boosted by panic. But they ran ceiling-high; no escape there.

His snap decision to hang around and await events almost crumpled with the paper of his pass as the old man wadded it and threw it down beside the brightly polished brown toes of his shoes. "They send their troublemakers here, to get them out of the way. They *try*. I don't tolerate mischief here."

He swiveled his head to stare at Tristan with those blind, blank eyes. Tristan found the sudden directness unnerving. "Well? What school are you from? Kennedy High? Bush? Gates?"

"K-Kennedy, sir."

The old man looked him up and down, blind-eyed. "You're big for the pitch of your voice. How old are you, boy?"

"Fifteen."

"No *sir*, this time? My, we're getting our confidence back nicely, aren't we?"

Tristan shrank.

"Are you a troublemaker, boy?"

Tristan's Civic Sciences teacher had packed him off during study period with a school-leaving pass, and a Library pass, and Brother Wind knows what other passes, in a thick envelope colored the gray of City business. Tristan had been doing his best of late to stay out of the way of Dirk Posten and associates. He suspected Mr. Higgs, mindful of his own efficiency rating, had decided to lend a pudgy white hand.

"No, sir. At least, I don't try to be."

The old man stared past him for a moment. He nodded. "You sound sincere anyway. I'm probably turning soft as I get older. What are you looking for?"

"Ah, I'm supposed to be doing a report on the upcoming mayoral elections, on the differences in platform between the Strength and Health Parties—"

The old man snorted. "Hogwash."

Emotions warred within Tristan, reflexes learned painfully over four years of captivity telling him one thing, his Plains pride telling him another. *I can't minge up now. I can't stand going back to the Dorms.* Or to the Black Gang, toiling in the mines beneath the lofty, treacherous mountains to the west, waiting for a quake to shake them down on top of him.

"Sir," he made himself say evenly, "I'm telling the truth. My assignment really is—"

"I know that, son. I was just snorting at the make-work they're passing out these days in lieu of actually teaching anything. It'd be dangerous to have the rising generation actually learn something, in the unlikely event they could find somebody who knows enough to teach it to them. Here, let me look at you."

Before Tristan could react the old man had put one of his hands on his face again. The fingers were long, hard, and brown, dry as sticks, and reminded him of a walking-stick insect he'd seen once years and years ago, when the Hardriders were cruising Osage country not far from the Big River. He kept himself from flinching and held himself erect.

"You don't pull away? Good, good. You've got backbone, and more important, you don't shy away from the unfamiliar." The old man smelled of some City liniment, a harsh, astringent odor that ran up Tristan's nostrils like a Sparrowhawk knife-blade.

"There's something different about you, boy. About your bearing, your accent. You're not from the City, are you?"

Tristan flicked a glance at him between knobbed brown fingers. "No, sir."

"Where then?"

"I'm . . . from the Plains."

"A Stormrider then?"

Tristan blinked, amazed that a mere Citizen knew the High Free Folk by that name. He almost forgot to answer. "Yes, sir."

"I remember now. It was several years ago . . . four. A nomad band raiding near Homeland was wiped out. A boy was the only survivor. You're that boy?"

Tristan nodded.

The hand left his face. "Well, then. I understand what's different now. They haven't had a chance to ruin you altogether yet. Come."

The old man walked away between the cliffs of books. He moved as confidently as if he possessed his sight; the only thing that seemed to hold him back was the arthritic knobbing of his joints. Tristan held back.

The old man turned. "Don't worry, boy. There's not a chit's worth of difference between Strength and Health. Both of them want to run our lives down to the slightest detail; Strength in the name of God, Health in the name of Psychiatry. It all comes to the same in the end."

Tristan still hesitated. "Come *on*," the old man insisted, with a rolling imperious wave of his insectile fingers. "This won't take long. I'll let you get back to your precious schoolwork soon enough. But first you must come with me."

Still doubtful, Tristan followed. Outside the storm rampaged like a wounded buffalo bull. Tristan could see the flashes of lightning through the high south-facing clerestory, could feel the rumble of thunder in his bones.

"What do you see around you?" the old man asked with a circular sweep of his hand. He walked without hesitation or aid, as if his muscles remembered every foot of path between the stacks.

"Books," Tristan said, wondering if this was a trick question.

"Books indeed. The sum total of the race's knowledge. Poetry, arts, science, history. A surprising amount of it's survived, all things considered. If anyone paid attention anymore."

They walked in silence punctuated only by the shouts of the storm, muffled by the Library's thick walls. Tristan kept turning his head dutifully right and left. There were a lot of books here, no doubt about it. But what did the old man mean by showing them to him?

They reached a clear expanse of floor paved in flagstones the color of a fresh-killed whitetail liver. A heavy wooden table was set here, surrounded by straight-backed wood chairs, under the irritable gaze of a portrait of a massive pink-faced man with poufy white hair, wearing outlandish clothes. The old man turned and faced him again.

"What are you thinking, boy?"

Tristan licked his lips, his mind seeking the familiar pathways of Dorm evasion. *Never tell the Man the truth.* The City boys down by law or psychiatry were a lot like bros in their outlook, but through harsh practicality rather than honor.

"You don't have to lie to me, boy. I won't punish you for the truth."

He'd heard *that* one before. Something defiant reared up in him, though, and he said, "Well, I mean—what's the point?"

The old man set his jaw, and leaned his skinny rump back against the edge of the table. "Remember," he said, apparently to himself, "this one has an excuse for being empty-headed. At least they haven't filled his brain to capacity with nonsense yet."

He looked Tristan in the face again, finding the boy's gray-blue eyes with his blind ones with unerring accuracy. "Where d'you come from, boy? Haven't you ever wondered that?"

"I know where I come from. I was born free along the Musselshell, in the year Valle Grande blew again, wiped out a whole band of Comanche in the Staked Plains near Rabbit Ears."

"And before that?"

Tristan's forehead creased. It took him a moment to make sense of the question. "Wyatt Hardrider was my father,

Hardrider of the Hardriders. Jen Morningstar was my mother. He stole her from the Smoking Mirrors. Of course, she helped a lot—"

"And before that?"

"My father's father was Anse the One-Eyed, the first Hardrider."

"And before that?"

"Before . . ." Tristan moistened his lips again. "Well, I can't rightly say. . . ."

"So. You know two generations of your own background. Who were your people before this grandfather of yours, this Anse the One-Eyed? Where were they? *What* were they?"

Who cares bubbled up behind Tristan's lips. He didn't let it out. He knew he didn't mean it, and that made it sound weak.

He still didn't feel he could let this blind old stick-man drive him into the ground without a fight. "What can your books tell me about a bunch of low-down scooter trash?"

To his surprise the old man laughed. "More than you could imagine, boy, more than you could possibly imagine."

He shook his head. "Well, enough for today. I don't want to overburden your intellect. Go on back to your newspapers, boy; mind you don't drip on them, or you'll get ink all over your hands."

His tone softened. "Come back anytime you wish, boy, and I'll help you find out who you are. My name is Bayliss."

In his bed that night in the upstairs room he hugged the bear to him and said, "Imagine, that old crazy-man expecting I'd come back. Shoot, the place gave me the creeps. Reckoned all those dusty old books would fall down on me *any minute*."

The bear listened in sympathetic silence. He was the closest thing Tristan had had to a confidant since Ferret left Dorm C. Tristan was a lot less self-conscious about doing things others might take as too young for his age, such as talking to a teddy bear, than a City boy would have been. With their sense of the totemic and talismanic, the Stormriders were used to talking to a lot of things, like birds and rocks and bushes, that City folk would never bother with. Some of the Folk even said they answered back, though this had never happened to Tristan.

Still, he felt a little self-conscious about the whole thing, so he had asked his father in a dream what a bro could keep.

His father and mother had not appeared on a regular basis for a long time, though the visions of the black wasteland and the ever-increasing glow were an almost nightly occurrence. But his father had come to him in a dream to answer: *"A bro can keep anything he pleases, so long as he rides an American bike."*

"What does that mean?" Tristan had asked plaintively. "What other kinds *are* there?"

"I don't know, son. It's just an expression."

Tristan's parents had been visiting him less and less often. When they did appear they said pretty much the same old things, his mother urging him to endurance, his father to patience—alien as that was to a Stormrider—so that he could one day gain his freedom and his revenge. They seemed to be fading somehow. In truth, Tristan was getting a little bored with them, though he would never admit it to himself.

Tonight they were back, though, strong as ever. "To survive in the City, you must learn as much of City lore as you can," his mother said.

"You got to know your enemy to fight him," Wyatt offered.

"But, Mom, Dad, I'm going to school," Tristan said.

"All the City's schools can teach you is how those schooled in them think," Jen Morningstar said. "You must learn this too, but it's not enough."

"What can I do then?"

"The Library. The knowledge the City doesn't even remember it possesses. Take what you find there."

In the background Wyatt was shaking his head. His long hair and sweeping mustache were heavily streaked with gray now, and the hard lines of his jaw had softened slightly. His jaw was set now, as if he disapproved of Citizen knowledge as much as Citizen ways. But, as usual, he deferred to Afrit Jenny's wisdom.

When they were gone, the jagged black landscape sprang into being around him. Out on the horizon the yellow glow blazed high like a bonfire. He could see something within now, bright inside brightness, that seemed solid.

As much by habit as anything else he tried to approach it, running, slowing to a walk when his dream self felt fatigue. The true form of the object within the glow eluded him.

11

Friday he was back with another pass signed by his Civic Sciences teacher. Mr. Higgs seemed bemused by his request to do research on his own. Initiative of that sort was officially discouraged in students. But Tristan's teachers regarded him as a piece of plastic with the fuse in place, ready to blow at the slightest jar. Of the possible irregularities Tristan might create, Higgs decided, this was the least irregular.

"After the talk I gave you last time, boy," Bayliss said, standing erect beside the work station where he'd ordered Tristan to sit, "it may seem paradoxical to tell you that not all knowledge can be found in books per se."

Tristan didn't know what "per se" meant, much less "paradoxical." But Bayliss still intimidated the hell out of him. Besides, one thing he had learned in his former life was to sit quietly with his mouth shut and his ears and eyes open, the way he'd sat by the hour watching Nick Blackhands as he lovingly stripped down a scrambler or a Kiowa sled, made a sick machine well or a whole machine a whole lot better.

Of course, if he didn't pick this up any better than he had the Wrench Art, old Bayliss the librarian was going to be mighty disappointed with him.

"The key," the old man intoned, reaching a stick finger

toward a button on the console in front of Tristan, "is that not all books come in the same form."

The large screen before Tristan's face sprang alight with a page of newsprint. The headline was huge, and read, "COMET SAGAN HEADED FOR EARTH: Experts Say Only Long-Banned N-Warheads Can Stop It."

"This is a reader," Bayliss said. "It holds the contents for newspapers and periodicals for many years—since back before StarFall, in fact."

Tristan drew in a sharp breath. "You mean it's not just a story after all?"

A humorless chuckle. "No, boy, it's not just a story. Only, it wasn't a star that fell; it was a comet, a great huge ball of ice and rock." He tapped the screen with a forefinger tip. "A comet named Sagan. The story's here, boy, all of it, as much as any-body knows."

Tristan sat staring at the screen. His eyes absorbed words. "The hunt continues for thermonuclear devices which might prevent Comet Sagan from striking Earth. As yet, no country will admit to having defied the long-standing UN ban, though informed speculation for years has claimed such violations were rife. . . ." But the words were slow seeping beneath the surface of his mind. He felt a strange free-fall sensation inside, like riding his scrambler over a buffalo-grass mound and being airborne for a handful of seconds. *StarFall!*

Bayliss demonstrated the reader's controls for Tristan, show-ing him mainly how to flip backward and forward a page at a time. "There are many things you can do with this, a world of things: search for dates, or names, or phrases, any word you want. But I don't want to put too much strain on your mind."

Tristan just nodded.

While Bayliss stood by, Tristan paged experimentally ahead one screen. "Don't try to read everything," Bayliss cautioned. "Newspapers were bigger in those days. You'd be here all day and all night trying to read a week's worth. Just look at those things which catch your interest."

Tristan frowned. In the years he'd been following City in-structions, he had never received such an open-ended assign-ment. Usually you were given a procedure, step by step, and told not to deviate from it. "But shouldn't I—"

"You should open your *mind*, boy. You should *learn*. Do you want to be a robot like the others out there, never questioning, always obeying? Do you not want to learn who and what you are? *Do you want to be an orphan all your life?*"

Tristan turned his head back to the screen. Bayliss tapped it. The headline beneath his finger read, "HOUSE, SENATE IN EMERGENCY SESSION; Comet Legislation Debates Continue."

"Use the headlines as stepping-stones, boy; skip from one to the next, and they'll take you where you want to go. See this, boy, and pay attention. While doom was rushing toward them, our ancestors debated whether or not to censure the comet, and whom to blame for its approach. In this one article is much of what you really need to know about this 'Civic Science.' "

"C-can you read this?" Tristan asked.

"I know these pages well, boy. Very well. I wasn't always blind."

Cautiously Tristan pressed the PAGE DN button a few more times. A headline caught his eye: "EXODUS CONTINUES; Thousands Flee Coasts, Cities As Comet Approaches." He glanced up at Bayliss.

Bayliss nodded, though Tristan had said nothing. "Go ahead. Read the article if it interests you."

In a stroke of insight Tristan realized the old man had felt the movement of air displaced by his face. There were many ways of looking at the world. The old man was definitely teaching him that.

Tristan let his eyes flick at the imaged page tentatively, as if too prolonged a contact might awaken something dangerous. He was accustomed to the mechanically based technologies of the Plains. A device like this, that could hold all the lore of all the bards and skalds of the Plains and still have room left over for dessert, could summon up any part of that lore at his whim. To him that was magic, was Power as potent as his mother's limited command over the Stalking Winds.

"In defiance of bans by local, state, and federal authorities," he read, "tens of thousands of people are fleeing urban and low-lying coastal areas, fearing the impact of Comet Sagan and the earthquakes and tidal waves certain to follow in its wake. . . .

". . . join forces with retreaters, people who have fallen under the sway of a revival of last century's outlawed survivalist movement, and who claim that the recent wave of volcanic and seismic disturbances worldwide presages a period of planetary unrest which will mean the collapse of civilization . . .

". . . expected clashes with participants in another late-twentieth century revival—outlaw motorcycle gangs—have yet to materialize in most places. An uneasy truce appears to be in effect among the new urban refugees, the retreaters, and the bikers. Spokespersons for the retreaters say their own harmony with the cosmic order is affecting the others and producing an air of love and cooperation. More skeptical observers speculate that both bikers and refugees are trying to insinuate themselves into the retreaters' good graces in order to learn the locations of their supposed illegal hoards of food and medical supplies.

"In a related story, the National Police report yesterday's wave of arrests in the Southwest and Texas has broken the back of a ring smuggling motorcycles and parts—long outlawed as safety threats—from Mexico. . . ."

Tristan shook his head. Bayliss was right. This was a lot to take in all at once.

Adolescent outrage seethed within him. The Man had made bikes illegal before the Star fell! It shouldn't have surprised him. Treachery was so deeply dyed in the fabric of the City that it had to have been going on for a lot of years.

Just the same, as he walked home that afternoon beneath skies filled with boiling mustard-colored clouds, his head was filled with lurid adolescent visions of rebellion and revenge. The Citizens had kept their boots on the bros' necks for centuries, it seemed, a longer time than he'd ever really suspected might have elapsed in the whole history of the world. It was time to take their tyranny and smash it to smoldering fragments.

He envisioned himself riding down Homeland's Main Street on a giant blatting hog, holding a torch high above his head as he led a howling throng of riders to the final reckoning. . . .

Mrs. Tomlinson greeted him at the door when he arrived at the neat two-story house, to wipe her hands on her apron and enfold him in a bosom that smelled of lilacs and supper cooking, and he forgot his violent fantasies.

● ● ●

The City was divided into quadrants, districts, and neighborhoods. The residents of each neighborhood were supposed to monitor one another as part of their civic duty—and themselves as well. The neighborhoods held mandatory weekly self-criticism sessions, in which those who had been turned in by their neighbors for infractions such as keeping their homes too warm during the harsh winter, or watching unauthorized broadcasts on their TVs, could confess their faults in front of their neighbors and be shamed. Ideally, people were also to confess misdeeds that they *hadn't* been caught at, out of civic duty. Tristan trooped dutifully to these with his foster parents, since only illness or emergency duty was an excuse. Even though his Dorm-honed instincts told him the meetings were bound to be rife with informers, the meetings were mainly excuses to exchange recipes and the latest gossip, and nothing was ever done.

It made him wonder if the City could really control its Citizens' lives as closely as it desired and claimed to.

Another control mechanism was the Neighborhood Watch Cadres, gangs of adolescent youths who patrolled the Blocks on foot and bicycle, to drive out criminals and, of course, report infractions by householders. The Cadres were also organized into quadrants, districts, and neighborhoods. Neighborhood Watch duty was considered a highly Civic activity. A lot of kids were very zealous in carrying it out.

Tristan sometimes helped Mr. Tomlinson at his hardware store. Mr. Tomlinson never asked him to. It was just something he started doing. The Tomlinsons treated him like a son, but he wasn't their son. He had been taught since childhood to be a burden to no one, and he felt guilty if he didn't do something to pull his weight—they *had* got him out of the Dorms, after all. Besides, helping out as often as he could helped him keep the distance he needed. To start thinking of the Tomlinsons as his parents would be disloyal to his real ones.

Strictly speaking, helping out at the store was one of those violations you were supposed to 'fess up to at the self-criticism sessions. Child labor was illegal, though that hadn't kept Tristan from being farmed out to arduous jobs when he was in the Dorms. That there were two sets of rules in the City, one for the City and another for its Citizens—Clients, as they were called here—was a fact he'd learned around the campfire in his boyhood. It was a fact of life, like ashfalls and lightning strikes.

One autumn afternoon he dawdled his way back from school afoot—motorcycles were illegal for Clients, though of course City military and police used them. Even Pure Engine folk like Tristan did not disdain to ride bicycles; they were quiet, good for scouting enemy camps or herding work. But the Tomlinsons could not afford one.

The air and the ground were wet, as usual. He kicked his way through mounds of dead leaves drifted in the gutters. The neat piles in front yards on the residential blocks tempted him—it was a lot of fun to take a run and dive right through the middle of them. But the householders who had raked the leaves together in hopes they could get them bagged before the winds came up and scattered them again took a dim view of kids preempting the wind. Tristan tried very hard to keep out of even minor trouble that would not send him back to the Dorms. He had learned the hard way that that made trouble for the Tomlinsons.

Suddenly the clouds swirled up black overhead, and a cloudburst announced itself with a peal of thunder. He ran the rest of the way laughing, with wet leaves clinging to the legs of his jeans.

At the store he let himself in through the alleyway in back, not wanting to drip on the linoleum floor up front. He'd be the one to clean up any mess he made.

Because flashfire storms were inevitable at any time of year, he kept a spare set of clothes stashed in the back. He stripped out of his sodden clothing and changed, then made his way to the front to say hello to Mr. Tomlinson—he never thought of him as his father, or even his stepfather. Anticipating, he picked up a push broom along the way.

There were voices from the front. Tristan stopped dead just inside the door when their familiarity struck him. One was his father's, normally mild, now edged. The other was Dirk Posten's.

He pressed his nose to the wire-reinforced glass square in the door to the front of the store.

They were all three there, arranged in their standard semicircle, with Mr. Tomlinson backed against a counter displaying electrical extension cords, trouble lights, replacement bulbs. Round-faced Mr. Tomlinson was not large—Tristan was taller than he. Posten and his henchman Halt Newsome were about Mr. Tomlinson's height, but the dark-haired Halt Newsome was broader in the shoulders. Blond Brace towered over all of them. The three boys wore unmistakable yellow and black Neighborhood Watch armbands.

Tristan frowned, as much in confusion as anger at the invasion. *They don't live in this neighborhood, that's for damned sure.*

Dirk Posten's voice came right through the door. Tristan had not noticed before how penetrating it was. "You're harboring trash off the Plains. That looks like antisocial behavior to *us*, Mr. Tomlinson."

"My wife and I adopted a boy out of the Dorms. We provide him a home environment, plus we save the City the money to support him. You can't get more social than that. The Neighborhood Living Counselor praised us to the skies for it."

"Must be some Health minge," sneered Halt.

"We don't care what the Counselor said," Posten said. "We've racked up a load of Citizenship Points for our Neighborhood Watch service. It's why we got promoted to District Watch. If we see things that are harmful to the City, we have the initiative to *take action*. Know what I mean, old man?"

Tomlinson squared his round shoulders. "The adoption was approved by the City, all right and proper. They're not letting teenagers make or revoke City policy quite yet, are they, boys?"

Halt turned dark under his olive complexion. "Listen, you," he said, poking Tomlinson in his ample canvas-aproned belly. "Tomorrow belongs to us! If you—"

That was it. Tristan firmed his grip on the broom handle—good hardwood, good to do some fairly serious hurt if you knew where to poke it or strike with it—and started through the door. You did not lay a hand on a member of a Stormrider's family. That he was carefully not considering Mr. Tomlinson family did not register on him right now.

The others were focused on the shopkeeper. Mr. Tomlinson alone was looking outside the semicircle. He saw the door begin to open. His blue eyes caught Tristan's over Halt's beefy shoulder as the Plains boy appeared.

The man shook his head once, not much but emphatically.

The gesture froze Tristan. *The Dorms. Rehab. The Black Gang.* You did not fling yourself on Neighborhood Watch Cadres with murder in your heart. You didn't even talk back to them, if you knew what was good for you.

That wasn't enough to stop him. His fury was too great for cost-benefit analysis. What stopped him was the sudden sick realization that if he jumped Posten and his butt boys *they'd take it out on the Tomlinsons too.*

He couldn't carry that freight. No way. A Stormrider didn't hang his bros on a line.

He saw Posten lay a restraining hand on Halt Newsome's arm. "The future belongs to us, yeah," he said, guiding the youth back away from his victim. "And if this Mr. Tomlinson steps just one centimeter out of line his ass belongs to us, too."

Tristan turned and ran. Through the piled dimness of the storage room, out the back door to an alley where the drizzle hung in the air like motes of dust in a sunbeam.

He ran two blocks, three, keeping to alleys. He didn't want anyone to see him. And if Posten and the others ran across him, the effort it had taken to swallow his rage and run would have all been wasted.

He slumped with his back to a poured-cement wall. The alley dirt was a slimy mulch beneath his butt, slick with oil, soft with decay. The smell of wet cardboard melting in a recycling bin filled his nose like batting. The drizzle found his face and flowed against it, over it, like a slug-slime trail.

He held up his hands and saw that he had broken the broomstick in two.

12

"FUJI ERUPTS; 40,000 Feared Dead In Latest Volcanic Outburst." "EARTHQUAKE LEVELS SEATTLE; TSUNAMIS SWEEP HAWAII." "RING OF FIRE AFLAME; Expert Sees End Of 'Quiet Earth.' "

The newspapers and magazines held within the reader went right up to the expected day of StarFall. Then they stopped dead. Other papers, looking far cruder even to Tristan in their onscreen reproductions, picked up again weeks or months later. Though they made plenty of references to the "cosmic catastrophe" there were no *details*. It left Tristan both agitated and unsatisfied. He had to know what happened when the comet actually hit. What did it look like, what did it sound like—what did it *feel* like? If he had been less leery of City girls—he grew up believing they were fickle and treacherous and would lure a man to his doom—he might have recognized that he had a case of the intellectual blue balls.

He was skimming backward from the Big Event, trying to get a line on things. What he was mainly picking up was that, even without the comet, it seemed the planet was in trouble.

He let his eyes skip the article like a stone on the stream: " 'Much of Earth's history has been far more violent, geologically and climatologically speaking, than what we've experienced during recorded human history,' says June-Ellen Tso, chairperson of Earth Sciences at CalTech. 'Now the glaciers are advancing, storms are becoming more and more powerful and destructive, and major earthquakes and volcanic eruptions are sharply on the rise. If you plot eruptions over the last few centuries, you see the activity increasing gradually since Tambora in the early 1800s. Now it's shooting up exponentially, and more than exponentially.

" 'What this translates as is, the party's over.'

"Not everyone attending the government-sponsored Ring of Fire Conference in Pomona, California, agreed with Dr. Tso's assessment, however. 'If there's a problem, it's purely man-made,' said Dr. Jeffrey Linstalk of the National Center for Atmospheric Research in Boulder, Colorado. 'We reduced greenhouse emissions, but we're still pouring tons of filth into the air to feed our consumerist habit. If the Earth is shaking and throwing up, we need to quit gouging at her and delving in her innards. We need more restraint, more restrictions—more laws.' "

Tristan's mind was drifting. Sometimes it seemed as if the people in the old days spoke an entirely different language from the English he'd grown up with.

He had more important things on his mind anyway. Not his actual schoolwork. That was easy enough to do, or easy enough to fake—it was like every other facet of City life: The authorities told you what the official line was, and then you parroted it back to them when they asked you. This was public education, and the City was enormously proud of it. It was something that set Civilization apart from the barbarians of the Plains.

The problem of Dirk Posten and his friends was what preyed on his mind. They were determined to get him. He could stay away from them indefinitely at school, he reckoned—the day a Plains rider couldn't give the slip to sag-nuts Citizens was the day to hang it up. But they could strike at the Tomlinsons too.

"You're distracted today, boy." He couldn't keep from jumping as Bayliss's voice cut the air like the ringing harmonic aftershocks of a pistol shot. "What's the matter?"

He turned in his chair. The tall man had materialized unheard at his shoulder. He did that, popping up at any random place in the stacks. Tristan was unsure how a blind man could navigate such a maze, let alone as silently as a Lakota warrior stalking Kiowa rolling stock.

Tristan sighed. "I . . . I have a problem."

"Tell me."

Tristan was not at an age when sharing information of any kind with adults came easily. And Bayliss was a City employee.

The old man read his hesitation. He had a disconcerting knack for seeing right through Tristan, eyes or no. He shrugged and turned away. "Suit yourself," he said.

"No, wait! I—I can't tell you about it, I really can't. But . . . what do you do when you can't fight and you can't run either?"

Bayliss turned his porcelain-blank eyes on Tristan's. "Two courses are possible boy. One: give up."

Tristan felt his lips press into a line. He realized in the pit of his belly that he'd been wishing for a way to do just that. It was cowardice. But he felt as if he were surrounded with the web of a giant spider from Plains campfire legend. It was binding his limbs, and every time he tried to dart it just got him tangled up all the more.

"I'm not sure I *could*," he admitted. "Even if I wanted to."

Bayliss nodded, and it seemed to Tristan that he took a small satisfaction at the boy's words. "Two," the old man said in his stick-breaking voice, "is to fight smart."

Tristan stared. The old man's phrasing was as unexpected as his meaning.

"It's the City you're talking about, of course."

Tristan tensed to run. *I knew it! He's going to rat me off! I should've kept my mingy mouth shut—*

Bayliss's hand clamped his arm with startling strength, holding him in his chair. "You have nothing to fear from me, boy. Believe it or not as you will."

The boy subsided back into the unyielding wood embrace of the chair.

"You are also wise not to tell me the details. Not because I constitute a threat. But as a matter of principle. You do not know that I *don't* constitute a threat, not for certain. You will live longer if you are careful whom you trust.

"You will also live longer if you keep remembering that you can't fight the City directly. Your father thought otherwise, and it cost him his life."

Tristan tore away and jumped to his feet, his eyes blurred with tears so hot they stung. "Don't say anything against my father, you goddamned blind old crazy-man!"

He regretted the words as soon as they'd blown out of his lips. He had meant them to hurt; only by striking at the old man with words had he been able to keep from lashing out with his fist.

Bayliss absorbed their impact without sign. Tristan had the sense he'd have ridden a blow the same way. There was more to this blind old walking-stick man than he had thought, or maybe could understand.

"You know I'm not lying," Bayliss said. "Can you say that I'm wrong?"

Tristan dropped his eyes.

"There is a third option I neglected to mention before: lose and die. That might be the heroic course. Of course, when Rehab burns everything but simple appetites out from behind your eyes, or the quakes shake half a Hellville mountain down on your back, the knowledge of noble defeat might not be so comforting. And the skalds won't sing your final battle around the campfires of the High Free Folk, because they won't even know. Any dog can die in a ditch, son."

For a flash Tristan wondered how Bayliss knew so much about the Plains. He didn't wonder long; it was probably because he knew *everything*. But Tristan's unrequited anger—not at Bayliss, he knew, though Bayliss had touched it off, let it off its leash for a frightening blood-singing minute—required an outlet of some kind. Or it would simply tear out the sides of his head.

"I'll do it someday!" he screamed. His voice bounced back and forth up the book-cliffs to the clerestory, beyond even their power to muffle. "I'll take the City on and win! *Someday!*"

It came to him then that he had gone too goddamn far at last. Bayliss would finally rat him off. Or—maybe worse—write him off as another adolescent pop-off.

He did neither. He nodded.

"Maybe you will, boy," he said. "Maybe you will. *Someday.*" And he turned and walked away.

Halt Newsome's father was Important. He had a lot of contracts with the City, and a lot of influence with the Council. But he was still a Client, not Staff—much less Admin. The gap was not wide, perhaps—you could see across it, talk across it, shake hands across it even. But while it wasn't wide it was impossibly deep, like the cut of the Rio Grande gorge near Taos, where the Hardriders had gone each year for Rendezvous.

Newsome Senior had pull, but it wasn't enough to get his adolescent son a permit to operate a motor vehicle, much less own one. Like most other kids his age he had to ride a bicycle. It wasn't that bad, he told himself; even Dirk and Brace were only permitted to drive on special occasions. He had an expensive bicycle, a good mountain bike with knobby tires and frame bonded of carbon fibers somewhere around the Great Lake.

This evening he was riding it home from football practice. The clouds were beginning to form a gray-white ceiling, and the smell and bite of snow were in the air. As he did everything else, he rode flat-out, as if to show he was as good as anybody and didn't have to look out for anyone or anything. He rode faster than usual tonight, to beat the storm home. If it got bad, his father's driver could drop him off at his meeting at Neighborhood Watch Cadre District headquarters.

He didn't shun alleys on his regular route home from school, no matter how narrow, dark, or dirty. Nobody would dare mess with him. He was a Big Man's son, and a Cadre member in good standing, and also he could beat the crap out of just about anybody who crossed him.

By City law he had a light on his bike. It wasn't enough to pick out the thin cord strung across the final dark-alley shortcut. It took him at the biceps and the chest just below the clavicle and whipped him backwards right off the bike.

He was very lucky in two ways. First, the line had not been piano wire strung at Adam's-apple height, in the traditional mode; if it had, his speed would have been enough to slash his throat open, though not decapitate him. Second, though none of Homeland's alleys was exactly well populated, someone must have been watching, because an ambulance arrived within minutes.

There was already a crowd around the unconscious boy. The ambulance techs shooed them back. They wondered aloud to each other how long it was going to take the goddamn cops to get their butts off the donut-shop stools and down here. Though the handsome homes of Newsome's father and his peers lay nearby, this was the Blocks, not a good neighborhood at all.

Even the least enlightened Clients generally left medtechs alone. One small kid with brown hair falling in his dirty face did have the nuts to dart forward and stick his hand in the injured boy's pants pocket. One of the techs ran after him—not too fast and not too far—while the others checked the victim's pockets. He still had his wallet and his key ring, so the kid obviously hadn't gotten anything.

"Ballsy little bastard," muttered the tech as he returned. His partners pulled the ambulance's double rear door shut behind them. He climbed in next to the driver and they wailed off to the hospital in a storm of colored light.

Hung on a wire.

It is by repute the very worst thing you can do to a Plains biker. Worse even than stranding him without his hog. In a pinch, a Plains-wise rider can survive a journey of hundreds of miles to help on his Nike wheels. No one could survive having his head go bouncing down the road alongside his sled.

Melodramas showing the extravagant brutality and squalor of the nomad biker gangs were a staple of TV shows, the amateurish homegrown efforts and the slicker productions made in larger Cities and bounced off satellites to Homeland's few carefully controlled dishes alike. Nothing was more guaranteed to produce a thrill of self-righteous horror than portrayal of the retribution the gangs were said to take on Diggers and Citizens who were crazy-bold enough to wire High Free Folk riders. The least you could expect, the TV shows said, was to be buried to your neck in a fire-ant hill or to have your arms and legs chained to trucks and be pulled to bloody sections.

There was more than a little truth to it, as there often is to clichés.

Halt Newsome came out of his experience of being hung on a wire with a concussion—the cruel schoolyard joke, which Tristan was careful never to repeat or even be seen smiling at, had it that they'd X-rayed his head and found nothing—and a few strained ligaments and cracked ribs. Nonetheless, his father *was* an influential Client, and he was a member of the police-auxiliary Cadre. The police announced a massive manhunt for the perpetrator or perpetrators. The City-controlled papers deplored the random violence of the act and called for new laws.

What nobody did was suspect Tristan Tomlinson. He had a perfect alibi for that night. He and his foster parents had had their names checked off the rolls of the weekly neighborhood self-criticism meeting a good ten minutes before young Newsome met his mishap. Everyone had seen them there, including the City informers off the Block.

But suspicion would have fallen on him dead last anyway, even though it was near certain school narcs had passed the word to the authorities that Tristan had had his differences with Halt and his friends. For once Tristan's status as a semi-civilized nomad brat worked in his favor.

No TV-watching Citizen could possibly *imagine* that a Plains biker would stoop to a low-down Digger trick like hanging someone on a line. Even his worst enemy. He'd sooner wear a helmet.

If suspicion conspicuously failed to fall on Tristan for the bushwhacking of Halt Newsome, he might well have been a suspect in the burglary of Homeland's biggest television store two nights later. It was a very slick job. The criminals made off with several thousand vouchers' worth of TVs and stereo equipment.

He might have been a suspect had not an anonymous tip led police to an unused back room of the District Headquarters of the Neighborhood Watch Cadre. Most of the stolen TVs were stacked there in neat piles. There was loot from other burglaries there, as well as dime bags of marijuana, coffee, and tobacco, and porn mags and videos from Brazil. It was the bust of the year, all told.

Pressed between a couple of boxes, as if it had fallen there from a careless pocket, was Halt Newsome's ID.

It might all have been hushed up, of course. Halt's dad was about as important as Halt liked to think he was, and Halt was inextricably tied in with both Dirk Posten and Brace Webbert, whose fathers were considerably more so.

But the owner of the television shop was Wade Tener, a powerful member of the City Council. He wasn't letting the theft of his TVs get swept under any rugs. Bob Posten was a rival for leadership of the Strength Party anyway. Tener hid his triumph behind a mask of concern, speechified about the need for sacri-

fice to maintain discipline and the integrity of City law, and
waited for blood.

Young Dirk had not had *his* ID turn up amidst any loot. Halt
Newsome, protesting his innocence to the last, was packed off
to the Homeland Defense Force—he was underage, but his father readily gave permission when it was made clear to him the
alternative was Hellville and the Black Gang. Dirk Posten and
Brace Webbert were forced to resign from the Neighborhood
Watch Cadre. They were also transferred out of Kennedy High,
strictly on general principles.

Tristan had been nowhere near that alley when Halt Newsome
took his faithful spill, but he wasn't innocent.

He hadn't set the trap or helped with the follow-through. He
had helped with the break-in at TenerVision, though. He was
also along when the copy of Halt's key to Cadre District headquarters, made from the impression taken of the key as Halt lay
stunned by the former Dorm rat who had actually set the wire
trap, was put to use. Tristan personally tucked the incriminating
ID card the ex-Dormie had stolen from Halt's pocket between
the boxes of hot merchandise. And the plan, of course, had all
been his.

The former residents of Dorm C were not his friends; he had
no friends anymore. But he had learned there were other bonds
than friendship. The comradeship of shared hardship, combined
with simple greed—not *all* Wade Tener's TVs were recovered
from Neighborhood Watch HQ—and a shared interest in giving
a black eye to the City's privileged and powerful, could serve as
well as friendship and possibly better.

It was a lesson that would stay with Tristan all his life.

13

Tristan discovered sports, or rather, sports discovered him.

Athletics were serious business for the Cities. Trade among the city-states came and went—though it had a habit of continuing right along even when it was at its most illegal—but the games went on. It was a way to act out rivalries, for one City to display dominance over another in an age in which outright military conquest was made prohibitively expensive by distance, hostiles, and the unquiet land and sky. Athletic competition was a fairly cost-effective surrogate for war.

Not that the Cities gave up plotting and dreaming the real thing. Nor did they stop their campaigns of intrigue, espionage, sabotage, and sponsored terrorism against their dearest rivals. Inter-City sports were a mask for all these things to hide behind.

Tristan had good coordination, and was as quick and fluid-strong as a catamount. The coaches loved him. He could run and throw, and in football he took savage joy in contact, whether hitting or getting hit. Everyone agreed he had the potential to turn pro.

Suddenly, Tristan did not have to watch his every step. If a schoolmate taunted him, he was free to destroy him, and the unfortunate taunter would suck up whatever punishment was meted out. Tristan was bullet-proof, within limits that he had a very shrewd estimate of. The City loved its prestige more than anything. Tristan had become a valuable Citizen.

He kept going to the Library. Because he was now a star of sorts his behavior was indulged. It did cause some concern. In his junior year an assistant football coach took him aside, mentioned his habit of spending long hours in the library, and asked Tristan if he was a queer. Tristan said he wasn't.

In school he continued to do well at the subjects that interested him and indifferently at the ones that bored him. Though the professionally concerned members of the Health Party wrung their hands about it, the academic performance of potential star athletes was a non-issue. Promising jocks were fail-safe.

Tristan's trips to the Library had nothing to do with school anyway. They were about his quest for knowledge. Another thing entirely.

His parents continued to visit him in dreams from time to time. They seemed less substantial now. The other dreams—the vision of the glow—came regularly.

The glow began to take on a hint of shape, evolving dream by dream into something suggestive of a cross.

The Tomlinsons attended the Church of Christ, Citizen—the official City denomination and a pillar of the Strength Party— every week without exception. Neither said anything to Tristan about going, but he knew it would thrill them if he embraced their religion.

The thought of following the Jesus Road made his skin creep. Some Stormriders were Christians, but no Hardriders. Tristan associated the faith with the City, its walls and straitjacket ways, and nothing since he had been sucked into the City had changed his mind.

He had no particular religious beliefs, other than the general Plains lore of Father Sun and Mother Earth, Brother Wind and Sister Moon. It wasn't much with him now, and he had a shame-faced suspicion that it was all just silly superstition anyway. His mother, Jen Morningstar, had been an adept of the StarLodge, the female secret society. StarLodge taught that the High Free Folk were offspring of the Fallen Star, and that everyone among them was not just of the stuff of stars, but actually *a star*: that each Stormrider had a star in the sky which was his or her soul.

Tristan didn't know what he thought about that. He knew now that the Star was also called Sagan, and was actually a comet, and that the stars were balls of flaming gas like Fa—like the Sun. Did that make any difference, did it invalidate his mother's beliefs? He didn't know. He had not found his Star, that much was certain.

He was years off the Plains, and the old beliefs had faded like the faces of his mother and father. He was learning about science and scientific patterns of thought—more from old Bayliss than his classes at school. But he could not act against his medicine. The dreams of the glow were dreams of Power. He would follow where they led regardless.

So he permitted himself to be cinched into a necktie, fighting down claustrophobic panic the while, and allowed Mrs. Tomlinson to pomade his unruly black hair into place, and wrap him up in a suit coat they'd bought which was now too small and bound between the shoulder blades, adding to his sense of imminent suffocation. And he followed them dutifully on the ten-block Sunday walk to church through a spring morning that was actually bright and clear, though windy.

He might as well have saved himself the trouble. As soon as he stepped into the cool antiseptic dimness of the church, his heart told him this had nothing to do with his vision. That meant nothing to do with him; and before the man in the collar could began his sermon Tristan rose and walked out without a word, moving quickly so he wouldn't see the hurt look in Mrs. Tomlinson's eyes.

During those years the City fought a sporadic but unending series of battles: against terror squads from Dallas, against Comanche of the renegade Kwahadi band, but mainly against the High Free Folk. The City's farmlands, trailing away like voluminous skirts eastwards from the Front Range of the Rockies, and particularly the City's rich trade drew them. As it had drawn Wyatt Hardrider.

Though his adolescent heart quickened when the TV showed battle footage for suppertime, Tristan could not watch. When fighting was in the news a lot he tended to go to his room early.

He wasn't sure why. Maybe he was afraid he might see his own face.

But when spring arrived in his senior year—later even than usual, delayed, it was rumored, by an especially violent series of eruptions in the FlameLands to the Northwest that had turned the snow black with ashfalls—the pressure of war news became so great Tristan could no longer shut it out.

It was a Saturday afternoon. Basketball season had ended, baseball season was about to begin. Kennedy had taken the City championship in basketball, and was expected to do well in baseball. Tristan was a major reason for both.

For the morning's warm-up drills there was still grimy snow patched around the fringes of the practice fields, looking like mounds of cement ice cream. The sky showed an intense eye-hurting blue beyond puffy cumulous clouds that banged against each other incessantly but didn't leak.

Tristan was pleased with practice and pleased with himself. He took an animal, sensual pleasure in intense physical activity, in challenging himself, driving himself. He enjoyed excelling.

He also enjoyed having the opportunity to vent the hot, frightening anger he didn't even realize he harbored until he had found a sanctioned outlet for it.

Tristan played dirty. Football gave him the greatest scope for it, of course. Kennedy had lost the City championship in that sport, but Tristan, as a linebacker, had set unofficial Homeland records for hospitalized opponents. Basketball was more circumscribed, but he could throw an elbow with such blinding speed even the victim was sometimes uncertain where it had come from. Baseball was a chance for spike-high slides—and because he alternated pitching with playing center field, as was not uncommon in high school, he had the opportunity to put opponents in the dirt for true, and bust them up some if they weren't quick enough on the dodge.

His teammates adored him, of course. And the coaches . . . from the dawn of time, coaches have felt *good sportsmanship* consists in winning. Tristan's on-field brutality made even them shake their buzz-cut heads sometimes, but they told themselves it was merely his keen competitive spirit, and wouldn't the ever-dominant Dallasite teams drop their jaws when they got a load of *him*. . . .

Tristan didn't care about any of that. He didn't really care about *winning*. He was just enjoying the opportunity to rack up some City meat for free.

He was enjoying other perks too, like Melodie Krebs last night and Kathy Setzer the night before. His earlier reticence about City women had long since gone with the wind. He was in such demand he could ignore any games any girl wanted to play with him.

He was seventeen, and he was immortal.

He came downstairs barefoot, in jeans and worn jersey, still toweling the hair he wore as long as regulations allowed and then some. His foster parents were in the living room staring at their small television.

"Mr. Tomlinson," he said in surprise. Since the afternoon when the man had stood up to Dirk Posten and his official vigilante thug friends, Tristan had acknowledged him as a bro, even though he didn't ride. But it was still beyond him to call him *Dad*. "What are you doing home?" Usually he worked at his store on Saturday, bending the labor laws.

Tomlinson gestured at the screen without even turning his head. His wife looked up and bit her lip. "It's the news," she said hesitantly. "I'm afraid it will upset you. I know how sensitive you are about violence."

Because he really did love her, he didn't laugh. What he was *sensitive* about was watching the City's faceless and efficient military machine chewing up brothers and sisters the way it had his own family and friends.

"This is too much to ignore," Mr. Tomlinson said in an uncharacteristically gruff way. "They're driving clear to Big Sandy Creek."

"The news people say they may even try to go as far as the Smoky Hills," said Mrs. Tomlinson, scrubbing her already immaculate hands on her apron. "Isn't it awful?"

Her husband made a neutral sound and shook his bald round head.

Tristan frowned, still not looking at the set. *It's a smart time to strike,* he thought, dead inside. The clans were hungry, stiff, and sluggish from a winter's forced inactivity. The last of the snows brought the High Free Folk their weakest time of year.

He glanced aside, quickly, fearing to look at his foster parents almost as much as at the television. Mr. and Mrs. Tomlinson were almost painfully average. Their outlook could not have differed too much from what most of their neighbors thought, or they would never have been approved to adopt a child. They had always refrained from making any anti-biker slurs or statements when Tristan was present, not even to grumble, "It's about time," or "They had it coming," when the Defense Force hammered a particularly troublesome band. Nor had they ever commented on his own rough-edged ways when he first arrived—they had sweetly but firmly taught him to say please and thank you, and eat with a knife and fork, and keep his room cleaned up, and never said boo about it. Still, he assumed they didn't care much for the High Free Folk. Citizens didn't.

But instead of being elated at the great and bloody victory over the bike scum the reporters were blatting about from the screen right this minute, they seemed glum, apprehensive. It didn't make sense.

"They're going too far this time," Tomlinson said, shaking his head.

Tristan looked then. It wasn't so bad, though the act made his scrotum suck up to a tight little ball between his legs. The screen showed an open-topped personnel carrier with armored slab sides and four huge cleated tires chewing up the tough, rain-slick prairie grass with a low hillside for backdrop—a Buffalo, Tristan knew, manufactured by Black Mountain Foundry, which also made bikes. He didn't like to watch it used against his own people, but he was an adolescent, and he knew the hardware. In the background a little open-frame combat car went skidding by, a machine gun flaring off from a roll-bar mount.

The picture cut away then to the broad concrete steps that led up to the mammoth bunker of City Hall. There was a crowd of maybe fifty to a hundred people there, waving hand-lettered pasteboard placards that read END THE MADNESS and BRING 'EM BACK ALIVE.

Mrs. Tomlinson clucked and shook her head. "How can they do that?" she asked. "It's our duty to support our boys."

"No matter what," her husband agreed. ''It's Good Citizenship."

"What are they doing?" Tristan asked.

"Protesting the war," Mrs. Tomlinson said.

"I've never heard of such a thing," her husband said.

"They should be careful," Mrs. Tomlinson said earnestly. "They could earn a lot of Antisocial Points that way."

14

"This is Neil Hansen. I'm standing on Cape Flattery, the northwesternmost point of the continental United States, beneath skies which are cloudy and ominous, as befits the occasion. Behind me the Cape Flattery lighthouse stands where Juan de Fuca Strait meets the Pacific Ocean."

The camera pans away from the neat, gingerbearded man, across a gray waste of beach with evergreens rising thick and black beyond. *"Cape Flattery lies on the tiny Makah Native American Reservation, whose residents have mostly fled, despite official assurances that they had nothing to fear.*

"Comet Sagan is expected to enter Earth's atmosphere any moment now. Experts at the National Atmospheric Research Center have predicted that it will strike far out in the Pacific Ocean. We have come to this desolate spit of land to see if we can catch a glimpse of the distant splash.

"I—wait, wait—" The picture shows him pressing fingertips over his right ear, as if trying to trap a gnat in there. *"We have a report of a huge flash in the sky on the East Coast. We'll give over now to our New York . . . no, no, New York seems to be off line. Oh, my, there may have been a misestimation . . . here, we'll go to satellite scan, see if we can get an image of the impact site from orbit."*

The camera eye watches him walk back inland to the boxy van and press his finger to something that looks like a shiny blackboard and shows swirling whiteness—a television, clearly, but not like the TVs stolen from TenerVision.

In the background, the whole eastern sky lights in a flash.

Hansen's head snaps up. *"What's this? Wait, that was inland! That was—oh, my God, Seattle, Tacoma, the people, the people—"*

Tristan punched off the reader and sat back. A breath he hadn't been aware of holding blew out of him in a long gust. *StarFall.* This was the only actual footage that Bayliss had been able to locate of a strike by a giant comet fragment. There may have been a dozen strikes in all across the Northern Hemisphere. Tristan never tired of watching it.

It's my world, coming into being. StarLodge is right about that much. We were all born then.

He heard Bayliss breathing at his side. For an old man the librarian breathed quite quietly. Tristan's prairie-honed senses were keen, though he was still generally unable to catch Bayliss approaching, especially when he was staring fascinated at words and pictures on the screen, or wrapped up in some dusty old book.

"What does it mean?" he asked. "I mean, all these people protesting at City Hall."

"It means, in part, that some people dislike the use of force under any circumstances."

Tristan's eyebrows went up. He rolled the concept around in his head like a morsel of unfamiliar food in his mouth, testing it for taste and consistency. His reflex response was that it was a pretty piss-poor idea. But it had been Bayliss himself— certainly not his City-certified "teachers"—who had instilled in him the idea that the unfamiliar was not necessarily *wrong*.

"What do *you* think?" Tristan asked. He knew better than to ask that—it was inviting a snarled response of "Think for yourself!"

But Bayliss compressed his thin lips tighter and nodded his head slowly. "I think that a man who doesn't defend himself against an aggressor makes himself an accomplice in aggression," he said slowly. "The same applies for women, of course."

A tremor passed through the massive cement bones of the Library—just a small one, more sensed as a deep-subsonic rumble than felt. A thrill of terror went through Tristan. He had learned to control the panic response, at least to the extent of keeping the terror off his face. But he retained a claustrophobic fear of being *within walls* when Mother Earth shook. He always would.

When it was safe to show expression again he felt himself frown. "So you think the . . . clans . . . are committing aggression against the City."

"I know they often *do*, boy, and you know it as well as I. But this current campaign . . . it's easy for our lords and masters to manufacture high and noble-sounding reasons for it. But it's not just crime, it's folly."

"You think this war is that? A crime and a folly?"

Bayliss nodded. "I do."

"Uhh—both, sir?"

"Both. It is morally wrong and a military mistake. The City is itself aggressing, and in the process overextends itself." His walking-stick fingers played thoughtfully on his chin. "I think perhaps some of the protesters realize that too—that the City government has gone too far. But then, I may be getting soft in the head and heart as I grow old."

If there was anything at all *soft* about the librarian Tristan hadn't been able to find it. Any of Tristan's assistant coaches— even the senior and head coaches, middle-aged men with crew-cut hair and cauldron bellies—could have knocked the librarian into a cartwheel. Yet when it came to toughness, Tristan felt somehow that Bayliss had it all over the swaggering athletes. Jen Morningstar had taught him that true toughness was not necessarily on the surface, and when it was most loudly proclaimed, it was most likely to be absent.

"Who's protesting then?" Tristan asked. "Are they Health?"

"Some, perhaps. Health supporters affect to be horrified by violence of any kind—though what else you can call chemical lobotomy and some of their other Rehabilitation techniques escapes me. They abhor self-defense above all. But at base they more than anything want to extend their therapeutic 'help' across the prairies, especially to the benighted bike gangs. And if the Strength hawks break a lot of eggs, well, ultimately both Strength and Health wish to dine on the same omelette."

He sighed, and his sightless eyes stared up to the clerestory windows, where white lightning flashes played like ripples in a stream. "I can hope that *some* of the people protesting can see the difference between people and eggs."

"So what's going to happen to them? The police keep breaking up the demonstrations, and the Council is always talking about sending them to the mines or Rehab on CityChannel."

"The City is winning, and is therefore magnanimous. In fact, that is another reason I doubt many of the protesters are Health. Health is as much a partner to Strength as a rival, if not more, and nothing succeeds like success."

Tristan looked blank.

" 'War is the health of the State.' A wise man said that, long before StarFall. Health is the State as much as Strength, though for the moment Strength holds the upper hand."

Tristan still looked blank, though he knew that was risky with Bayliss. He hastened to ask the new question he was struggling with. "Who are the protesters then? If they're not Health or Strength, what are they?"

"Think, boy," Bayliss rapped. "You're not that inculcated with City nonsense. Which are your High Free Folk, Health or Strength?"

Tristan laughed, instantly sobered. "Neither one . . . sir."

"You needn't 'sir' me. I wasn't offended that you laughed; the question was intentionally absurd."

Tristan bit his lip. "So, the protesters are—they sympathize with the—the Plains people?"

"Are they biker-lovers, to use the phrase Strength loves and Health deplores? Probably not. There are other possibilities still, my boy."

Tristan licked his lips. He hated to sound stupid. But Bayliss always said that if you were afraid to *sound* stupid by asking questions, then not only *were* you stupid, but you were going to remain that way. And he would say it at any minute too; blind Bayliss could read Tristan as easily as Tristan could read the books ranked all around in silent rows.

"Like what?" he made himself ask. He remembered a strong, heavy face then, seen on weather-scrubbed posters on an alley wall years back. "Like Reconciliationists?"

A corner of the old man's mouth quirked up. "*Reconciliationists*. It's been a while since I've heard that word. They're

underground, now, of course. The Council ruled them antisocial.

"Them and others, boy. Liberty-lovers. Are you familiar with
the word liberty? No? They don't teach it in school. It's a bad
word, to the ears of the City.

"But if I've taught you anything"—he swept his arms around
an encompassing circle—"it is how to *learn*. The books are
here. Jefferson. Tom Paine. Frederick Douglass. Lysander
Spooner. Bastiat. Mencken, Lane, Nock, Hayek, Friedman,
Rand. Heinlein, Smith, and Snodgrass. Rothbard. O'Rourke. In
fact and fiction, satire and dead seriousness—though nothing is
more serious than true satire—these men and women have de-
lineated *liberty*. And try as they might, the powers of the City
have not extirpated knowledge of it."

He chuckled, a sound as dry as his yellow-brown knuckles
rapping the oak study table. "Of course, they could if they ever
came here to see for themselves what sedition I harbor on my
shelves. But they don't, and won't. The Library is an ornament,
something the City maintains to prove it's civilized. No one
comes here but you and me."

Tristan was still wrestling with what Bayliss had said before.
"You mean," he said, breathlessly, because it was the designa-
tion the City said was deadliest of all, "the protesters are *rights
addicts*?"

"Yes," Bayliss said. "At least I hope so."

For four days Homeland was saturated with coverage of the
great offensive in the east. Big-screen televisions from
TenerVision—available for purchase only to those who could
show need, which was to say highly placed Admin people—
were brought into the study halls. Nonessential classes—
everything but Phys Ed and Civil Sciences—were canceled so
the students could watch the succession of glorious victories.

Tristan almost lost it the second day, when the cameras
showed a nomad camp that had been hit by the deathstorm of
the offensive. The tents, torn and faded under swirling black
skies. The scooters and pick'em-ups, flying pennons of pale
yellow flame that the downpour didn't dampen. The bodies,
showing few visible injuries to the all-intrusive camera eye, not
looking really human, resembling instead plastic dolls, care-

lessly strewn, clothes awry, drawn up to reveal wax-pale bellies, pulled-over faces, all appearing to be melting in the rain.

Tristan had seen it before. Had lived it.

The others crowded into the darkened classroom cheered and pumped their fists in the air: "All *right*!"

"They really kicked *ass*!"

"They gave those scooter pukes what they *deserved*!"

No, he told himself, *I've come so far. I can't blow it now. . . .*

The hateful images were gone, replaced by images of City armored cages rolling across the endless rain-fed swells of grass, occasionally letting their weapons go in balloons of flame against the sky. And then a press briefing with General Carmody and his aides congratulating one another on their wonderful campaign.

Tristan relaxed, slowly. He turned his fists upright, let his fingers uncurl. His nails, cut short, had drawn blood from both palms. But he had survived again the greatest challenge: mastering himself.

15

It seemed to Tristan that for all the noise the advance went pretty damned slowly. A hundred miles in four days. Even off the Hard Roads, a nomad raiding party that couldn't cover that in a day would be pretty sag-nuts. The City soldiers seemed to think they were the hottest thing this side of the FlameLands. Tristan, who knew not just the ways of the Plains but the exploits of men with names like Chingiz Khan and Napoleon and Patton—names never mentioned in Civic Sciences class—had his own opinion.

By the fourth day it struck Tristan that the news coverage was showing the same footage of rolling armored vehicles and combat cars that it had since about day two, and the images of slump/sprawled nomad bodies were so familiar they barely caused a hitch in Tristan's pulse anymore. Air time was eaten up more and more with those self-congratulatory briefings, with lots of broad colorful lines drawn on maps and bar charts of casualties. He wondered why no one else, fellow students or teachers, appeared to notice that all the news was old news, and that the briefings now were all about themselves.

On the fifth day the plug was pulled.

"What do you think's going on?" the catcher hissed.

"Shh," Tristan said without looking back. The season began next week. He wanted his batting eye as sharp as possible by then. Even though you got to hit people more and harder in football, baseball was his favorite sport, and the one he thought he was best at.

The pitch was a curve, high and outside. "Strike!" called the assistant coach playing umpire for the intrasquad game. He was a math teacher doing double duty, seemingly not much older than Tristan, with a fresh-scrubbed Evangelical look and ears that protruded widely from the close-cropped sides of his head. Tristan turned around and gave him a glare, and gave the catcher one too for good measure.

"Seriously," the catcher said, as he lobbed the ball back to the pitcher. "I heard Carmody got chopped to shit near the Cheyenne Wells. Bikers cut him off and jumped all over him."

"Say!" the math teacher exclaimed, voice cracking adolescent-like. "What's going on here? Are you spreading rumors, Toland? That's antisocial! You, you could be . . . you could be expelled!"

Toland went white behind his mask. You could be worse than expelled. He was so rattled he signaled for a fastball over. Tristan extended his arms and swatted it over Mayor Hunt's stern face painted on the low wall in left.

As he trotted the basepaths he felt nothing but satisfaction in making contact. He'd long since learned how much rumors were worth.

"Oh, my God. It's terrible. It's just so terrible."

Mrs. Tomlinson was weeping into her apron in the living room. Her husband stood beside her with one hand on her shoulder.

The television showed a line of transport trucks rolling back down the Hard Road toward Homeland in the never-ending rain. Bearded, haunted faces stared out over the tailgates.

The rumors had been worth something after all.

The news blackout had continued until routed elements of Carmody's invasion force had hit the wire-and-cement-tangle perimeter of Homeland itself. Military police roadblocks had been set up on the road to prevent them mingling with the civilian population. But the fleeing soldiers had hit off cross-country, infiltrating through the wire singly or in groups or simply blasting paths through with plastic. By some sixth sense they had immediately located all the bootleg booze and smuggled-in grass in the City, sucking down the intoxicants and telling the horrified populace that the Barbarian Horde was rolling down upon Homeland like a steel tsunami.

Faced not with defeatist rumor-mongering but immediate evidence of real live *defeat*, the City government fell back upon the last, most desperate expedient of the State: the truth. Or at least some of it. The controlled media were now acknowledging that General Carmody's glorious offensive had flashed off to Jesus like a scrap of paper dropped in a lava flow, along with the general himself and somewhere upward of a thousand of Homeland's five-thousand-man armed forces. The spin was that, in the hour of crisis, it was the duty of all Citizens to pull together to support the boys.

"Those poor boys," sobbed Mrs. Tomlinson, shaking her head. Tristan was fascinated that she seemed more concerned for the welfare of the scared, bedraggled troopies than afraid of the imminent arrival of the reeking shaggy biker hordes, red-eyed and bent on rape and plunder.

"There, dear," her husband said. "They'll make it." He nodded his bald head at the screen. "*He'll* bring them through."

"Captain John Masefield—'Black Jack,' to the adoring troops he has extricated from the Cheyenne Wells disaster—has taken command of a rout and turned it into a fighting retreat. . . ." the reporter was breathing.

Tristan looked. A bomb of cold went off in his stomach.

There were more wrinkles around and behind the dark sunglasses, and a hint of loose skin hung beneath the still-firm chin. But the face was the same.

It was that face which had kept Tristan alive and sane during the years of his captivity. Given him a reason for going on: *vengeance*.

It was the face of the man who'd murdered the Hardriders.

Homeland police opened fire on demonstrators outside the toad-squat of City Hall. Ten people were killed, at least forty injured, either by bullets or the panicked stampede away from them.

The Administration could have contained the damage either

by calling the shooting justified or immediately deploring it. It did the worst possible thing: both.

Tristan found Bayliss in his beloved Library with his coat off and his shirtsleeves rolled up, bending over a boxy metal mechanism that emitted rhythmic thumps and pulses of unearthly green light. Tristan stopped in shock. He had never seen the librarian without his coat before.

"Sir," he said, not wanting to creep up and take the preoccupied old man by surprise. "Mr. Bayliss—what are you doing?"

The old man raised his head and turned blind eyes toward the boy. "Something I should have done a long time ago," he said.

Tristan stood there in his letter jacket, unenlightened. One of Bayliss's favorite saws was that there were no stupid questions. Like all the other adults of Tristan's acquaintance he contradicted himself without self-consciousness, though, and Tristan reckoned he'd get his head bitten off if he asked the same question twice.

"What's that machine?" he settled for asking, after a few breaths. He had known it was there, off by one wall under the painting of Samuel Johnson, but Bayliss had never touched it or referred to it, and Tristan had just come to accept it as one of the inexplicable fixtures old buildings tended to possess.

"It's a copier. A duplicating machine. They're illegal for private citizens to have, of course. The Library has one because the City Council thinks it would be ill-equipped without such a machine, even if it's never used. It's what used to be called a status symbol, you know."

"Oh," Tristan said. He still didn't get it, but what the hell; he had come here with something bubbling inside him like lava in a fumarole.

"Did you hear?" Tristan said. "About the cops shooting all those people?"

Bayliss nodded.

"At practice they even said they're going through the hospital looking for people who were wounded. They're just dragging them away."

"Be cautious of rumor," Bayliss said, lifting a plastic sheet and removing a book that lay open facedown on the mechanism's glass top. He picked it up, studied it as if he could see it, then lay it down on a cart, picked up another, opened it by touch, and laid it down where the other had been. "Though in this case rumor is perfectly correct."

"Why'd they do it?" Tristan asked breathlessly. "Did the Mayor order them to shoot?"

"Rumor says that too," Bayliss said. In the years he had known him, Tristan had never seen Bayliss exchange a word with any other human being, had only seen others in the Library once or twice a year. But if Bayliss claimed to know the rumors, Tristan never doubted it. Bayliss had his ways.

"In this case the rumor is incorrect," Bayliss said, as the machine commenced its thump-and-glow routine again. "Or so I believe. An individual policeman panicked or lost control of his temper and started shooting, and his fellows spontaneously followed suit; this is what happened, you may depend on it."

He shook his head. "Fear and anger are always the products of defeat," Bayliss murmured.

"On the TV Admin said the crowd was harboring deserters who were probably armed and dangerous," Tristan said excitedly. "Then they said it was all a terrible tragedy. Then they said the demonstrators were traitors and had it coming. It don't sound like that all can be true."

" 'Doesn't,' " Bayliss corrected. "And it all cannot be true. The Administration is panicked. It fears that it's gone too far for even the docile and obedient populace of Homeland. May they be correct."

Tristan frowned. The librarian's conversation was showing a tendency to pull off in a certain direction, like a cage with its steering out of alignment. It was starting to unsettle him.

"Uh, just what *are* you doing, sir?"

"As I said, something I should have done a long time ago. Making copies of ancient words, in hopes the time has arrived when people will be prepared to read them once again."

He picked up another book, held it open before him, gazed with his blind eyes at a point above Tristan's forehead, and recited. "We hold these Truths to be self-evident, that all Men are created equal, that they are endowed by their Creator with certain inalienable Rights, that among these are Life, Liberty, and the pursuit of Happiness—That to secure these Rights, Governments are instituted among Men, deriving their just Powers from the Consent of the Governed. . . ."

The breath left Tristan in a rush. *Consent of the Governed?* "But that's—" he began.

"Wait," Bayliss rapped. "That whenever any Form of Government becomes destructive of these Ends, it is the Right of the People to alter or abolish it . . ."

He smiled thinly at the dumbstruck youth. "It is seditious, boy. It is antisocial. It is the most revolutionary political document ever devised. Far more revolutionary than the reactionary nonsense of 'revolutionary' socialism which attempted to succeed it."

"Wh-what are you going to do with it?"

"Disseminate it, boy. Hand it to folks on the street corners. A futile gesture, to be sure, but one that this old man cannot live with himself any longer without making."

He smiled again, making it twice more than Tristan usually saw him smile in a week. " 'Life, Liberty, and the Pursuit of Happiness—.' I'd say our current Form of Government has become amply destructive to those ends. It's *based* upon destroying them. Perhaps one or two people will read and understand. Perhaps a few seeds will be planted and will germinate."

He shook his head. "But most likely is that I'm a softheaded old fool."

"Why are you doing this?" Tristan asked.

"I wasn't born old, boy," Bayliss said in a dry-stick whisper. "Once I had ideals, energy. But I was weak; when I lost my eyesight, I lost those things too. I've hidden here in the Library for thirty years, taking the City's gold and keeping my nose clean.

"But now: enough. I'll never get my eyes back, but I will regain my integrity. My *pride*."

Tristan quickly lowered his head, just as if the old man could see the tears gathered in the corners of his eyes. Six years of captivity had done nothing to lessen his Plains-bred contempt for the smug, cowardly Citizens. But sometimes—Mr. Tomlinson facing down Dirk Posten and his butt boys in the hardware store, the ancient librarian among his books preparing to take his stand—the most unexpected City dwellers showed honor the equal of any Stormrider brother.

• • •

Tristan had found Bayliss at the copying machine on Tuesday. He did not get back to the Library until Thursday.

Friday was the opening game of the high school baseball season. Tristan was pumped with anticipation, and he wanted to share his excitement with Bayliss, even though the old man lacked his enthusiasm for sports.

He was also eager to discuss the latest news with Bayliss. Monday's shootings had brought a shocking end to the demonstrations in front of City Hall. But Wednesday night they had broken loose again with redoubled fury. Tristan wanted the old man to explain why that should be, or at least to steer him in the direction of understanding.

The Library's double bronze doors were locked.

Tristan stood there with a chill wet wind whipping his long black hair. Library hours were nine to nine, every weekday. Never in his years of coming here had he found the doors locked during those hours.

Panic flashed inside him like a shooting star. *Is the old man sick?* He'd never known Bayliss to be ill, but he knew age had a way of catching you up no matter how fast you ran.

He pounded on the door, first with one fist, then with both. "Hello! Hello? *Mr. Bayliss, are you in there?*"

"Hey. Hey, kid."

He turned around at the shout from behind. At the foot of the broad weather-spalled cement steps stood a big-bellied man in a hard hat. He was obviously attached to the crew of the panel truck parked toward the end of the block, fixing power lines downed by an early-morning onslaught of spring's inevitable fist-sized hailstones.

"Save your knuckles, kid," he called. "Library's closed."

"Where's Mr. Bayliss?"

The lineman shrugged. "Cops came and took away some old geezer this morning. That was him maybe?"

"Where's Mr. Bayliss?"

The police station foyer smelled of old sweat and illicit tobacco products. "Hold on, kid," said the heavyset sergeant standing behind the counter. "Who's Mr. Bayliss?" He glanced aside to buzz a couple of patrolmen out through the partition. They wore bulky riot gear, with the visors of their helmets up.

"He's the librarian. From the Public Library. Somebody said you took him away today. Where is he?"

The sergeant shook his head. He had a wad of something in his cheek and was chewing it. It might have been legal chicle, or it might not. "Are you next of kin?"

"No."

"Then we don't give you nothin'. You got no need to know."

Tristan turned red. "Listen—"

"No, *you* listen, junior. We're the law. We don't got to account to no snot-noses for every old piece of puke we scrape off the sidewalk for pushing subversion—"

Tristan vaulted the barrier. The sergeant dropped his jaw, staring in disbelief before grabbing for the not particularly well-worn grips of his Shawk & McLanahan service revolver.

Tristan caught him with a straight right to the mouth. He put all the happy anger of adolescence and six years' captivity into the blow. If the sergeant had owned more of a neck, or if what he had wasn't so well bulwarked by muscle and fat, the blow would've snapped it clean.

As it was the punch splintered teeth and busted the first two knuckles on Tristan's hand. Adrenaline blanked Tristan's pain. The sergeant went down.

The two riot cops turned and tried to get back in the door, but it had already locked behind them. The sidehandles of their *kubotan* nightsticks clashed as they hammered at the door.

There were plenty more cops where they came from. They came at Tristan in waves, to fall beneath his joyously flailing fists and feet. But the Law of the Gang-Stomp inevitably kicked in. It doesn't matter how tough you are when the odds are forty to one.

At last they swarmed him, and the nightsticks fell like Front Range hail. Tristan's vision became like the old newspapers he viewed on the Library's reader: black and white and red all over.

Tristan Tomlinson was a budding sports hero. But cops were cops; they were the backbone of the City's Administration, and Tristan had put a round dozen of them in the hospital. The City needed law'n'order even more desperately than it needed prestige.

Given Tristan's background, the judge wasn't inclined to be

lenient. But along with his proven athletic ability he had shown amazing fighting spirit that afternoon in the cop shop. Given recent events, the City had need of a combination like that.

The mine bosses lusted after his back and wind. The Therapists drooled over the prospect of unraveling his barbarian psyche. Neither the Black Gang nor Rehab got him.

He was sentenced to pay his Civic debt in the Green Machine: the Homeland Defense Force.

PART TWO

OUTLAW ONE

16

The trooper seated across from Tristan swept his coal-scoop-shaped helmet off his head. "Nothin' happenin'," he said, mopping his forehead with an olive-drab handkerchief. "Another wasted day sweating our asses off for nothing."

Then his forehead exploded out between his fingers and all over Tristan.

The six-wheeled Buffalo personnel carrier ran second in the column, right behind an armored car armed with a 20-millimeter quick-firer. The lead car veered right off the dirt track to stop when its sharp snout plowed into the base of the hill the column was running past. The vehicle commander blew out of the turret hatch on a pillar of yellow fire.

Staff Sergeant Tristan Tomlinson's hand clutched at his throat. His thunderstone arrowhead wasn't there, of course; hadn't been since he was eleven.

He had a feeling he'd miss it today.

There were a lot of men named Davis in the Homeland Defense Forces. Tristan's determination to find the right one was as strong as his memory was long.

The Davis he was looking for lived off base, as veteran troopers got to. Under a sky the color of sodden paper, Tristan walked toward his home, a prefabricated dig-and-drop-in semi-subterranean burrow on the outskirts of town. It was basically a big old piece of cement culvert sealed at both ends like a giant pipe bomb. A pick'em-up rode blocks in the yard, and a big V-twin Osage bike sat its stand at the end of the rutted drive.

An end of Tristan's mouth twisted beneath his neatly trimmed service mustache. He knocked on the door.

The girl who answered didn't look as if she could possibly be more than fifteen. Beneath the zits she was reasonably cute in a round-cheeked, pouty, vacant-eyed way. Dishwater-blond hair hung to the straps of what looked like a man's undershirt, laundered almost transparent over her sad pointy white-trash adolescent breasts, but not laundered any too recently to judge by the stains. The butt of an illegal cigarette smoldered between her fingers. She raised it to her lips for a defiant puff and said, "What the fuck do you want?"

"Is Sergeant Davis in?"

She showed teeth as stained as her shirt in an expression that might have meant anything. "Bud," she called over her shoulder. "Some sag-nuts grunt here to see you."

Tristan grimaced. There was no shining on the HDF hair regs. The white sidewalls gave his status away.

Davis shouldered the girl aside and slouched in the doorway. He was shorter than Tristan remembered him, but nobody was really that tall. Tristan could look him in the eye now. His gut was bigger, though. He wore an old OD blouse open over his own undershirt. A leather thong hung down into the undergarment, out of sight among the graying thatch of his chest. Tristan kept his eyes away from it.

Davis took a drag on his own cigarette. It looked machine-rolled, not a hand job. "What do you want, shavehead?"

"You're Sergeant First Class Walton Davis?" Tristan already knew the answer.

Davis's black eyebrows came together until it looked as if they'd been drawn on his head in a single lampblack swipe. "What if I am? Don't waste my time, shavehead."

"You have something of mine."

"Not fuckin' likely."

"Remember seven years ago? You delivered a prisoner to the Sedgwick Youth Hospice? Boy about eleven years old, only survivor of a motorcycle clan you wiped out that morning?"

Davis had his smoke to his mouth again. A smile spread either side of it, onto his stubbled cheeks. "Times sure do change, don't they? You grown a packet since then."

"You took something from me then," Tristan said, looking him in the eye. "I've come to ask you please to give it back."

Davis blew smoke in his face. "Fuck off, scooter puke."

Tristan's hands knotted to fists. "Bust him up, Bud!" the girl shrilled around the sergeant's biceps. "Break his face! I *hate* bike trash!"

Davis's brown eyes met Tristan's, now the merciless pale blue of midwinter sky. Davis had the weight on him, but it wasn't exactly all muscle. And Tristan excelled at Empty, the martial art practiced in barracks the way knife-fighting was in Dorm C, so-called because it used the unaided hands and feet. It was thoroughly against regulations, but unlike the Diagnostic & Developmental brass, the HDF higher-ups knew about it and looked the other way. It was brutal, but that was the way Command wanted its soldiers, no matter what rules the candy-assed Therapeutic types wrote for them. Any time lost from injuries suffered in all-out Empty practice could be written off to training accidents.

Davis shut his girlfriend off with a backhand across the face. "Don't yell at me, bitch," he snarled over his shoulder. *"Ever."*

He turned back to Tristan. "The amulet's mine, tramp. Right of conquest. Spoils of fuckin' war. Maybe you can take it off me, and maybe you can't. But we got rules against shavehead public troopies taking off on their superiors in this man's army. No candy-ass judge is gonna let you off light like when you busted up them City pigs. Make a play for me, court-martial'll have your ass in Hellville before you can unclench your asshole to shit."

"Someday," Tristan said, and walked away.

"Anytime, motherfucker," Davis said to his back.

Sergeant Davis had thought Tristan was just blowing wind, that much was clear. It was a mistake. Tristan was stone determined to get his father's amulet back.

But right now he was faced with the problem of surviving

long enough to take another crack at it. Or at seeing tomorrow's sun.

The gunner of the stricken armored car reared up out of the turret, screaming, bathed in a skyward torrent of fire. Muzzles flashed their pale semaphores from the hilltop to the column's right. Bullets pounded on the Buffalo's slab sides like hail, and tumbled away with shrill hawk screams. Ahead, a derelict flatbed truck came thumping out of a brushy draw between two hills, banged into a jumble of boulders that just happened to be lying beside the dirt road, and came to a stop blocking the column's path.

Lieutenant Hamilton stood up in the front of Tristan's Buffalo. "Out of the vehicles!" he shouted, waving his arms. "Ambush! Stop the column! Everybody out!"

As the Buffalo slowed Tristan jumped to his feet, ignoring the fact that it exposed the upper half of his body to the slanting gunfire storm. "No sir, wait!" he shouted. "We can't stop here! It's suicide!"

As if to emphasize his words the carrier behind them cranked to its left, off the dirt road into the scrub. An explosion lifted it immediately into the air and dumped it on its side. The squad within tumbled out, willingly or otherwise—and began to scream in agony as the tiny plastic butterfly mines sowed in the dirt began popping parts off them with ringing vicious cracks.

The rest of the lead squad huddled below the slab walls of the Buffalo. Their eyes ratcheted back and forth between their lieutenant and his much taller squad leader as though they were watching a tennis match. Hamilton kept yelling for the platoon to stop and unass, and Tristan kept yelling no and trying to get his attention.

"Sir, please," Tristan begged. "They've got AT rockets, they've got the high ground, they've got God knows how many mines scattered through the available cover. If we get pinned here, we're meat."

"God damn it, Sergeant, you'll follow my orders! The rules of engagement say we hunker down and wait for reinforcements."

"Rules of engagement my ass, sir. We're all going to die."

It was a beautiful ambush, well-laid and lethally executed. The cycle nomads lacked many military virtues—in fact, almost all of them—but they gave great ambush. And there was no question this was a nomad ambush. The broken country where the Arkansas busted out of the Rockies south of Homeland was too far north and west for Dallasites in such concentration, no other City had enough of a hard-on for Homeland at the moment to try a stunt like this. Besides, the gunfire had the stop-and-go popcorn-popping quality of massed single shots, not the chainsaw rip of full-auto bursts such as all Cities taught their grunts to fire.

It was a big group, and extremely well-organized for a one-percenter clan, there was no doubt about it. Lethally well-equipped too—though a half-dozen shoulder-fired antitank rockets and a couple crates of mines cost less and were far less bulky to transport than the truckloads of ammo a City platoon routinely blazed off in a minor skirmish. The High Free Folk weren't frugal about much, but hard experience had taught them to make the most of their killing resources.

Tristan had read a book that was banned by the City Council, but which the Library had a copy of anyway. It was by a man called Sun Tzu, who may not have existed in spite of having written it. In it, the possibly nonexistent philosopher wrote, *"In death ground, fight."*

If this wasn't death ground, Tristan didn't know what was. He'd absorbed his ambush lore even before reading Sun Tzu, around the Hardrider campfires. Quicksilver Messenger was a master of ambushes, and loved them. When he was happy, he told stories of successful ambushes he'd been on; in his black despairing moods he spoke of failed ambushes, or ambushes he himself had ridden into.

Tristan knew in his marrow what kind of a fix First Platoon of Bravo Troop was in. And here he stood jawing with a shit-for-brains looie while bullets cracked past their ears.

A nasty look of triumph twisted the lieutenant's face. "That's mutiny, Sergeant. I've waited a long time to get the goods on you—"

About that time his right clavicle came popping right out of his chest, propelled by a slug from a looted storm carbine. It looked like a twig that had been used to stir red paint. Lieutenant Hamilton looked down at the mess his camouflaged blouse had become, and passed right out.

If you rode with a man, you never let him down, no matter how big a shitheel he was. So the first words out of Tristan's mouth were, "Somebody see to the lieutenant." The next were, "Driver, step on it. Drive us right up the goddamn hill."

The driver's position on the Buffalo was a little cab with heavy sloped armor-glass stuck on the front of the vehicle like the cab of a caterpillar. It was open to the rear so that a replacement could easily get to the wheel if the driver sucked a round. The driver turned around and instantly started showing attitude: "The lieutenant said—"

"Lieutenant's out of it. I'm in command now." He stuck the muzzle brake of his M52 storm carbine in the driver's left ear. "Follow my orders or I put your brains on the dashboard."

The driver turned white, and around, drove the vehicle uphill, and gunned it straight into the teeth of the ambush.

17

As the armored carrier went groaning and bouncing up the slope in first, Tristan glanced back. The crew was bailing out of the second armored car at the tail of the column; whether it had actually been hit or they had panicked, Tristan couldn't know. The two surviving Buffaloes had stayed on the road; they either hadn't gotten the lieutenant's message or they'd had their doubts after seeing what happened to the first carrier to follow his orders. The nearer one had already pulled up into ragged echelon with Tristan's vehicle. As he watched, the second followed laboriously. Of the two light scout cars in the escort, one was shooting up the hill with its machine gun erupting from its roll bar. The other was nowhere to be seen, though a billow of black smoke from the scrub across the road hinted it might have run afoul of a mine.

Tristan turned forward then, and did the thing that Plains warriors most derided City soldiers for: held his M52 two-handed over the Buffalo's little armored cab and let a whole magazine go blind. He disapproved viscerally and intellectually of the City doctrine of substituting indiscriminate full-auto bullet-launching for marksmanship. But this was maybe the one circumstance in the world where it was called for. In the killzone—old Sun Tzu's *death ground*—the enemy had fire superiority from the get-go; if you tried to play cool and pick your target you got dead. The only thing to do was to try to put enough lead in the air to make the other guy blink and *charge the bastards*.

The Buffalo was well suited for that. It looked like nothing so much in the world as a big armored dump truck, with its tractor cab and slab sides and open top. Its mass and shape directed the force of mines upward and around the vehicle—what took out the second Buffalo was probably not just a mine but a big-ass command-detonated explosive, something like fertilizer soaked in fuel oil, and it hadn't *destroyed* the carrier; it had merely knocked it over. The Buffalo's thick sides shed small-arms fire. It offered no overhead protection, of course, but you could get out in a hell of a hurry if something did go wrong, which the crew of a hardtop couldn't as the fate of the lead armored car had shown.

From his reading Tristan knew personnel-carrier design had been a dilemma for a long time. Smart troops didn't ride inside a closed APC for fear of burning; green or lazy troops wouldn't get *out*, to avoid effort and the occasional stray round, and they did burn. The open-top Buffalo kept most lead off if you stayed low, and blind-firing over the rim wasn't a lot less accurate than shooting out the firing-ports of closed armored vehicles.

Once headed up the hill, the Buffalo protected its passengers from the slanting fire that had blown the first trooper's brains out. The outlaws' fire hammered on the hull with insane ferocity, but it could no more penetrate than so many fists.

Smoke blossomed, and an AT rocket came rushing at them from a bush to their left at the top of the hill. The driver made a keening sound through his nose. The rocket buzzed harmlessly overhead, a quick dark streak against a dirty-linen sky, and then the carrier was bouncing over the crest of a hill.

"There's a man—" the driver yelled, starting to swerve.

"Run the fuckard down," Tristan snarled.

The driver did. He cranked the wheel and sent the Buff bucking into a bush. A bearded man dropped a bolt-action rifle and turned to run. The Buffalo's nose bumped him and threw him to the ground, and the big honeycomb tires took him.

Behind the bush stood a big cruiser bike, a full-dress Kiowa sled. *These are some ballsy sons of bitches,* Tristan thought. He winced as metal crumpled beneath the tires. *To bring their big scooters on an ambush like this.*

"Left!" he shouted at the driver. "Crank it left!" He straightened and gave the arm signal for the rest of the column to follow his lead.

The numbers, discipline, and bonehead arrogance of the ambushers were starting to rattle together into a recognizable shape in Tristan's mind. With a fresh box in the well of his M52 he straightened up, ready to do some serious table-turning. The brush-churning wheels of the Buff flushed another ambusher. The snarling-puma colors on the back of his sleeveless denim vest told Tristan what he knew already.

"Catheads," he said. "Fucking Catheads."

He had always wondered what he'd do if, the first time he got in a serious hassle with a Plains clan, it proved to be with blood brothers of the Hardriders. Instead Father Sun or Brother Wind or somebody had arranged that his first face-to-face shoot-out should be with the 'Riders' blood *enemies*. The Hardriders hated the Cats worse than the Smoking Mirrors, and the feeling was mutual.

He aimed past the cab and put a short burst right through the embroidered catamount face.

"Stop it here," he yelled at the driver. Because it lacked overhead armor, the Buff could carry heavier protection on the front, back, and sides than the armored cars did. But you still didn't want to stay boxed in a huge waddling missile-magnet longer than you absolutely had to.

He turned to the squad. "Everybody out of the pool. It's time to kick butt."

The heavy tailgate of the Buff fell open with a squeal of hinges. Struggling with their helmets, packs, and storm carbines, the squaddies began to spill out and flop on their faces in the scrub and tough bunchgrass.

The sky looked like a stained sheet that had been slashed with a knife, showing blue beyond. "Get the MG up and going in that bush," he told the machine-gunner and his assistant. "The rest of you, get off your dead asses. Forward by short assault rushes, rolling overwatch."

One fire team, short the ambush's first victim, whose brains were drying on Tristan's cammies, stayed down to give covering fire while Tristan led his three men forward along the crest line, firing from the hip.

There was a big sage bush ahead of him, chin-high, with pale-leafed branches spread wide. From the middle of it a flower of light bloomed, flickering erratically as if blowing in the wind that had come up from nowhere, whipping stinging bits of sand and rain against his cheek.

Time slowed. *He's shooting at me,* Tristan thought. *I'll be damned.*

He was out in the open, not ten feet from the muzzle now. He'd been under fire before, but never at this range—he had no idea on earth how the outlaw could *miss*. The nearest cover was the bush with the gunman in it. It was the ambush all over again. If he tried to run or go to ground, the Cathead would put the hurt on him sure.

He blitzed straight into the dusty-green bush. A young face fringed in sandy beard raised toward him, an astonished expression rounding eyes and mouth and making the Cathead look like one of those faces all of circles of various sizes drawn by the little kids in Sedgwick. The outlaw started to rear up, trying to bring his carbine to bear on the charging Tristan.

Tristan helped him along with a running kick that lifted him up to his knees. His arms flew up, the Osage carbine spinning away. Tristan stuck the muzzle of his M52 between the front flaps of his colors and shot him twice.

With the immediate danger dealt with, external sound once again began to override the roar of pulse in his ears. A sound like drawn-out prairie thunder was rising about him: the blatting of scores of big outlaw bikes revving up for fight or flight.

Right now it was Option One. A burly nomad with blond hair in flying braids was bearing down on him on a rangy scooter with far-extended front forks and a gas tank painted in bright geometric patterns, holding an aluminum pole with a catamount skull mounted on it in one hand and steering with the other.

Isn't that just like the Catheads, flashed through Tristan's mind. The bastard was trying to count coup on him. Well, the Cats had a way of showing class, even if they were animals most ways.

The nomad raised the cat's-head standard. Tristan whipped his storm carbine to his shoulder and fired two semi-auto from one knee, a pure Plains-warrior move. Two fist-sized splotches of red appeared on the rider's grimy T-shirt.

Tristan had always kind of thought the .243 round used by the M52 to be a tad underpowered—the Hardriders used the flat-shooting .243 as a light-game rifle, taking pronghorn and small whitetails at long range in open ground. But in practice it served just fine. There was little muzzle jump between rounds, and the Cathead went right over the rear tire of his big old Iron Mountain sled.

The Cathead standard landed practically at Tristan's feet. Without thinking he stooped, caught it up with his left hand, and raised it over his head with a hawk's scream of triumph. Coup had been counted big-time, but not by the Hardriders' ancient enemy.

Already the chug of outlaw bikes had begun to Doppler deeper as the Catheads turned tail. There was nothing deadlier than a busted ambush—for the ambushers. Tristan's dismounted troopies were all down in the scrub blasting merrily away at the Catheads as they ran for their scooters. The surviving combat car had had the sense to bust the ridge line at full speed—speed was what they had in place of the Buff's massive armor—and was now running flat-out parallel, while the gunner played Rat Patrol with the .30-caliber roll-bar gun. Nobody knew where the expression *Rat Patrol* came from, but it was the scout-car crewman's universal phrase for driving and firing flat fucking out.

That the upper-Arkansas country was pretty broken up was all that let any of the Cathead war-band get away. The troopies blasting away with their storm carbines set on full rock 'n' roll didn't hit much. But the bikers' unbreakable reflex was to go for their scooters when the wind of battle blew against them; it was a major disgrace to get killed afoot, passed only by being captured that way. And once mounted, they were easy targets for the scout-car gunner and the two squad automatic weapons that had made it up the hill. Especially with their cruisers wallowing across broken ground and bogging down in drifts of sand; that Cathead vanity in bringing the full-dress sleds instead of agile scramblers was paying off in blood.

Tristan just stood there with the Cat standard raised and the wind whipping rain and the smell of gunsmoke and spilled fuel against his face, watching his boys chase the outlaws over hills and down arroyos with their bullet-streams. The rider he'd

downed was lying nearby. His breathing had reached the rat-
tling stage.

Something made him look down. The dying man's bloodshot
eyes locked his. "You—" the Cathead croaked. "You ain't—
ain't no minge Citizen."

Tristan laughed. The head rush of victory was inflating him
like a balloon. "No. I'm not."

"What . . . are you?"

"I am Tristan Hardrider. Last of the Hardriders."

The man's eyes bulged. "The Hardriders are dead!" Blood
gushed from his mouth. His head fell back against the hard-
packed caliche.

"Not yet, they're not," Tristan quietly said.

He had known he was dead when he first saw the president of
the court-martial.

"You, Staff Sergeant Tristan Tomlinson, stand accused of
rank insubordination; of mutiny in the face of the enemy; of—"

The room was small and airless and deep underground. The
smell of sweat and mildew and confined air Tristan always associated with the cloistered City was overlaid with the tang of
shoe polish. The tables and chairs for use of the prosecutor and
Tristan's thoroughly intimidated defender had been removed.
For verdict and sentencing the chamber was bare of decoration
or furniture except for a short standard bearing the red, white,
blue, and gold Homeland flag and the judge's table.

Tristan tuned the warrant officer court-secretary out. The
specific charges he was rehashing prior to judgment being delivered didn't matter one damned bit. What they added up to
was death by firing squad, or life in the mines, which came to
the same by a far more agonizing road. *If* he was found guilty,
and that was one thing he never doubted.

His platoon lieutenant might have been able to forgive him if
Tristan's bold action had gotten the unit washed away. But victory was inexcusable.

The lieutenant was well-connected. He came of old Admin
stock, with a handful of Councillors and one Mayor in his
bloodline. But even that didn't count for a pinch of dried buffalo
flop.

Tristan didn't know the faces of the captains sitting left and right behind the table in front of which he stood stiffly at attention. He wasted no time looking at them. Despite his gold major's leaves the man in the middle obviously didn't pull enough rank to wear his shades in court, but Tristan didn't need them to recognize Black Jack Masefield.

For his part in saving the City soldiers from themselves after the Cheyenne Wells debacle, Masefield had been given command of the Strikers, the City's motorcycle-riding scout force, as well as a promotion. Tristan wondered if this was another bone his masters were tossing him: the last of the Hardriders for dessert, as it were.

"—and, finally, conduct unbecoming a member of the Homeland Defense Force, in that you willfully and maliciously did mutilate the bodies of fallen enemy personnel—"

Well, all right, he *had* scalped the Catheads he had downed. His ass belonged to the HDF, but he knew where his duty lay. He noticed that the City court-martial wouldn't dignify the Plains scum with the name *soldiers*, even though they'd come within an ace of wiping out half a hundred City troops.

The court secretary finished and glared at him. Masefield folded his hands on the blotter before him. His eyes were gray, so pale they seemed colorless against the boot-lather tan of his face, even buffered by the pale raccoon-mask from wearing the sunglasses all the time. They looked surprisingly weary. Tristan wanted to believe the bastard's conscience kept him up at night, but he knew in his heart that Masefield would sentence him to die and never lose a wink.

"On the charge of mutilation of enemy dead," Masefield said, his voice baritone and sure, "this court finds you guilty as charged, and orders that you be stripped of noncommissioned rank and returned to the status of civic soldier."

All right, you mingy bastard, be that way. Play it out. Tristan summoned every scrap of Plains pride. He would not let the fuckards see him so much as break sweat.

"On the other charges—"

Tristan stiffened. *This is it. All those years of eating City shit and biding my time go washing down the gully.*

"—this court finds you not guilty, and finds instead that you acted in accordance with the proudest traditions of the City of Homeland and her Defense Force."

• • •

Tristan drifted down the corridor outside, buffeted by the back-slaps of the survivors of his platoon. He couldn't have been more stunned if somebody'd bounced a Kwahadi lead mace off his skull.

A hand gripped his shoulder. He turned, feeling the stupid look on his face like a coat of drying mud.

Major John Masefield stood there, looking up at him with a slight smile.

"City needs men like you, son," he said. "It'd be a criminal waste to send you to the mines."

If there was anything in the world to say, Tristan couldn't think of it.

"Damned near as big a waste leaving you in the Regulars," the slayer of the Hardriders told the last of that line. "I want you to join us. I want you in the Strikers."

"Do—do you know who I am?" He felt drunk, and knew he sounded the same way.

"Of course. You're the nomad boy we captured, the day we wiped out that marauding clan. I've had my eye on you ever since."

If he hadn't been so stunned by the way events were blowing, Tristan could never have said what he did next: "I'm sworn to kill you."

Masefield grinned. "Of course," he said. "You'll just have to put it off awhile."

18

"Southern exposure isn't very romantic in midsummer," the young woman said. Back-scatter moonlight turned the hair that fell to shoulders left bare by her Empire-waisted evening gown metallic and pale. "Even when the moon is full, it's so far north you have to crane way out to look at it."

Tristan laughed. His dress uniform was a blue so dark it looked almost black even in good light. It made him look dashing as hell, and he knew it. Hell, it had been designed that way.

"At least the sky's clear enough to see the moon tonight. Be grateful for what we have." He caught her smooth hand in his scarred hard one, twined fingers, turned the back of her hand to his lips, and kissed it gently.

Her father's house was built in the foothills south of town—literally *in*. It was sunk into the flank of a hill, back and sides surrounded by earth to the level of the roof, the front an artificial cliff two stories tall. The Plains stretched away before them, undulating shortgrass land, contours smoothed in shades of silver, gray, and black by the full but invisible moon.

Tristan stared out over the nighttime land. He sighed, smoothing a wing of his ferocious handlebar mustache with a thumbnail. To her a night like this was pleasant, even pretty. Nothing more. She had led a sheltered life, protected by walls from the worst violence of an angry Earth. She knew a peaceful evening such as this was rare, but she didn't *truly* appreciate it for what it was.

"A gift of Mother Earth and Mother Sky," he murmured.

With a cool smile she disengaged her fingers. "I hate it when you talk like that," she said in a dry, half-bantering tone. "I never know whether it's a sign you're reverting to barbarism, or simply the delight you Strikers all take in playing the barbarian."

He showed her his patented devil's grin. "Maybe it's both."

She didn't melt at his smile. Maybe that was one of the reasons he found her so damned desirable. "I'd certainly never think of marrying anything but a civilized man," she said.

She tipped her face back, lips parted. He kissed her.

He became aware of *presence* behind them on the balcony. He raised his head and turned, hand dropping to the ceremonial holster flap of his Bolo.

Quanah stood there, his backlit bulk making the tall and broad-shouldered but rangy Tristan feel like an adolescent again. The Comanche ex-caravan guard's great jack-o'-lantern face was masked in shadow, but even in good light Tristan would never have known if the big bastard was amused or not. Indians made the best poker players. They knew how to show nothing when they wanted to.

"Colonel wants you," the Comanche said. "In the study."

"Your father's timing is either terrible or perfect, Ellie," Tristan told the woman. "I'm not sure which."

She smiled thinly. "It's terrible timing. Father is too untraditional to care what you and I do."

Tristan made a noncommittal sound and followed the big Indian.

"So how come you can always sneak up on me like that? I've been a Striker five years now. If my hearing wasn't pretty fair some blond-haired Son of Odin son of a bitch would've sneaked up and given me a second smile by now."

"Day an Indian can't sneak up on a white-eyes, it's time to bag it, go into space, and let you have the damn country."

Tristan showed a sour grin to Quanah's wide back. From his long-lost Library days he knew people really *had* gone into space, way back before the Star fell. If he hadn't known that, he would have chalked the phrase up as just one of those enigmatic things Indians say, probably to rev up the white man and make him look silly.

Of course that was probably still what it was. But you could never be too sure what the Comanche's sometimes employers, the Osage Nation, might have up their denim overall sleeves. . . .

"Some Purity boys here tonight," Quanah said.

"Here? At a party celebrating Mayor Schenk's first year in office?" Tristan shook his head. "They're showing some balls. Think they'll cause any trouble?"

Quanah stopped at the oaken study door, shrugged like a mountain with a tremor rocking through it. "They do, I throw their white asses out."

The study was lined with shelves of books. Nowhere in Homeland except the Library itself had Tristan seen so many books. Tristan walked between the book-lined walls, down a long hardwood table to where a leather chair sat in a pool of light at the far end of the room.

He stopped a respectful distance from the chair, on the light's fringe. "You sent for me, Colonel."

"Sit down, Lieutenant," said Lieutenant Colonel "Black Jack" Masefield. "Care for a glass of wine?"

Tristan paused. He was leery of alcohol; he tended to overdo it. He didn't like to lose control. Then he shrugged and sat down. "Sure. It's a party. Sir."

Masefield laughed softly and poured from a bottle. He wore regular Defense Force dress greens, with the jacket off and tie loosened. "Here's to the Reconciliationists," he said, raising his glass. He never referred to Mayor Schenk's party by its modern official name of Sanity. "A year on the job, and Homeland's already showing signs of something that looks a lot like liberty."

Tristan sipped. He knew a lot of people in the HDF didn't feel that way about Sanity. "Quanah says there are some white-jumpsuit types downstairs."

"Why shouldn't they be? It's not a free City yet, but we're working on it."

"Purity doesn't see it that way."

"No. They think the City's gotten too free, and want to make things the way they used to be, only more so. It's the Newtonian nature of politics. The success of Reconciliationism has provoked a powerful opposite reaction. And we tolerate it."

He raised his glass to the light of the single standing lamp, swirling the yellow fluid and studying the way the light played in it. "That's what happens in a free society; it respects the rights of even its bitterest foes."

"These Purity bastards aren't going to settle for speechifying and passing out handbills forever, sir."

"No. Probably not. But that's why Homeland needs men like us, Lieutenant. Not all the enemies are outside the walls."

They sat for a moment in silence. The sound of a Vivaldi concerto came up through the floor.

"Is it true, sir?" Tristan asked. "What they say?"

"What *who* says? I haven't trained you very well if you can't be any more precise than that, Lieutenant."

"Mr. Breeze." It meant he'd heard a rumor. Tristan grinned suddenly. It was a Plains phrase from his childhood. The Strikers had caught it from him, and it had spread to the rest of the HDF. "He says when Mayor Schenk steps down you'll run to be his successor."

Masefield cocked an eyebrow. "He says that, does he? He's a little premature. Unless this Purity backlash gathers momentum quicker than anybody thinks possible—most of all the Purity leadership—John Amos is going to be in office a good many years yet."

"But someday?"

Masefield tipped the glass, shrugged. "Someday, perhaps. I don't think soldiers belong in politics. But some people feel differently, and John Amos has let it be known he's one of them."

He gave Tristan a lopsided slight smile. "You're my best man, not to mention the leading candidate for my son-in-law. Maybe I'll make you *my* successor. Think you can handle it?"

"Sure." Tristan rubbed his long chin. "Uh, you said this *would* be sometime in the future."

"Indeed I did. I won't be thrusting command of the Strikers into your capable but twenty-four-year-old hands just yet."

He set down the glass. Its base tunked decisively on the hardwood tabletop.

"So the Catheads are back," Masefield said, "and they've gotten religion."

Tristan nodded. "That's the word out on the Plains, sir. Folks say they're even meaner than they used to be."

"Ah, yes, the blessings of the higher, spiritual cast of mind. Fortunately religion isn't famed for making people *smarter*." His fingertips played the tabletop briefly as if it were the key-board to the grand piano downstairs. "It's hard to see a bunch of outlaws going for the Fusion, though."

The Fusion was a mystery cult arising somewhere east of the Big River, in a part of the continent that was itself mysterious to the nomads and Citizens of the Plains. The Eastern Seaboard had been more extensively remodeled by StarFall and unquiet earth than even the FlameLands of the Northwest.

The first missionaries of the Fusion had arrived in Homeland a little over five years ago, not long before the ambush that re-sulted in Tristan's court-martial. They taught that humankind should tear down the walls that kept people apart; not just the barriers of race and politics, but the boundaries of individuality as well. They claimed that adepts of their faith were in constant telepathic communion with one another, joined in an ecstatic Fusion of minds.

Despite its emphasis on discipline, the Fusion had a lot of ap-peal among the wiftier elements of Health. The Evangelical zealots of the Church of Christ, Citizen denounced its mission-aries as agents of Satan. Dallas banned the cult entirely. It wasn't anything Tristan paid much attention to.

"You're going out in two days?" Masefield asked.

"Yes, sir." It was a rhetorical question. In the years since Cheyenne Wells Masefield's handful of Strikers had done a bet-ter job of keeping the human-based violence of the Plains from washing into the City than the more numerous HDF regulars ever had. The Strikers were chosen for their initiative, and al-lowed to exercise it. They exercised it when Masefield directed, on tasks he set them. He knew when Tristan was taking his scrambler out again.

"Go east as far as you can."

"Is this side of the Mississippi okay, or do you want me to press on farther?"

"If the Cats are on as much of a tear as we're hearing, even you'd have your work cut out for you getting past them. I hear they have a contract out on you."

Tristan shrugged. "It's nothing I'm not used to. I'm a Hardrider. We've been their enemies since before there were Hardriders."

There was a moment's unspoken acknowledgment of why there were no longer Hardriders. Then Masefield said, "You're damned near as good as you think you are, boy. But sending you on an information-gathering mission does me no good if the Catheads tack your hide on the wall of some Digger's barn to dry. And remember, the Cats aren't the only clan with a grudge against Outlaw One." Outlaw One was Tristan's radio call sign.

"What information are you looking for, sir?"

"I want you to find out just how a bunch as crazy as the Catheads turns into two-wheeled missionaries for a super-regimented cult like the Fusion."

"Tristan Tomlinson! You're not thinking of going downstairs with those things over your shoulder." The tone of Elinor Masefield's voice made it clear she was not *asking*.

"Not for a moment, honey," Tristan said. He had the buffalo-hide panniers from his scrambler over his shoulder. The butt of his Saskatoon Mark V patrol carbine in its buckskin sheath stuck up behind his ear. Quanah had retrieved the saddlebags from the locked storeroom where Tristan had deposited them on arrival.

She crossed her arms under her breasts. "Then how are you proposing to get out of the house?"

He walked out onto the balcony, pulling out a coil of rope as he did. He broke the coil in two, tied one end around his waist, tossed the other end out between the wooden balusters to snake down into the night.

"Like this," he said. He kissed her on the cheek, then jumped up on the railing. He reached down for the free-hanging rope and began to lower himself hand over hand.

She ran to the rail and leaned over. Her breasts—large for her slim frame—threatened to pop out of her low bodice. "You are completely crazy!" she yelled.

His feet dangling inches above the seat of his parked bike, he laughed up at her. "I know," he called back. "That's why you can't get enough of me."

He dropped lightly beside the motorcycle, coiled the rope back in his panniers, slapped them on the bike behind the seat, and rode away laughing.

19

"Home so soon, Outlaw One?" Leo asked, leaning against the interior door with a beer in his hand.

Tristan dropped his panniers on the rump-sprung couch, plopping down beside them. Dust swarmed up around him like a cloud of gnats. "I'm going out day after tomorrow. Big job. Have to get ready tomorrow."

He and three other Strikers rented a house on the eastern outskirts of Homeland. It was all aboveground, built like his foster parents' house in some long-lost time when things were made to *last*, and could bear up to a few hailstones and a few tremors without having to burrow into Mama Earth's capacious bosom for shelter.

It was showing the years, of course, as everybody must. But it was a gracious old age, able to tolerate the antics and shoddy housekeeping of four healthy young men.

Tristan's second housemate, Mal, emerged from the kitchen in shorts and a sage-green T. The fourth man, Billy, was out on a mission.

Mal grinned wickedly at Tristan. "The Ice Princess still isn't putting out, in other words."

Tristan frowned. "Hey. I didn't say anything about that."

"No. But you're here. That means you're not dipping your wick in any wells of ice water—"

"Slack it," Tristan growled.

Leo laughed. "Juan never knows when to back off." Mal's call sign was Juan Mo' Time, for reasons no one knew. *Ask the ladies* was his unvarying answer when asked. "It's his style. You remember how he kept needling those seven Kiowas in that trading-post bar down to Wagon Mound?"

Mal winced under the shock of light brown hair falling almost in his eyes. "Ouch. That's hitting below the belt, Leo."

"Some of that was involved, as I recall." Leo was watching Tristan out of the corner of his eye, and Tristan saw the big man relax as he sensed Tristan's quick tension flowing out of him.

Leo was like that. For one thing, he didn't have the customary one-syllable hard-sounding City nickname. "It's short," he'd say, "but it's definitely polysyllabic."

He was not your average Striker, if you could say there was any such animal. The average Striker was small, like Mal, or at least whip-lean and panther-lithe after the fashion of Tristan. Leo was neither. He was a great big black bear of a man, with curly dense hair all over his body, as you could see right now, thanks to his propensity for hanging around the rented house in his underwear: on his chest and arms and legs, in a spectacular walrus mustache under an old potato of a nose, even on his cheeks, which were perpetually blue and bristly no matter how recently he'd shaved. The only place it was sparse, he would point out ruefully when he'd had a few, was on top of his head.

His call sign, of course, was Big Bear.

He was also a born diplomat and peacemaker. It was a good thing. When something torqued his nuts, which was *extremely* rare, his fury was so volcanic even Tristan gave him plenty of highway.

Mal padded in, sat on an overstuffed chair across from Tristan, pulled his bare feet up, and began picking at the stuffing bulging out of one threadbare arm. He was a quick, cunning man, never still. He reminded Tristan of Quicksilver Messenger, but without the savage mood swings. In his own odd prairie-fire way, he was stable; not *predictable*, but stable. Fire is always hot, and so was he.

"Didn't mean to wire you up," he said to Tristan. "Everybody in the Strikers's been drooling after the old man's only child since she was about fourteen. You're the first one of us sag-nuts bike tramps she's ever given time of day to. But nothing in your behavior has exactly given us any reason to stop calling her the Ice Princess, if you know what I mean."

Tristan smiled wryly and accepted a glass of apple juice Leo had padded into the kitchen to bring him. Maybe that was part of the reason Elinor had such an effect on Tristan. She encouraged his attention—she said she loved him—but she made him keep his distance.

With most of his growing days behind him, Tristan was a pretty impressive specimen, if he did say so himself. Six-four, long-muscled, graceful in a big-cat way. He wore his hair in a brush, as a nod to regs, but like most Strikers—Mal was a clean-shaven exception—took advantage of the slack allowed the scouts in the matter of facial hair. With his long chin, a nose that several good bustings had turned into a hawk's beak, his Fu Manchu mustache and the wildfire grin beneath, and most of all his eyes—smoke or springwater or burning like vents into a forge, depending on his mood—few women wanted to keep their distance from him.

"It's not too late, guy," Mal said, watching him in that sidelong way he favored. "You've still got a black book the size of the HDF Manual."

Tristan tipped his head back and gazed at the yellowed peeling paint of the ceiling. "Don't think so. Gotta hit the road early."

Mal laughed. "Listen to this! Call the papers! When you first came into this chickensquat outfit, you'd have stayed at that party soaking up the booze till dawn, and then snuck off with a politician's daughter or two—or their wives, if they were cute enough—to do a little exploration in the bush. This is not the Outlaw One of old. What do we see happening here, Leo? Is the boy sick?"

"He's turning respectable," Leo said from his doorway.

"Respectable?" Tristan said, feigning outrage. *"Respectable?"* He shook his head and stood up.

"Sister Moon help me if I'm catching *respectability* at the ripe old age of twenty-four," he said. He hitched his panniers over his shoulder and nodded his way past Leo's furry bulk to go back and hit the rack.

• • •

He didn't sleep with the stuffed grizzly Mr. and Mrs. Tomlinson had given him anymore. The boys back in barracks had learned to be respectful of his little foibles, especially once he tempered his berserker rages with some Empty proficiency, and his fellow Strikers, like the High Free Folk they spent so much time among, inclined to habits that were weirder than that. He had just up and quit.

The little grizzly was snug in his accustomed place in the panniers, though. He was never far from Tristan. He'd ridden in his ruck the day of the ambush near the Arkansas. Tristan didn't have his thunderstone's protection; that bear was his luck.

Tristan felt a certain discomfort that he hadn't exactly been used to in the days before he and Ellie Masefield fell in love. But he'd had an active day, as usual, and had been a soldier of one sort of another for seven years. He fell asleep quickly, remembering the feel of her hair, the soap-clean scent of her skin.

His parents did not visit him. They hadn't in almost five years.

His father's eyes were terrible and bright. "You've betrayed me, boy. You've betrayed the Hardriders."

He made himself hold Wyatt Hardrider's unblinking stroke-victim glare a few heartbeats longer, then turned to his mother. She hung back, dim in the mistiness of the World-Behind-the-World. Her normally proud gaze was downcast.

Black Jack Masefield had killed her too, after all.

"When you signed on with the Butcher, we thought it was a good scam, to get close to him so you could carry out your vengeance. 'A good scam's worth a whole MC'—remember how Quicksilver Messenger always used to say that? Or have you forgot the Messenger too, like you forgot what you owe your blood and your clan?"

Tristan dropped his eyes.

"But no." Wyatt Hardrider's words tolled like a death sentence. Which in a way they were. "It was a scam, okay. It was a scam on us."

Masefield's a good man, *he longed to say,* a great man. He can end the fighting between City and Plains. We're losing in the long run, don't you see? The nameless little massacres like the one that washed you away happen every week, somewhere

on the Plains. Every week another clan goes down. The Cities
are going to *win.*

Besides . . . it's been so long. And killing him won't bring
you back.

*Of course, since this was the Dreamworld, his father heard
his every thought.*

"You low-down little turncoat!" *his father thundered. His
hair and mustache bristled, as if a charge was building in him
before a lightning strike. In fact blue flames did crackle among
the coarse hairs. Being dead gave you some unfair advantages
where histrionics were concerned.*

"The City got to you, boy! Your mother and I have visited you
faithful, year in and out, to help you keep your center and keep
true."

He seemed to deflate then. The crackling fires died. "But it
didn't do no good. The City turned you."

"No," *Tristan said.* "No!" *he screamed, when Wyatt and Jen
began to fade.*

"No, I didn't! I'm still your son! I'm still a Hardrider! I'm
doing what's best—damn you, don't you see?"

*His parents were gone. For the first time in his life, he was
truly alone.*

Sometimes he dreamed yet that he was a small boy, blood
drying on his face and chest, black braids flying in a stinking
wind, screaming for his mommy and his daddy, who would
never answer again. He'd driven off more than a couple of
girlfriends that way, and once he'd woken up sobbing hysterically while Leo cradled his head in his lap. In barracks that
would have won him a raft of shit, but even if it hadn't been Leo
who woke him from his nightmare, no Striker would've said a
word. You were assumed to have a fair amount of craziness in-
born if you were a Striker, and Strikers were hanging out there
on the fringe days, weeks, months at a time—unlike the Regulars who, given the hit-and-run style of their usual antagonists,
didn't have to stay on the line for any length of time unless it
had terminally hit the fan. Strikers woke up screaming all the
time, in bivouac anyway. Just part of the job.

He was spared that dream tonight. He had the other one,

though. The vision of the black wasteland, with the blobby cruciform glow on the horizon. For whatever reason, it had never forsaken him.

Tonight the strange shape blazed up brighter than he had ever seen it before. He ran toward it until his legs quivered and his lungs burned. It tantalized him with hints of shape, but in the end his vision held itself as chaste as Ellie Masefield.

"Enjoying the clean night air? It smells better now, I imagine."

She whirled. A young man had come into the room. He was of medium height for a man, about her own in fact, dressed in a jumpsuit so uncompromisingly white that even the butter-colored lamplight could hardly soften its starkness. He wore his brown hair cropped to a stiff widow's-peak brush. It looked as if all the softness had been baked out of him somehow. Perhaps by the inner fires you could see shining out his dark eyes.

"You could knock," Elinor Masefield said. In the light she had her father's eyes, steel gray, and ashen-blond hair.

"At least I come and go by way of the door. Like a *civilized* man."

"You have a magical way of reminding me just how boring civilization can be."

He made a show of looking around, as if probing the corners and shadowed places of the room for bugs or informers. "At one time, statements like that might have been taken as evidence of marked antisocial tendencies."

"They still are in places. By you, for example."

The man in white barked a laugh. "Not me. I know you're joking; I know your heart."

"You'd have purged me a long time ago if I weren't a woman, and beautiful."

He slid forward with a fluidity surprising for one so taut. He grasped her hands in his. They were not calloused like those of a worker from the Blocks, but they felt like wire wound over steel. "Not so. Not so at all. We value your incisive mind, your unbreakable will—"

"Also I'm well-connected," she said, holding her face averted and head well back on her long slim neck to avoid his attempt to press a kiss on her.

He laughed, let her go, and walked out the open French doors to the balcony. "It doesn't hurt your standing with Purity. That the daughter of the traitor-in-chief is one of us, dedicated to restoring discipline and strength—Purity—to our City before its slide into decadence is complete . . ."

"You can save the speeches. Also, I'll thank you to watch what you say about my father. He's misguided. He's a total romantic, though he thinks he's the world's biggest realist. That doesn't make him a traitor. How many times have *you* been shot at for the City?"

He turned back from the railing. "I'm at risk every day. My beliefs aren't popular right now."

Elinor laughed. "Nonsense. Sanity guarantees your right to say what you please. And the poor fools even mean it."

"You see how unfit they are to rule? They don't have the iron in their spines even to preserve themselves against seditious foes like me."

"Do you ever stop orating?"

He came forward and caught her hands again. "I might. If you came away with me, Elinor."

"What? Are you quite serious?"

His eyes burned her like coals. "I've never been more serious in my life," he said in a quiet blade voice. "Come with me. Away from here, away from this doomed capital. *Marry* me."

"Wherever would we go?" she asked, pulling back. His hands were like iron claws on hers.

"Away. Anywhere. Fort Hammond. Missouri City. Dallas, even."

"Dallas? What happened to your patriotic love for Homeland?"

"Dallas isn't riddled with corruption, at least. It's no threat to the City, never has been; if we were wise we would have embraced them as brothers long since." He shook his head urgently, as if trying to fling drops of water from his hair. "But it doesn't need to be Dallas. I don't care. I'd give up politics completely, if I could be with you."

At last she managed to disengage.

"Now you're straining my credulity," she said, walking

away. "You'd never give up politics, Dirk Posten. It's in your blood."

He watched her go. His shoulders subsided slowly, like a truck sinking in a bog. "You're right," he finally said to an empty room. "And soon you'll see how right you are."

20

Tristan was in the midst of a vague dream of falling when he hit the floor and realized it wasn't a dream at all.

He came awake resting with his forehead against the hardwood floor of his bedroom and the dirty shag of the throw rug rasping his cheek. Thunder reverberated in his ears.

Under normal circumstances he took a good long time to come fully awake. Quicksilver and the other adults had given him wads of grief for it; Jamie never had, because Jamie knew his heart and only got on him for important things. His three housemates called him the Zombie in the mornings, when he staggered around bashing into things and swearing until they funneled coffee down his throat.

When it hit the fan, though, he woke up *now*.

He snaked his broom-handle Bolo out of its holster, which was tucked between mattress and box springs of his fancy brass bed—once Angels of Death MC booty from a raid on a homesteader caravan, and then Tristan's after that particular band of Angels had had no further need of beds for their sleep.

He had landed between the bed and the window. He jumped up, ready to risk a three-second look over the sill, and he heard bare footsteps in the hall.

He swung the long slim-barreled pistol to cover the door. Mal Veeder appeared, skidding slightly on the wood. "Column comin' up the road. Rags in boxes, can up front."

Translated, that meant *HDF Regulars in Buffalo carriers, with an armored car in the lead*. "Coming for us?" Tristan asked.

The house shook again to a sound so loud the ears just gave up trying to take it in. Dust rolled from the ceiling, up from between the planks of the floor, from everywhere. The glass of the window behind the crouching Tristan, fly-specked and streaked with the tracks of ash-laden rain, cracked and slip-slid inward all over him, slashing his bare back like claws.

"—the fuck do you *think*, scooter tramp?" Tristan heard Mal yell when his ears emptied enough to hold sound again. "They designated our front porch a firing range?"

Holes splintered open in the bedroom wall. Mal's chest erupted in double fountains of blood and bone chips. He flew forward against the bed and slumped to the floor, leaving Tristan's sheets sodden red.

"Shit," Tristan said. That was a .50-caliber, chiming in with the three-and-a-quarter-inch mortar that had just dropped a couple near the house. Whatever the specifics, they were in some serious lava.

He snagged his holster out from under his mattress, stuffed the Bolo back in and buckled the belt around his waist as he risked a glance out the window. He was still up on his knees—if the gunner thought to lower aim on his big fifty, it didn't matter how much cover Tristan was behind, since there was nothing in the isolated old house the machine gun couldn't shoot through a block of.

He could see nothing outside but a gray predawn sky so loaded down with moisture that it drooped all the way down to the foothill roll in places, like a long-neglected ceiling. The smell of dew-wet grass and earth and burned explosives rolled in the violated window to mingle with the smell of Mal's expelled body fluids.

He heard the growl of engines, not too close yet, and the sudden ripping snarl of City small-arms fire.

He spun from the window. "Leo! Big Bear! Where are you?" He snaked his bolt-action Saskatoon Mark V Scout from its scabbard and scrambled out the door.

"Out here. Living room."

Tristan hit the end of the hall, came to one knee and around to cover the front door with the Scout. It was still closed, though a pair of .50-caliber holes gaped in it.

"This way, Outlaw One." Leo was crouching in the glass of the blown-out window with a Tallahassee Arsenal 12-pump in his furry hands. Storm-carbine rounds were coming in the window with thin savage cracks. Like Tristan he was dressed only in his OD skivvies. His shaggy gut hung over the band. Tristan joined Leo via an elbow-belly-knee crawl, disregarding the damage the glass shards did him.

This time a peek showed him a Marauder armored car laboring up the dirt road toward the house on its low lonely hill, still a good two hundred yards distant. Behind it, a pair of Buffaloes had stopped and were spilling squaddies into the weeds. Some had gone down in a firing line and were busting caps at the house.

"Frogwits," Leo said under his breath. "Only Rags would think of trying to sneak up on somebody in armored cars."

"Wouldn't've done 'em any good to tiptoe, the way their mortar squad jumped the gun."

Big Bear shook his head. "Rags," he said simply, summing it up. There was a reason the Strikers had a grossly disproportionate success rate against the nomads, compared to the HDF Regulars. Now, in case Tristan had any doubts, he could tell their situation was totally screwed and getting worse by the second by Leo's use of "Rags" for Regulars. He usually avoided derogatory words, and chided his housemates for using them.

The world exploded.

When Tristan's brain stopped flywheeling inside his skull he was sprawled over the end of the sofa. The front wall was bowed inward, the porch sagged drunkenly into the field of view, and the air was thick with smoke that stung the eyes and throat and riled the stomach.

Leo lay on his side clutching his left thigh. A six-inch wood splinter projected from it, just above the knee.

Tristan got his feet under him, started to come off the couch. A burst of fifty crashed in, smashing the sofa inches from his left hand.

"Outlaw . . . clear out," Leo grunted. "Leave me and go."

Tristan started toward him. "I'm not going without you."

Leo glared at him. His bearded lips were skinned back from his teeth in agony. "Then you're not going at all. You want the bastards to make a clean sweep? Who's going to . . . avenge us?"

Tristan squatted there staring at him for three breaths.

"Watch your topknot," he said.

"Mind yours, cousin," Leo said. The pain flashed in his face. "Now *go!*"

Tristan turned and ducked back through the hall door. A .243 burst chewed up the sofa where he'd been.

In his bedroom he picked up his panniers, swung them over his shoulder, and went out the window. The Rags were unassing their carriers too far away to have flanked the house yet.

The house was set at an angle to the approach road. The bikes were parked on the north side of the house, masked from the road. Tristan ran around the back. He dropped his panniers into place over the rear tire, vaulted to the saddle, and kicked the Black Mountain scrambler awake.

The Marauder crew had gotten smart. The sneak assault was blown wide open; the car had taken off across country to try to cover the north side and rear of the house and prevent the alerted occupants from fleeing.

They were just a little late. A burst of .50-caliber smashed Mal's and Leo's bikes into booming flames and twisted metal, and Tristan was down the back slope of the hill and into a handy arroyo—they hadn't picked this location by accident— and gone.

Black Jack Masefield's house crawled with HDF soldiers like a week-dead man's head with maggots. They were obviously not there to safeguard the inhabitants; they had the lazy surly arrogance of an occupying army. Watching from a brushy draw a few hundred yards away, Tristan felt a stab of panic—*Elinor!*— but he wasn't surprised.

The Rags were all wearing white armbands. He might have wondered just what that was supposed to mean, except the force was sprinkled with a handful of young men in white jumpsuits. *Purity* white.

He wasn't really surprised with that either. The old-line Administration types had never been graceful about being voted roundly out of office. Their sons and daughters missed their privilege, and had never made any bones they intended to take it back with *beaucoup* interest.

Black Jack didn't make many wrong calls. But the Catheads and their new love affair with the Fusion hadn't been the biggest threat to Homeland after all.

Did the fuckards catch you at home, or did you get clear? With a pang of guilt he realized he was more concerned about his boss than his almost-fiancée. Elinor was in small danger; Purity had an exaggerated regard for women, highborn ones in particular. They hated her father more even than John Amos Schenk, because they feared him. They'd kill him like a dog if they got the chance.

Tristan made himself breathe slow and deep, through the mouth. Fury threatened to wash out his vision and his judgment, send him forward with a banshee cry to kill as many of the bastards as he could before he fell.

That had been his father's way. His father's death. It had been ballsy as hell, and just as futile. Had Wyatt lived, there was a chance—however tiny—that the Hardriders might have been reborn, and eventually avenged. But Wyatt had taken the easy way, the spectacular final charge.

Tristan would not shrug his blood-debts off so lithely.

He turned. And stared up the muzzles of half-a-dozen storm carbines.

White coveralls were not ideal for Halt Newsome. They made his barrel-like frame seem bulky and graceless. An early paunch didn't help.

"Dirk was right again," he said, shaking his head and grinning.

The open combat carryall crawled between the cement masses of the Blocks, tall square old apartments and the newer warrens, low and squat. The tenements stood as dark and quiet as if deserted. The Citizens were keeping their heads down, watching without letting themselves be seen, awaiting events.

Newsome was turned around to taunt his prisoner over the passenger seat. Tristan noted he was showing some extra meat to the jowls. His father hadn't scored many City contracts since the Strength regime had been sent packing, but Halt apparently hadn't missed too many turns at the table. His black eyebrows were growing together in the middle.

Tristan made himself sit as relaxed as he humanly could with his hands cuffed behind his back; it was his way of not giving in to the muzzle brake of the Water Horse M52 storm carbine screwed into his right ribs. Tristan wore only his boots and a pair of tan whipcord Striker pants with stripes down the legs and leather padding at crotch and butt.

Bags, bike, and guns were stashed in the carryall's rear cargo compartment. The boys were taking them back to HQ as trophies. The muzzle brake was mighty cool on his bare skin.

"But that Dirk, he's always right," Newsome said. "We set up where he said to, and you plopped down right in front of us."

"Where is the little bastard?" Tristan asked.

Newsome slapped his face, but without conviction, almost playfully. "I'd teach you to have a little respect, but when we get you to City Hall Dirk'll teach you a *lot*." He laughed as if he'd just told a terrific joke.

"Commander Posten's got bigger fish to fry," the driver said. He and the other escort, the one making love to Tristan with his piece, wore Rag cammies with Purity brassards. The driver gestured toward the radio, crackling sporadically with reports. "He just laid the hard arm on John Anus Skunk in person. But he'll get around to you, scooter trash. Don't sweat it."

"Yeah," Newsome said, as if he could barely contain himself. "And then your goose'll be cooked!"

"Masefield's still holed up in the warehouse," the radio said. *"Fucker's pretty badly hurt, over."*

"White Knight, be advised, watch your language. We're building a new order here."

21

Tristan let himself grin. It was a nasty, lopsided affair that just hiked up one end of his outlaw mustache.

"Yeah, Halt. And here you are, taking out the garbage, right? Some things never change, do they? Once Dirk Posten's butt boy, always Dirk Posten's butt boy, hey?"

Newsome's face started to clump and darken. "Watch that shit, you mingy—"

"I'm glad I had you hung on a wire back when we were in high school, Tubby." Newsome gaped at him. "Only wish I'd strung it myself."

"What the fuck are you talking about?"

"That wire in the alley that knocked you off your bike. The kid that took the impression off your key and planted all those TVs in your Neighborhood Watch clubhouse. Major disgrace. What, you don't remember? The fall off your bike must've scrambled that teaspoonful of buffalo shit you call your brains."

The escort on his right gouged him under the arm with his M52. "Watch your mouth, scumbag."

Halt Newsome was turning all kinds of dark, like Mother Sky when she was fixing to pitch a major cloudburst. "I should have had my pals run the wire a little higher and roll that pumpkin head right off your shoulders. But I guess it was more fun watching your good buddy Dirk let you suck the rap—"

Old Halt came right over the back of the seat at him, one huge

158

hand wrapping Tristan's neck, the other piling punches into his chest and belly. "You fucking son of a bitch, you spoiled my dad's chances to go Admin. You fucker, I'll kill you!"

Tristan grinned into Halt's flared nostrils and Dutch-courage breath and slammed his forehead into the bridge of Halt's wide nose.

Bone snapped. Halt screamed. Tristan flattened his spine against the seat and threw himself sideways with all his strength.

The M52's muzzle brake scraped a red groove on his bare belly. The storm carbine went off. Tristan grunted as the muzzle flash seared his skin.

Holding both hands over his streaming nose, Halt reared up, away from the sudden shattering noise of the storm carbine. Tristan brought a knee up under his chin, hard. He turned sideways and pushed with his powerful legs until he was practically sitting in the armed escort's lap. The Rag was trying to fend him off with one hand and disengage his weapon with the other.

Tristan snapped his head sideways into the trooper's face, breaking his nose with the thickened bone above his own right temple. The chief rule of Empty was that there aren't any rules. Hitting somebody with your head was not the ideal thing to do—it was hard to scramble your enemy's brains more than you did your own—but if you were desperate you could go strength against weakness and hope you held out longer.

With the strength of anger and desperation Tristan hammered the soldier with the blunt instrument of his skull, closing an eye and caving in a cheek. The soldier let go of his carbine to whale at him blindly.

Halt was back in action, eyes red, nostrils flared, squealing like a pig who smells the slaughter as blood poured down the lower half of his face from his nose and his tongue, which he'd bitten through when Tristan kneed him. He grabbed Tristan by the throat again, thumbs digging for the windpipe.

Tristan whipped both knees up, clipping Halt on the chin again. The Purity conspirator hung on. Tristan flung his knees apart, breaking Halt's grip, and then wrapped his legs around Halt's neck.

The driver had a pistol out. The carryall wove hysterically as he twisted in his seat to try to bring the weapon to bear. As much for a shield as anything else Tristan hauled Halt over the back of his own seat, halfway into the rear.

The escort, now pinned behind the sideways Tristan, grabbed Tristan by the throat. Tristan slammed his head back, gashing his scalp and caving in the soldier's teeth. The fingers left his neck.

Tristan had vague notions of throttling Halt with his legs. But while the wildly flailing Newsome couldn't escape, Tristan couldn't seem to find a grip to block his wind with his thighs, powerful as they were. He began cranking his hips wildly left and right, left and right.

Newsome clawed at Tristan's legs. His dark eyes rolled. His neck broke with a pistol crack.

His body convulsed furiously. The carryall veered and hit a light standard. It stopped.

Tristan let go of Halt's suddenly quiescent bulk, started shoving with his feet against the back of the seat in front of him. He got his butt up onto the back of his own seat, perched in front of the rear cargo compartment. The escort, his face a red ruin, grabbed at him. Tristan heel-stomped him in the throat. He fell into the well between the seats, face purpling beneath the blood.

The driver had split his forehead open on the wheel. Groggy, he turned again, waving his big Griswold & Grier Government .45.

Tristan had been inexpertly cuffed, and was busy skinning his bound wrists forward over his butt. Had the driver turned an eyeblink later he would have caught Tristan with his legs pinned together. As it was Tristan kicked the big handgun from the soldier's hand.

The collision had buckled the carryall's frame. The driver fought the door as Tristan pulled his legs up and slipped his cuffs off over his boot heels. The driver finally got the door opened, bolted from the car.

Tristan launched himself off the seat back in a flying leap. He landed square on the driver's back as the soldier tried to run. He clamped his long legs hard around the man's ribs, dropped his arms over his head.

The handcuff's short chain pulled taut around the trooper's throat.

● ● ●

The warehouse lay in the business district south of Homeland's center. The area at large had begun to pick up, as the triumphant Sanity Party had encouraged trade with other Cities, in contrast to the paranoia of Strength and the distrust of commerce that characterized Health. This section was rundown anyway, with boarded-up windows and doors sealed by locks that had long since turned into lumps of corrosion. *Maybe Black Jack didn't discount the Purity threat as much as I thought,* Tristan thought. The location suggested that the colonel had been on his way to a secret early-morning meeting with his good friend Mayor Schenk, probably to discuss that very subject, when the ambush hit.

Walls were splashed with the graffiti of Purity's initials and the initials of its slogan: "Purity+Discipline=Unity." They had probably been whitewashed on by Purity beavers last night in preparation for The Day. They didn't usually last more than twenty-four hours before being defaced by Homeland's impure youth.

The street was full of Marauders and troops in white brassards, hugging the armored vehicles and pointing their M52s at the large block-shaped yellow brick building where Purity's new Civic Enemy Number One had gone to ground. As Tristan pulled the carryall to the curb, well back of the combat lines, he noticed snipers silhouetted on the rooftop of a nearby structure.

Smart, Tristan thought. *Trust the Rags not to think anybody can shoot better than they can.*

He got out of the vehicle. He let himself give it a quick, casual once-over. His traps and bike were out of sight under a tarp. The bodies of his former captors were resting in an alley in a part of the Blocks, where people never saw anything and the Block Wardens didn't either, if they liked breathing from above the chin rather than below. He hadn't been able to do anything about the bloodstains on the vehicle itself, but like the spatters of red on Halt Newsome's borrowed coveralls, they might lend a touch of realism on this violent uncertain day.

A steady drizzle fell, glistening on otherwise dull metal and cloth and pavement. He strode forward as if he were Dirk Posten himself, with the same arrogant stride that had carried him into a score of outlaw camps, through throngs of men and women who'd sworn to slit his throat and hang his hide to dry.

Nobody paid him any attention. They had other things on their minds. Like surviving the impending confrontation with the Devil Himself, a.k.a. Black Jack Masefield.

He walked right up to the street before the building's front entrance, where an obvious officer was hunkered down with his nervous staff behind the comforting bulk of a Marauder. The man looked at him as if he were crazy for not keeping his head down and scuttling like everybody else on the street.

"Good morning, Captain," he said, making a thumbnail judgment—HDF Regulars never wore rank badges in the field, a lesson learned by generations of hassling with sharpshooting nomads who could read the insignia as well as the squaddies could. "What's the situation here?"

It was a totally insane gamble, which made it about dead-center for a Striker, and more so for the notorious Outlaw One. It was also quite calculated. For one thing, Tristan's face was far less well-known within the City's perimeter than without—no news conferences for Black Jack's handpicked elite. His hair was cut as short as any Purity member's, even if it had a pink tinge and was tending to spike from the blood he hadn't managed to sluice off in the stream of a handy hydrant. Though it hung like an old tent on his athletic frame, Halt Newsome's outfit hit him high at ankles and wrists, but not everybody in Purity was as image-conscious as their leader.

The white jumpsuits seemed to be in charge of the whole fandango, no questions asked. The issue was whether he could convince the Rags he belonged in it also.

"Good morning—sir," the officer said. The hesitation in his voice seemed no more than the usual reluctance a soldier felt to call a civilian "sir." "One of our teams successfully ambushed Lieutenant Colonel Masefield's personal car about two hours ago. His driver was killed."

He nodded across the street, where Masefield's vehicle sat with its right wheels up on the curb. Its front end looked as if it had run into a shoulder-fired antitank missile. A huge form lay covered by a bloody sheet beside it, one copper-colored hand outflung.

Tristan tried to turn the grimace he couldn't suppress into a sneer of satisfaction. *Well, Quanah, you fought your last fight. May the Road stretch clear before you.* To judge by the other forms still lying around like farm buildings hit by a Stalking Wind, some covered with sheets and some not, the Comanche and his boss had given a good final accounting of themselves.

The officer looked back to him, then glanced at the Lakota Bolo cinched to his hip. Tristan felt his scrotum retract. It was a distinctive piece, with its straight "broom" handle and the box magazine before the trigger guard. It was also a characteristic Striker weapon.

"Trophy, huh?" The captain grinned. Tristan grinned back. "You fell into some good hunting."

"It's been a great day for the City," Tristan replied, trying to get just the right crazy gleam in his eye. He was trying to get the old Block reflex to kick in. Nobody with all his marbles wanted to say a word more than dead necessary in the presence of a True Believer. A closed mouth gathers no Civic Demerits, not to mention Hellville vacations.

''We're, ah, we're waiting on reinforcements,'' the officer said, pretending to stare at the warehouse entrance while his eyes kept a sideways hold on Tristan's face. "We should be ready to make the final assault in a matter of minutes, if you care to stay and watch. . . ."

There was no acting in the look of contempt Tristan gave him. There were a hundred mutineers surrounding the structure already. Still, they didn't think themselves strong enough to overpower a lone, injured man.

"The plans are changed," he said brusquely. He drew the Bolo, racked the slide to check the chambered round. "I'm going in."

"Wait! You can't—" But it was too late: Tristan had whipped around the butt of the Marauder and was running bent over toward the door.

22

The door had gone the way of the space program, salvaged for metal probably—old habits died hard, and scrounging in the rubble was still a main source of income and raw materials for all the Star's children. The boards that had sealed it indifferently shut had been wrenched away, not recently to judge by the weathering on the faces of the breaks. The blood spattered freely on the boards was clearly much fresher.

Tristan ducked under the remaining boards, ducked around to put the wall at his back, held the Bolo ready, switched to full-automatic. He waited for thirty heartbeats, in case the putative captain either sent men to try to save this loony white jumpsuit from his own zeal, or found his stones through Tristan's sterling example and ordered the assault to begin.

Neither happened. Tristan grinned. *Score one for the visiting team.* He clicked the Bolo back to single-shot and holstered it.

He moved through the building, feeling its vast emptiness, smelling the mice and mildew, seeing dust and accreted ash floating in air in beams of weak sunlight that fell down from high places. He walked quietly as any Blackfoot stalker, knowing the slightest sound he made would be magnified a thousand times.

He paused by a fall of wan light, put out a hand to touch scaffolding. There was a lot of wood in this building, in scaffolds and interior partitions and crates of goods so decayed or intrinsically useless that even the few persistent derelicts who managed to avoid being scooped up by City Welfare to be improved in Rehab or the mines hadn't stolen them.

It was a different world to him still. Out on the treeless Plains where he was born, and in the Cities between here and the Big River—Fort Hammond, Misery City—the crate wood would be more valuable than almost any contents could be. Here, near the lushly forested Rockies, they took wood for granted.

His nose led him to the spot. Blood and burned gun-lubricant and seared flesh and cloth. Strong unequivocal smells, plain to him as any signpost—and ominous as reading *Bridge Out!* by lightning's last flash as you roared full-throttle between abutments. He homed on the stinks.

He came around a pile of crates filled with sodden rotting paper, to judge by the smell, to sense a rustle of movement, see the dance of weak stray light on blued steel. He stepped into the light.

"It's you," a voice croaked. "I knew you'd come."

"No you didn't. They got you, they could get me."

A death-rattle chuckle out of the dark. "They did too, to look at you. But you're younger than me, more physical than I ever was. *Better* than I ever was. They couldn't *hold* you."

"I got lucky."

"That's—" A cough, with blood in it, thick as tuberculosis. "That's part of being good. Don't ever doubt that.

"Besides—" A scraping shuffle, as of a body being dragged. "Luck is all in what you make of it."

Black Jack Masefield came into the light. What was left of him. He was bad. But he kept it out of his face, Tristan saw.

"Yeah, I know. I look like Hell on a bad day. That's why I'm running on. Dead man's entitled to a few last aphorisms. Man needs a good exit line."

"You took a few with you. That's the best one." Tristan knelt beside him to examine his wounds. "Besides, it's too early to talk about—"

"*Bullshit.* I took more of that rocket's blast than is good for a man. Caught a couple of bullets while Quanah was pulling me out—maybe one for every three he caught, which was more than enough for this old man. He accounted for most of the deaders anyway."

He grunted, trying to sit up. Tristan caught him, tried simultaneously to hold him back and support him. "What the hell do you think you're doing?"

"Sitting up."

"Forget about it."

Masefield strained briefly. The feebleness of the effort tore at Tristan's innards like marten's teeth. Black Jack Masefield had never had the sheer power of body of Tristan or any number of his Strikers—he was just too small. But he had always possessed a startling wiry strength. No more. And what he had left he was losing as Tristan watched.

"All right. You talked me into it. But I have something for you." The ruined face contorted with effort as Masefield tossed his sidearm up, caught it reversed, presented it butt-first.

"What's this?" Tristan asked.

"It's the piece that killed your father, Tristan Hardrider."

"What do you want me to do with it?"

"Take it. Keep it. But first . . ." The remaining eye caught his and held it in a fierce grip. "First—kill me with it."

Tristan's hand shied away. "No way."

"D—ahh!—*do* it, damn you! *Do it.*" Supporting the sidearm's weight took a killing effort, but he kept it wavering in the air.

"Take a good look at me, soldier. If you even got me to a hospital, would they be able to patch me up enough so I could stand on my own to face the firing squad?"

"No."

"Then do it. As a last service to a comrade in arms. Don't leave me for *them.*"

It wasn't torture Masefield feared, Tristan knew; Purity would have a hard time dreaming up pains to inflict that were half as bad as what he was feeling now. He just couldn't stand the thought of falling into their filthy hands.

It was a thought worthy of a Stormrider.

"Take the pistol. Kill me with it." A ghastly smile. "Avenge your father. Just as you swore so many years ago. Kill me with the gun that killed him, so his spirit can travel the Big Road and leave you in peace."

How did you know? Tristan wondered. But Masefield didn't know everything. He didn't know that, in his own spirit at least,

Tristan had laid his father's ghost that morning, when he refused the choice his father had made, the last charge into glorious defeat.

He accepted the weapon. It was a Dance Brothers & Park Vindicator, a Wonder .40. Not a brute, no Comanche or Thunder Dog. But quite effective. A piece well suited for an officer who was also a gentleman.

Tristan leaned forward and kissed the seared forehead. "I have my own," he said, and straightening, drew his Bolo and shot Black Jack Masefield through the center of the forehead.

He could hear the Rags yelling to one another outside. The gunshot had stirred their hive, unavoidably. The captain, if that's what he was, was figuring that if he let a Purity wheel walk unescorted into a building with a dangerous fugitive, and the jumpsuit got washed, his own personal ass was going to be hanging from the flagpole come reveille. But the Regular dither factor, the old reliable, had kicked in; he obviously couldn't wait for word from Higher Command, but he was none too eager to stick his chicken neck out further.

The rich edgy smell of wood and paper smoke told Tristan that the flares he'd placed throughout the derelict warehouse, quickly but deliberately, were having the desired effect. He smiled. He drew his Bolo from its holster with his right hand and the Vindicator from his belt with the left.

"Help! Oh, sweet God Jesus, *helllllp meeeeee!*" Tristan wailed. He ripped off two staccato bursts from his Bolo, then loosed off three quick rounds from the .40, because even Rags might get suspicious if they heard what was supposed to be a firefight played solo.

That got them. He heard the captain yell, "Oh, shit, oh, dear. Go, go, go!"

He faded back down the main aisle, slipped behind a stack of crates he hadn't left a flare in. In a moment half a dozen troopies hit the door in a flying wedge. Naturally they jammed up tight. The captain's voice whipping them from outside and behind—no flies on this boy, nosiree—made them forget whatever building-clearing procedures they might have learned and just all come spilling in like schoolkids off a bus.

Tristan, watching with just one eye around a corner, was startled to see five uniforms followed by the gleam of a white jumpsuit. *No wonder the captain decided to get off the stick.*

The jumpsuit was waving a fancy little Green River machine pistol of the kind favored by Kiowas and yelling contradictory instructions. Tristan pulled a final flare from his pocket and tossed it unlit into the depths of the warehouse.

"There! That way!" the jumpsuit yelled, waving the MP. Three of the squaddies ran straight down the aisle, as much to get away from the McTen as to obey.

Tristan waited with his back to rough wood until they passed. Then he chopped them with one long burst from the Bolo: *rip* left to right, letting the natural muzzle jump slash the weapon upwards.

"Payback begins now," he said aloud as they fell with a clatter of unfired arms.

"Oh God oh God oh God!" cried the white jumpsuit. "You, go right. You, go left. Damn you, don't just stand there like you got shit in your mouth! Do it. Do it! *God damn you—*"

A spasm of fire, a scream, a thump. "You made me do it," the jumpsuit's voice whispered, torn like a Digger's long johns. "The New Order is about obedience, you fucking bastard."

Tristan was laughing silently, off playing tag in the dark. Though the gunshots still echoed in his ears, he could hear the stumbling gait and desperate open-mouthed breathing of the surviving troopie. The sound of a man who pursued, even though he understood full well *he* was the prey.

Tristan could almost feel sorry for him. But he was fresh out of sympathy today.

He made sure to scuff and bump things now and then, loud enough so the trooper could hear them over his own sounds. The man followed. The air got thicker with smoke.

He circled right, waited until the man passed a side passage, and whistled. The man had good reflexes, or maybe was just wound. He snapped back around the corner blazing away from the hip, so fast he almost caught Tristan before Tristan could dodge to relative safety around another crate stack.

The man started down the passage, poking the M52's barrel in front of him like a beetle's feelers. Tristan ran to the next passage, down it, then around until he was looking at the man's back.

"Behind you," he said softly.

The man yelped, wheeled, fired. A .243 slug punched splinters an inch from Tristan's left ear. *Better not get too smug.*

He let the man hear him running, deeper into the warehouse. The woodwork was burning seriously here, frame structures of flame rising into the cathedral dark. The stink of burning flesh was sickeningly strong.

It was like walking through Hell's antechamber. The trooper followed, face pale, flames reflected in the sweat enameling his face. Doomed but determined.

A demonic figure laughed at him from atop a fiery scaffold. The trooper shrieked, turned, and let go with a shuddering burst.

The figure dropped lithely to the cement. Above his head the platform where he had stood *whumped* into flame. The figure walked toward the soldier, tall and purposeful.

The trooper shouldered his storm carbine, centered the sights on the dark approaching torso, squeezed the trigger.

Nothing. Loud as thunder.

"You're empty, soldier boy," the tall figure said. He grabbed the M52 by the barrel, yanked it away, cartwheeled it into the flames rising from three crates set end to end in a blazing catafalque. The trooper snatched at his issue bayonet. The figure shot him in the right thigh, just above the knee.

He collapsed. His helmet rolled away. A rough hand caught his close-cropped head by an ear, lifted it.

"See that?" To his horror, the trooper saw the figure of a man lying prone in the flames. At least he wasn't kicking and screaming.

"The funeral pyre of Lieutenant Colonel John Hancock Masefield," his assailant said. The hand twisted his ear painfully, forcing his face upwards until he looked his captor full in the face.

"Outlaw One," the demon visage said. "I'm leaving you alive on purpose. Tell the City: They'll be hearing from me."

He released the trooper and stood. The trooper's head bounced on still-cool cement. Down there the smell of urine and mildew were as strong as roasting human meat.

"If you crawl for all you're worth you can save your ass from frying. Do us both a favor and *move*."

Painfully but vigorously, the trooper obeyed.

• • •

"Ohhh. Oh, *God!*"

At the drawn-out soul-lost moan, the white jumpsuit jumped up from the rusted hand truck by the door and covered the approaching figure with his McTen.

The eerie ghost-shine of white cloth in the gloom kept his finger from spasming around the trigger. A Purity jumpsuit. *It's the man we came to rescue! I did it!* He rushed forward to help hold the staggering man erect.

There wasn't much white left in the suit, in all fact. What wasn't red was mostly black. The man's face was a gory mask. He smelled *much* worse than he looked.

"It's terrible," the apparition moaned.

"What? In God's name, what?"

"They're all *dead*."

"What happened?"

The figure straightened, took a step away, squared off facing him. "Me," it said. It raised a Vindicator and shot him between the eyes.

Half a hundred storm carbines snapped to the ready as Tristan emerged from the warehouse in a billow of gray smoke. The sight of the white jumpsuit, blood-splashed and charred, and his face completely hidden in the blood-wash from the wound he'd carefully reopened in his scalp, was even more dramatic in the light of what passed for day in Homeland.

Soldiers rushed to his side, keeping out of line with the doorway, just in case. He allowed himself to be led behind the Marauder.

"What happened in there?" the captain asked as a medic dabbed at his face with handfuls of gauze. The snafu sweat stood out like clear nail heads on the officer's face. This wasn't going to look good on his quarterly efficiency report.

Tristan let his head loll on his neck. "It's . . . it's a *trap*," he gasped.

The captain jumped as if he'd been jabbed in the nuts with a cattle prod. If this were all a setup, he could possibly be forgiven for losing half a squad and a whole white jumpsuit, plus getting another Purity boy smoke-damaged.

"Jones! Get on the horn and find out where the hell those reinforcements are! I want them ten minutes ago. Waldrop, Ford—get this man to an ambulance immediately. Can't you see he's hurt?"

Maybe he was getting soft, maybe his blood lust was sated, however momentarily. Tristan let the two ambulance crewmen live. He didn't need to kill them to convince them not to try to slow him down or follow. He didn't even have to do them any lasting hurt.

By late afternoon the warehouse had pretty much burned down. The discovery of the bodies of Halt Newsome and his two HDF escorts in one seedy part of town—and their combat carryall in the very exclusive southeast section of town, where the legendary Broadmoor Hotel was reputed to have stood—had sparked a City-wide manhunt, not to mention some serious interrogation of an HDF captain who until then had been pretty much the man of the hour.

But it's a law of nature that there are always more places to hide than the Authorities know to look. Tristan and his bike and gear stayed in one of them until well after dark while the search raged like a thunderstorm.

The Homeland perimeter wasn't perfect. It was too long to be rigorously patrolled by the City's limited manpower. A lot of arroyos ran through the wire tangles, with new ones being cut every time there was a serious downpour, which was about seven days a week this time of year. It was impossible to keep all the rain-cut gullies blocked.

Smugglers knew that—not that the smuggling trade had been booming lately, with Sanity allowing imports of goods like coffee and liquor and slashing tariffs. The Strikers knew the best smugglers' routes.

Tristan Tomlinson blew out of Homeland down one of those arroyos at oh-dark-hundred in the morning following the Purity coup, and no man or woman saw him go.

23

He stumbled across the blackened waste. The lava rock turned beneath his boots, twisting his ankles and cruelly gashing his feet. He ran unflinchingly onwards, toward the light.

It was growing larger now. He could make out a central mass, a something winging out to either side, a hint of upward sweep. But recognition eluded him, dancing away from his mind like a butterfly dodging a child's grasping pudgy fingers.

He vented a hawk-scream of frustration, launched himself in a flying leap. The glowing vision eluded him, taunted him with its silent untouchability.

He fell facedown toward cold lava like broken glass. . . .

He awoke with a shrill cry echoing in his ears. He remembered screaming in frustration, but he thought it had been longer ago in the dream. *Well*, he thought, *time flows differently in that world than this.*

Again the scream. It seemed to fall from above, like the strange white pressure on his eyelids. He opened his eyes.

They filled with pain and dazzle. It took him a moment to realize it was *sunlight*. He looked away from Father Sun's hot eye, which both gave and robbed sight.

He was lying by a gentle-voiced creek, with the earth warm on his back, the sun on his face, and the wind in his hair. One leg was drawn up: a long leg, the leg of a tall adult, encased in dust-colored trousers and knee-high tan boot.

He looked around. He could not move more than his eyes, or maybe he was afraid to try. He could see that he was wearing a faded olive-drab vest or T-shirt. A harness of some sort constricted his left side; he smelled leather and lubricants, and saw the butt of an unfamiliar kind of pistol jutting from his left armpit. Almost around the corner of his vision he saw a bike propped against the same slope he was lying on. The butt of a scabbarded carbine protruded above the far side of the seat.

He sighed. He was safe. He was free.

He tipped his head back. The sun was almost overhead. Almost between him and it a black shape wheeled, round-tipped wings and short broad tail outspread. A hawk. Red-tail.

Tristan laughed. His voice was deep, a familiar voice, yet somehow strange. As if he'd expected it to crack with the stress of incipient adolescence.

I'm here, he knew. *The vision-place, where I came while I was in the Hole in McGrory.*

Slowly he sat up, ran his hands down his body. He was solid. This was real then. As real as anything outside the World-Behind-the-World got.

His vision had been true then. He really *was* free. In the wind again, for the first time in thirteen years.

It seemed at least that long since he had seen the sun shine. At least like this.

The bonfire leaped high against the star-clad sky in a defiant hilltop dance. Tristan did not care who saw. City soldiers or outlaw clans: let them come. If they meant ill to Outlaw One, they'd curse their mothers for not aborting them.

He stood by the fire with arms folded and the heat washing over his face and bare chest like rain. He had spent most of his first day of freedom gathering the makings of the fire, driftwood, weeds, cow chips, none of it very dry, but convinced to burn nicely enough by application of a jerrican of real gasoline. He could spare the gas. His Black Mountain scrambler wasn't a thirsty machine. Besides, he knew where to get more.

Why he did it, he didn't know. He only knew that it was the right thing to do, at this place, at this time.

Slowly he raised his arms above his head, until his hands met. He threw back his head, brought his arms down and out, like the wings of a soaring hawk.

I rode my own Road, Father. And I won.

I'll live on. I'll go on winning. I'll build a new clan, bigger than the Hardriders, stronger, more feared—stronger and more feared than any clan in the history of the Plains, before StarFall or after. And I'll take my revenge. I'll avenge Mr. Bayliss and Colonel Masefield and Leo and Mal. I'll avenge you and Mother and the rest of the Hardriders. I'll take the biggest vengeance ever known. And I'll take Ellie Masefield too.

All because I chose to live.

If you can't accept that, Father—then good-bye.

He began to dance. It was no particular dance. It was a dance without form, without plan, leaping, spinning, kicking, jumping high, round and around about the flames.

Why he did it, he didn't know. He only knew it was the right thing to do.

Henry Two Tractors tugged the brim of his black and silver Raiders cap, adjusted the headphones to his little portable tape player so it didn't mash his thick black braids into either side of his head quite so much, and cussed the new Homeland City Administration as he drove along in his rig.

In the old days, when the Sanity people ran things, they treated a man right. Let him come into their City, stay in their hotels, drink in their bars—hell, let you drink stuff *worth drinking* in their bars. He thought they were goody-goody and on the crazy side even for white-eyes, but they were all right by him.

Now, your old Strength people were pricks, who strip-searched you when you rolled into town, made you stay in a special compound in town—no mingling with the locals, *especially* their women—and really gouged you on prices because what choice did you have? Health did the same things, though they gave you different lines of shit as to why. He'd long since given up trying to keep the explanations straight.

But even Strength and Health you could do business with, even if you always got the feeling they wanted to go wash their hands whenever they shook with you. But these new Purity dudes . . . what a bunch of assholes. Talk about segregation, they wouldn't even let your red ass *into* the City; you signed your rig over to a City driver in a white jumpsuit with his head trimmed to a goofy burr-head plush, and you cooled your heels at what the drivers had dubbed the Trail of Tears Motel outside the wire.

Worst of all, they didn't even let you keep your own outriders. They claimed they kept the countryside abso-wanking-lutely safe, and they didn't want armed outsiders within thirty miles of their precious City. Two Tractors had six good riders, Kiowa like himself—two of them his wife's cousins—loafing on the payroll at a checkpoint five miles back.

His black eyes sidled left and right, scoping the surroundings. The land looked pretty smooth here, ramping up toward the Front Range, but he knew the land was furrowed with invisible folds that could hide whole armies of bike tramps bent on snagging his tankerload of gas. The escort riders promised by the white pajama buttholes, meanwhile, had failed to materialize. Two Tractor's rusty ass was swinging in the wind for true.

And him without even his trusty McTen tucked in the door pocket beside the seat. Those assbite Purity regs again.

He fiddled with his cap brim some more, checked the wing mirror. There was a motorcyclist overtaking him fast on the left. He tensed, but instantly relaxed, recognizing the rig of an HDF rider.

"What game do these butt-brains think they're playing?" he asked aloud. "Sneaking up on a man like that." There was still no sign of the rest of the escort, ahead or behind.

The lone rider pulled up alongside, looked up at Two Tractors with those big old cicada-eyed goggles, and waved a gauntleted hand. "Pull over!"

Two Tractors said, outraged, "Your white *ass*, pull over."

But of course if he didn't jump when their bike soldiers said frog, the Purity pricks would probably cut his head off on the *Evening News*. He pulled over.

After he got the rig stopped beside the road he clicked off his reggae tape, took the headphones off, and tucked them and the player discreetly out of sight under the dash. Purity probably had all kind of horse-hockey laws about driving with a headset on too.

He opened the door, stepped down to the pavement, and immediately found himself peering up the long barrel of a Lakota M96 Bolo.

"Oh, shit," he said, raising his hands. "You're kidding."

"Afraid not." The motorcyclist pulled off his goggles. Belatedly Two Tractors noticed his sweeping handlebar mustache. Facial hair made Purity as crazy as sex, drugs, or rock'n'roll. Two Tractors sighed.

"You're not the owner-operator?" the hijacker asked.

"You kidding? Rig belongs to the Nation."

"Kiowa?"

Two Tractors made a face. The Kiowa called themselves a Nation, and their employers, the Osage, did too, but it was just to humor them. The Osage were the only actual Indian nation on the south Plains, and really anywhere, and screw what a bunch of Blackfeet or Absaroka thought.

"Osage," he admitted.

"Well, that's good and bad. I'm glad you don't eat the loss. On the other hand, I'm not too eager to win pride of place on either nation's fecal roster."

"Why don't we just knock back a couple tallboys and walk away then?" Two Tractors suggested brightly.

"You're carrying beer in that thing, the white pajamas would have confiscated the whole rig and tossed you in the jug anyway. I'm doing you a favor."

"Some favor."

The bandit grinned. "I'm offering you a trade. Your clothes and the rig for these leathers, the bike, and a couple extra cans of gas."

"Not much of a bargain."

The bandit clicked back the ring hammer. "Got any other offers?"

Two Tractors began to strip. "What the hell kind of highway robber are you anyway? You could just shoot me in the neck and cruise."

"You complaining?"

"No. Shoot, you seem okay for a white-eyes. But the Osage are gonna be hunting your ass big-time for this."

"Osage just have to understand that this is what happens when you try to run a blockade."

Two Tractors stopped with his jeans halfway down his legs. "Blockade? Who the fuck is blockading Homeland?"

"Me."

Two Tractors had to laugh. He almost fell over. "What do you think you are, a crazy dog wishing to die?"

"No. I'm Outlaw One. Remember the name."

He gestured with the Bolo. "Oh, and I'll take the Kiowa Raiders cap too."

The picture on the driver's ID didn't look too much like the driver, but the clerk at the transit camp didn't pay it much mind. Nor did he care much that the driver had quite a facial brush, and looked more like a lean North Plains hawk than a burly badger-shaped Kiowa. Lot of younger bucks sported 'staches these days, if they could muster a half-decent-looking one. And also the clerk didn't give a rat's ass. He wasn't grateful to Purity for creating this job. He was pissed at them for saddling him with it.

Also, the outrider team had never rendezvoused with the rig, and the driver was minded to bitch about it. Better to process him through and let him bend some other poor asshole's ear. Hell, he was wearing the same cap as in the picture.

An hour before dawn, the Osage-owned gasoline rig, parked in the yard awaiting a driver to take it inside the wire, blew up. The fireball destroyed half a dozen other tractor-trailers and their cargoes. A vigorous search for the driver began almost the same minute firefighting measures did. But he had vanished from the transient drivers' dorm sometime after bed check.

About that time a patrol found the bodies of the six-man patrol sent to escort Henry Two Tractors, with five of their bikes. A wire had apparently been strung across the High Road out of Homeland. The escort had consisted of HDF Regulars rather than Strikers—the Strikers had been disbanded with extreme prejudice, the survivors going to Rehab or the Black Gang—and the bike soldiers had been blitzing down the road full-throttle.

Three full HDF companies were sent to the truck park, one to pull perimeter security, the other two to pitch in fighting the blaze. At the height of the conflagration a voice broke in on the emergency band: *"To the cowardly plotters of Purity and their traitorous toadies in the Homeland Defense Force, a very good morning. I hope you're enjoying the fireworks display I've put on for your benefit.*

"I'm putting the City of Homeland on notice: I have no ill will toward her Citizens, who are bearing the brunt of Purity tyranny. But as long as Purity continues in control, a state of war will exist between myself and Homeland.

"I will make every effort to avoid doing harm to noncombatants. You have nothing to fear from me. On the other hand, members of the Purity Administration and their lackeys . . ." A deep chuckle. *"You have* everything *to fear. I can strike where I choose, without warning, and without mercy. I will do so.*

"Sleep well. This is Outlaw One . . . out."

24

A season in Hell.

The bus ground up the grade between the thin red boles of Ponderosa pines. The driver kept it prudently to the middle of the blacktopped road. There wasn't a lot of traffic up here, but tremors were lethally frequent.

Ferd and Buff were making the weekly grind up to Hellville and the mines with a load of the latest recruits for the Black Gang for the two-hundredth-odd time. The ancient flat-nosed bus, with its windows covered with heavy-gauge wire mesh and its body stuccoed with gray paint in so many coats it seemed clotted, despite the smells of piss and puke and general despair, seemed almost homey.

The prisoners—wailing, bitching, or catatonic—Ferd and Buff ignored as just part of the circumstances of their job, like flies on this hot summer afternoon, or the rockslides that often blocked the road. But today they had a cargo that they couldn't ignore, not for a country minute. It wasn't just irritating. It was like having a rude uninvited stranger in the house.

Matt Weller was a Purity weenie to the ends of his short blond hair. His jumpsuit practically glowed with its own white light. His black shoes were polished to such a finish that he could easily use them to look right up a woman's skirt, provided he was interested in what he'd see there, which Ferd and Buff privately agreed he was not. He was on his way to Hellville to screen the political opinions of the mine workers up there.

"What's the dang fool gonna do if he finds some as got some bad ideas?" asked Ferd from behind his wheel. He was a sawed-off little party with big belly and forearms and razor-cut side-burns that pushed the limit of Purity facial-hair regs and a ducktail that might have graced a carved-wood decoy, it was so hard and shiny. "Send 'em to the mines?"

Buff laughed. He was a ways younger than Ferd, a ways leaner, and a good ways longer; he was upwards of six and a half feet tall, when he bothered to stand all the way up, which was seldom. He didn't have a lot by way of a chin, and his straw-colored hair was already thinner than his partner's. His teeth were bad. He was riding in his customary place, sitting in the door well up by the driver's seat, kind of leaning on his 12-gauge Cherokee pump.

"Haw, Ferd, that's a good one!" He thumped the butt of his pump on the dust-encrusted rubber runner that ran up the aisle and down the steps. "What's the dang fool gonna do, send 'em to the mines?" He didn't get off a lot of good lines himself, so he liked to always repeat the ones he heard.

At the back of the bus, Weller looked up sharply from the pamphlet he was encouraging a distraught former court clerk to read to ease his mind. "What?" he asked in that edged grating voice of his. "What's that?"

Buff sniggered and bobbed his head. His head was plumbed funny, and when he did that a whistling noise came out his ears. Ferd said it was because he didn't have anything between them. Sometimes when they were both liquored up they'd pound on each other awhile over that one. They didn't *like* each other, rightly. They were more accustomed to one another.

Weller persisted. "What are you saying? What are you say-ing?" The bus leaned into a curve. "I insist that you tell me what you're laughing about."

"Now look what you've gone and done, you moron," Ferd murmured to Buff, who snorted and whistled more.

"What? What?" Weller shouted.

"I said we got to stop and hustle the hole bunnies off the bus."

"Why? Why do we have to stop?"

The bus's brakes groaned. "Because there's a slide blockin' the road."

Boulders, dirt, and random clumps of vegetation had slid into the right-of-way. Weller leaned across the court clerk and stared up the slope to the right that had disgorged the fall. Suddenly, the peaceful tree-crowded slope seemed threatening.

The driver and the guard seemed to take it all in stride. The guard parked himself in the door well, his shotgun in the crook of his arm, while his partner matter-of-factly went down the aisle, threading a strong, flexible cable through the prisoners' manacled arms. Then he took an axe-handle from a rack behind his seat, which was covered in black and white cowhide, and rowdied the prisoners off the bus with curses and cracks at legs and backs.

Weller followed the coffle into the sunlight, blinking up at a painfully blue sky. It was an unusually clear summer. The two Clients—impossible to think of them as anything else—got the captives to working on cleaning the obstruction away. He found a clump of rock by the roadside, deposited in some earlier slide, and perched on it to read the most recent works of Purity's youthful Chairman, Dirk Posten.

The Chairman wasn't yet Mayor. But he was the real power behind the throne, instrumental as he had been in the coup, and one day he would have his rightful recognition, Weller had no doubt. He stopped and reread a phrase that took his eye: "Obedience is what we owe the City. Discipline is as natural and necessary an environment for us as water to a fish."

He set the pamphlet down on his thighs, momentarily overcome. As he gazed along the road to the rockfall he saw dust puff out from between the shoulders of the shotgun-carrying guard's red plaid shirt.

The guard dropped to his knees. The chubby driver spun round and ran for the bus as fast as his short legs could pump. What was going on here?

Weller realized he had heard a shot. Loud and nearby—but so unexpected it took his mind time to process it. On the heels of realization came a second shot. The driver fell down kicking in the dirt beside the pavement.

Down the slope came a tall man, who held a small rifle

trained on Weller from the hip. Weller raised his hands and stood, spilling the words of Chairman Dirk into the grass at his feet.

"Don't kill me," he said. "I'm unarmed."

Keeping the weapon trained on the Purity commissar one-handed, the intruder knelt beside the now-still body of the driver, went through his pockets. He came up with a set of keys, grinned, tossed them in the air, and snatched them out of it.

He walked to the string of prisoners, who had stopped work and were staring at him with looks of incomprehension and alarm or just plain apathy. He began to open the locks that held the cables looped through their manacles.

"What are you doing?" Weller demanded, outrage momentarily overwhelming self-preservation.

"Freeing your slaves," the stranger said. "What does it look like?"

"That's antisocial!"

"Damned straight. I'm Outlaw One. Antisocial is what I'm all about."

The name made Weller weak. "Don't kill me, please," he said again.

"Oh, I've got no intention of killing you," the bandit said, tipping his rifle up to his shoulder. "But what *they* do to you is strictly up to them."

He gestured at the newly freed prisoners, who were staring at Weller with a strange fixity and shuffling forward. The disgraced court clerk was in the lead, the ungrateful bastard.

"This is Outlaw One. So sorry about that truckload of ore from Hellville. Maybe you can send a new busload of convicts to pick it all up off the canyon floor for you. Of course, you remember what happened to your last *busload of slaves. . . ."*

"This is Outlaw One. Condolences to the families of the members of that patrol on Cheyenne Mountain. . . ."

"Outlaw One here. Aren't you starting to wonder what's happening to the tax assessors you're sending out to lean on the farmers? This is three you've lost this month. . . ."

• • •

Summer wore on, hot and dry. Homeland set patrols to chase down Outlaw One; he eluded them. They set traps for him; he slipped through. They set teams of specialists on his trail; they were never seen again.

And always he struck, and always he taunted.

His one-man blockade was never enough to choke off trade to the City. But it laid some major hurt on. Homeland's trade partners were already disgruntled by Purity trade restrictions and tariffs higher than Pike's Peak. A random madman waylaying their valuable vehicles and scaring the shit out of their highly paid drivers did not encourage them to do much business with the Purity Democratic Union. It did offer a welcome pretext for jacking their rates; the price of imports had doubled by the equinox, and was still on the climb.

Down in the Blocks new slogans were appearing on the crumbling cement walls, in spite of the heavy penalties for even the most innocuous graffiti. The phrasing differed, the message was always the same: *Outlaw One kicks ass!*

Master Sergeant Walton "Bud" Davis woke to see a sliver of brightness hovering above his face. It took his sleep-fogged mind several seconds to realize it was the blade of a huge knife.

There was no sound but the wind, stalking between tall shadow-black firs like a beast intent on prey. His first thought was that the assholes in his platoon were playing tricks on him. Somebody would pay. "What the hell do you think you're doing?" he asked the form he sensed crouched over his bedroll.

Under the covers one hand went searching for his Leech & Rigdon .44 Mag revolver. Discipline was going to hell these days, with all this Outlaw One crap. A man could never tell. . . .

He felt a pressure across the back of his neck. The leather thong he always wore around his neck parted over the upturned blade. The heathen arrowhead of black glass tied to it dropped toward his clavicle. A scarred hand plucked it from the air.

"Reclaiming my property, Sergeant Davis," a voice said. It didn't belong to anybody in First Platoon, that was damned sure. But it was familiar, somehow. . . .

"Spoils of war, Sergeant," the voice said. "Only this time,

you're the loser. Don't move that hand any further, by the way, or I'll pin it to the ground."

"Hayes! Miller!" Davis hissed frantically to the men lying in their bedrolls beneath the stars to either side of him. "Wake up! Intruder!—"

The intruder chuckled softly, reached over to the man on Davis's right, put the tip of his Bowie under his cheek, and lifted.

Public Soldier Leed Hayes's head flopped over like a sack of grain falling open. His eyes stared half-lidded into Davis's. His throat had been cut to the spine.

Davis had thought he was a hardcase. Now he gulped, tasted sour vomit. "Oh, Jesus. Jesus God. Did you kill everybody in the platoon?"

The figure held a finger to his bandit-mustached lips. "Just your pals to either side. I wanted this to be a very intimate reunion."

Davis stared at him with eyes like hard-boiled eggs. "What— what *are* you?"

"A little boy you robbed," the stranger said. "A shavehead you bullied. The little boy got big; the shavehead went over the hill. They both turned into Outlaw One."

Davis's bladder let go into his cammie pants. The panic lasted for only a pulsebeat. Davis was a brute and a slob, but he was one proud son of a bitch. He raised his head to jut his chin defiantly. "Why don't you just go ahead and kill me?"

Outlaw One stood up. "I'd rather let you live with the humiliation," he said, and walked away.

Davis stared after him. Thoughts bubbled in his head like lava in a live vent. A minute ago he'd thought he'd never live to see daylight. Thanks to a crazy-man's shitheel bravado, he could now see his way clear to his long-deserved commission, and who knows how much more?

Quick as a shock wave his hand darted, came up with the Leech & Rigdon with the slightest whisper of sliding cloth.

Outlaw One pirouetted pretty as a dancer. His Bolo was already out of his break-open Striker shoulder rig. Davis's eyes bulged, and he put everything he had into bringing the .44 on line.

The broom handle cracked once. Walton Davis's right eye imploded, and his brains blew all over Trooper Miller. Miller was beyond minding the mess.

"Then again," Tristan said, "maybe I wouldn't." He ran into the night as those of the platoon who could came awake around him.

25

The mule put its foot in a hole concealed in the three-foot drift and stumbled. From the other end of the tether Tristan turned and glared. His hair had grown out, and now hung into the wolf-skin he wore thrown over his white, yellow, and red Hudson's Bay blanket coat.

"You suckers are supposed to be surefooted," he said reproachfully. The mule pinned its big ears back at him and clambered out.

He grinned and scratched the bridge of the animal's nose affectionately, watching the while in case the mule tried to take off one of his fingers to teach him to give *it* a hard time.

He'd bought the mule off a stray Pawnee horserunner for a few M52's. It was cheap for an animal this good, but the Pawnee was desperate. He was running a string of Chihuahuence ponies the long way round the Jornado del Muerte and the BlackLands, risking killer ashfalls, Smoking Mirrors, and Dallasites for a big-time payout. The mule he'd got off a Digger for a bad debt. The Bloods, Piegans, and Siksika, along with their sometimes friendly rivals the Absaroka, loved those white-nose Mexican nags, and would pay commensurately. They didn't give a green buffalo chip for mules. Graze wasn't hard to come by, what with the rain and the ashfalls, which, while they could be immediately fatal, were good long-term fertilizer. But the mule was still a money-loser, and Pawnees hated that more than anything.

Tristan had been a proud Pure Engine man, disdaining any power but that produced by his own muscles or internal by-God combustion. But he was something more than he had been, as well as something less. He was something that had not been seen on these prairies and in these mountains for many, many years. Maybe ever.

He had plenty of supplies skimmed from his many successful raids. But a diet of canned goods and Rag rats wearied a body in mighty short order. The young whitetail buck slung over the mule's back would keep him in meat for months. If you were going to try to survive a Rocky Mountain winter solo, a mule was a damned handy thing to have, if not a necessity.

He and the beast understood each other very well. Both of them were smart, tough, and contrary. And the mule was neither horse nor ass, but half of both and more than either. What old lost Mr. Bayliss's books would call a *hybrid*.

Tristan could identify with that too.

Reflexively he scanned the trees, and the rocky promontories jutting from the slope above him. Nothing stirred that he could see. He made sure his Saskatoon Scout was comfortably tucked into the crook of his left arm and trudged on, back to the tiny cabin he had built himself in a hidden draw.

He had begun work late in the summer. He knew he wasn't going to continue his one-man war against Homeland very actively during the winter. You didn't ride in wintertime; you were lucky to stay alive. Little moved on the Plains. The Citizens stayed snug between their walls, the Diggers cowered in their burrows, the High Free Folk hunkered down in their lodges to wait out the snow.

Obsessed with his vengeance, Tristan refused to stray far from Homeland's wire. He was also too cunning a wolf to den out on the Plains. Mobility and unpredictability had been his shields against the lumbering but mighty forces of the City. Winter stripped him of both. The HDF sent out regular mechanized sweeps throughout the snowbound months. The troopies were even slower and slacker than usual, but the chance of a patrol stumbling across a prairie hideout was just too great.

On the other hand, the HDF stayed out of the mountains in the winter, except for the vital roads to the logging camps and the Hellville mines. Movement was too difficult, and summer dangers were joined by the threat of avalanche.

Tristan was a comparative stranger to the ways of the mountains. But he'd picked up rudimentary mountain survival training in the Rags, more detailed and reliable information from his fellow Strikers. He'd absorbed some knowledge on the subject during his compulsive reading of Bayliss's books. And there was the ever-handy campfire lore of his childhood days; there was a breed of men, hunters and trappers and general loners, who lived by preference in the mountains. The High Free Folk ran into them at Rendezvous, or sometimes one stumbled across the other's camp. They didn't ride—or when they did, rode *animals*—but they and the Stormriders had a lot in common.

Also, Tristan was a survivor. He put stock in that.

Picking a site was the simplest part; that was just good tactics, with a dose of common sense. Access to water. Approaches he could watch from cover. Escape routes. Most of all, a location in which discovery, accidental or deliberate, was well-nigh impossible.

Just as not every man who forked a bike was your brother, not every pair of mountain eyes was friendly. With the Strikers suppressed, the risk of accidental City discovery was nil. But there was always the risk of bandits or scavengers, or a band of adolescent Blackfeet scouting for a cheap blooding so they could get initiated into a warrior lodge. A motorcycle clan that had run crosswise of Outlaw One before he really was an outlaw might have chosen to winter in the mountains; stranger things had happened. There were mountain men who were unscrupulous or desperately hungry or just generally homicidal. Besides, Stormriders weren't the only ones with bad memories of Outlaw One in his Striker days. One or two mountain men had made themselves apparent threats to the good people of Homeland in his time, with results fatal to themselves. No doubt they had kinsmen or blood brothers who remembered his name.

He found his site, in a notch tributary to a narrow cut in the hip of a bald-topped mountain, down which a small stream ran. Soaring Douglas firs almost hid the valley itself from the outside; Tristan's niche was further screened by an accidental stand of quaking aspen saplings, battling scrub oak for survival. It was most accessible from below, but you could also come on it from above—*if* you knew where to look.

That suited Tristan fine. Unless you're on the very summit of the highest peak—the most exposed point of all—someone will always be able to look down on you in the mountains. Tristan liked having a place where he could come to scope out the cabin before returning to it.

He had built by trial and error, mostly error. He tried gathering stones to build with—you didn't have to chop them down—but they tended to fall in even without the help of the frequent tremors. He resigned himself to chopping and trimming trees with tools looted from the City, or bartered for with stolen City wealth.

It was grunt labor of the rankest sort. The sort of thing most Stormriders disdained to the literal point of death. They were riders, poets, warriors, free spirits. Not drudges.

But he found something soothing in the work, a quality like that induced by the meditation Jen Morningstar had taught him as a child. When he worked to the point of total exhaustion he slept like a dead man. It was not enough to keep him from dreaming of that ever-unreachable vision. But if he were well and truly wasted, it kept him from dreaming of Elinor.

He worked between raids until the leaves in his little screening grove began to turn, and the air to bite. Then he moved himself there full-time with his brand-new mule.

The walls were peeled logs, chinked with handfuls of lichen. The windows were top quality double-paned glass, meant for an Administrator's summer cottage, far finer than the rude random way he forced them into place. The door was oak, carved in Mexican rosettes.

The ceiling was a bitch. He had plenty of tools, planes and adzes and Father Sun knows what, but he didn't have the skill to dress planks that didn't look like botched attempts at canoe-building. He finally settled for notching and fitting round beams—*vigas*-across the tops of the walls, front to back, and dropping liberated sheets of City tin over them. Because the corrugated metal held heat the way his cupped hands held water, he piled a layer of fir boughs on the roof for insulation, and covered them with earth. Then he stuck clumps of grass, its short roots still holding balls of dirt, on top of that, which didn't add much insulation but made the shelter *much* harder to see from above.

While he was at it he extended the roof a little extra ways and built a small covered annex for his Striker bike.

He finished the roof by the time the first snow fell, late this year. It kept him inside a couple of days, but then he was able to get out and finish constructing much ruder shelters out of brushwood—for his mule, whom he'd named Dr. Johnson, after the portrait in the Library, and the grain and alfalfa hay he'd bought for him.

When that was done the snows came back to stay. Tristan kept himself occupied digging a back entrance to his shelter. That, interspersed with occasional hunting trips, took up the time until the days began to lengthen and Father Sun began his northward journey all over again.

For the first time in years, Tristan was content. For the first time in his *life* he had a sense of home, of a place that truly belonged to him, and to which he truly belonged.

He had a fine home, a little cramped for a Plains rider, but comfortable. The walls and earth-sheltered roof kept out the wind and snow and chill. The potbellied stove was another spoil of war, and getting it up here had been a lot more heroic an undertaking than taking it in the first place.

Like his father before him, he lacked the gift of Wrench Power. He had learned enough to keep his scrambler running well enough—spare parts were no problem, as long as Homeland persisted in sending out half-trained Rags on bikes, imagining them to be mobile patrols. But the artistry that it took to build a bike from scratch, to make it a piece of art, a WildFyre, a beautiful potent monument to oneself, was denied him. He had never made anything with his hands, though he had destroyed plenty.

Until he made this house. And it was a good house. The best he'd ever known.

Tristan felt the engine vibrate between his legs, offered his face to the wind and sun, and laughed out loud.

The front wheel of his bike was kissing a sheer drop of six

hundred feet full on the lips. A wide valley stretched south before him, ridges ranked with Ponderosa pine slanting down into it from the right, drifting cloud-shadows dappling it green and gray and mauve. A free wind blew his long hair back like a black banner.

Winter was over. Or at least, the sky was mostly blue—except for the ugly black plume of a truly monstrous eruption, away down south where the Rio Grande became the River of Fire. And there was enough open ground for his wheels to bite, and carry him out in the wind again.

One thing he had forgotten during his long years of captivity: just how *boring* winter was. In the City, life just put on a couple of sweaters, a muffler, and a heavy coat and went about its business. Work went on, and classes, and television. The Library still had books, even if he was the only one to read them.

Out in the wilds you basically sat around. If there were minor indoor crafts you could do, you did them. If there were other people around you could talk, or sing, or fuck—if you were paired up right. But after a while you ran out of things to talk about, and sang all the old songs threadbare, and there were only so many times even lusty Plains bucks and babes could make the sign of the pink spider. After that, you just sat and stared at each other for a month or two.

Every year, along about the time the ice on the rivers was starting to break up, folk commenced to kill each other. Your lodge mate snored too loud or picked his feet one time too often, and out you went to the woodpile for a handy little hatchet. Not *always*, at least in smaller bands—it had happened only twice among the Hardriders in Tristan's memory. But every spring at Taos Rendezvous a few old faces were missing, erased by cabin fever.

Tristan caught himself going out to hold long conversations with Dr. Johnson. He had always talked to the mule; it was a natural thing, the way you'd talk to your bike. But in the last few weeks, when the snow still lay like white tyranny over the mountains, he had begun to believe that the mule answered him back in his mind. If he were a more traditional sort of Stormrider, he might have believed that this was true, that he had obtained the Power of animal communication.

He suspected it meant he was going crazy.

But now he was out, and the world was open wide. It wouldn't necessarily last—almost certainly wouldn't. Midsummer snowfalls were not uncommon in the mountains, as they were not unknown on the Plains. The remarkably early thaw meant it was almost certain winter had a couple of good rounds left in her magazine.

He'd had a good ride. But now it was time to be getting back. Daylight didn't hang around long this high up at this time of year, and sudden storms were always possible no matter how blue the sky was.

It's too early for any kind of berries, he thought, *but I'll scout around for some nice green shoots to take back to the Doctor.* Like any bro, the mule got tired of preserved food after a while.

Tristan turned the scrambler. There was another balloon of gray smoke hung in the sky to the north. A lot smaller than the volcanic plume, but also a whole lot nearer.

The only thing that near was his house. He slammed the throttle wide and went bouncing down the slope.

It was his unchanging routine to approach the cabin from above, to survey it and make sure it hadn't been discovered. That changed today. The fear was rolling around inside him like a big metal ball, clanging off his innards when he laid the bike over to go around a tree. A sense of violation stung his eyes like a road wind without goggles.

When he brought his bike snarling up the cut and through the little thicket he saw everything he feared made real.

The little cabin was burning merrily. The sod-covered roof had already caved in. Out in the little coral Tristan had fashioned the last few weeks so that Dr. Johnson could stretch his legs a little, the mule lay on his side. Red stained the patches of snow around him.

Tristan stopped, stood astride his bike, staring. Tears began to erode his vision like spring rains eating at a cutbank.

Thunder rose around him. The unmistakable blaring of big outlaw V-Twins.

26

The fist rocked Tristan's head back hard. He staggered backwards a few steps, started to go down. Hands seized his bound arms and held him up. Helpful-like.

Tristan's face felt as if it was swelling like a balloon. The rangy Lakota kid had a ring on the index finger of his business hand, a big gold affair with diamonds, looked like some Admin wheel's wedding band and probably was. Tristan figured you could take a pretty fair cast of it from his cheek.

He spat blood. "Fuckard," he said.

The Lakota smiled. His teeth were perfect. *He* was perfect, a real pretty-boy, wearing only jeans to show off his ridged flat stomach and muscular chest.

"That'll cost you," he said. Moving deliberately, with self-conscious grace, he spun around and slammed a reverse heel-kick into the side of Tristan's head.

Tristan sagged. *Up* and *down* got kind of tangled up.

"Boys," said the tall thin woman leaning with her butt on the seat of a huge gleaming cruiser and her arms crossed under her breasts. She had a stiff brush of brown hair and features of the sort of fine-chiseled kind that would not look out of place above an off-the-shoulders Admin evening gown—except for the eyes. Her eyes were the color of boot leather, and every bit as soft. "Don't you think you've spent enough time playing with your food?"

Instantly the pair holding Tristan's arms released him. It wasn't exactly a favor. He thudded down to his knees. His upper body just kept folding forward, without his arms to check it, until his forehead smacked. Laughing Boy wasn't done. "I'm not done, Jovanne," he whined.

"I say you are," she said. In the dirt, a tripod of misery, Tristan had the mental picture of her studying her nails as she said it.

A hand caught the hair at the back of his head, lifted his face from the dirt. That wasn't a favor either.

"Outlaw One," the Lakota said with a sneer. He hocked, spat full in Tristan's face, and walked away.

Though he couldn't see either of them, or anything at all except the little shaded patch of soil he had his nose in the middle of, Tristan could feel the sidewash heat of the woman's eyes as they burned holes in the Indian's back.

He heard the crunch of her boot heels as she walked up to stand over him. He toyed with the idea of throwing himself against her shins, trying to take her down, maybe rip out her throat with his teeth. He didn't take long to discard the notion. He wasn't on speaking terms with his dad of late—he wasn't on speaking terms with much of *anybody*, come to that—but he hadn't forgotten Trickster Charlie. Dead coyotes slip no traps.

He heard her sigh. "All right. Get him cleaned up, make sure little Johnny didn't break anything important. The Catheads won't pay as high for damaged goods."

"So you're Outlaw One." The cruiser veered alarmingly as the rider turned his head to speak over his leather-clad shoulder. "You don't look like so much."

He said it in a matter-of-fact way, the way you'd say, *You're not as old as I thought you'd be.* Tristan flinched away from the skinny gap-toothed outlaw's breath. The toughest part of joining the Strikers wasn't the intensive physical training, which he enjoyed, or the discipline, which was nominal, no more than a Plains warrior would expect from his own clan. It had been the discovery that his beloved High Free Folk weren't always as clean as his memory had them.

"Reckon you'll fetch top dollar at Rendezvous, though." The rider, whose name was Tooth for what he most conspicuously lacked—though on that basis Tristan figured he could be named Height, Wit, or Hygiene as well—spoke without any rancor. Like most of the clan that had captured him, Tooth regarded the infamous Outlaw One with more curiosity than anything else.

Their colors read Jokers. He didn't know them. The patch on the back of his keeper's leather vest showed not the familiar guy in the colorful tentacled cap from the deck of cards, but a dude with some sort of trunk instead of a nose, and a hand at the end of it. The rider—Tristan was shackled to his sissy bar—didn't seem to have a clue to the significance.

No response seemed called for, so Tristan made none. He had gone through a phase of being stunned, and another—after the beating John Badheart, the Jokers' renegade Lakota warlord, had dished him up—of frothing rage. The Jokers had gathered around him to laugh and pour bootfuls of piss over his head.

In this chill morning, with the clan picking its way overland beneath a low and lumpy white sky, he mainly felt ache and watchful resignation—overlying an unbreakable determination that, no matter what, he'd make somebody eat turd before he snuffed.

The bike's front tire bounced over a clump of bunch grass. Tristan set his teeth. He was bound loose enough that his arms didn't get wrenched from their sockets every time they took a bump, but the bars bit his arms.

They had come down out of the mountains north of Homeland and south of a ruined pre-StarFall City, a treasure ground that still drew scavengers like a lodestone, to be hunted by eerie and dangerous things, some human, some—legend said—nearly so. They were working their way southeast to skirt Homeland before making south for Taos, thirty–forty bikes, almost all cruisers, with maybe three scramblers in tow, Tristan's included. There were no auxiliary vehicles of any kind, no cages, no wind buggies. He judged they were twenty miles out.

"Aren't you cutting pretty close to the City?" he asked.

Tooth laughed. "Those sag-nuts cage monkeys don't come this far out 'cept on the Hard Road. Not that they could catch us if they did."

Tristan shook his head. Even in Tristan's Rag days, a band of this size couldn't move that close to the City in daylight without being challenged.

A dyspeptic growl drew up alongside them. Tristan looked left to see Johnny Badheart forking his gaudy Big-Twin hand-built, with the flames on the gas tank and a dozen scalps flapping from his sissy bar. It was an ace, no question, low and nasty, and Tristan admired it, but with its *long* extension up front it handled like a twenty-four-foot truck. It was far less use out here busting bush than Tooth's spare-parts V-Twin rat bike.

"It's too bad we have to turn you over, City shit. Maybe whoever buys you would let me give them a few pointers. It's kind of my *heritage*, you know?"

He noticed where Tristan was looking, snapped his Bolo out of Tristan's break-open holster, which he had strapped under his arm. "You like my new gun? It's definitely cool. Got a fine new scrambler bike in tow too."

He showed Tristan a grin. His teeth were startlingly white against his lean dark face. He fed the sled some throttle and putted away.

"Don't mind him," Tooth said. "He's an asshole. Thinks he's shit-hot, a real samurai."

"How come he rates my ride and my traps?"

Tooth laughed. "Was his plan to fire up your hole to draw ya in."

Tristan clamped a heavy hand on his spasm of anger at hearing the home he had so painstakingly constructed with his own hands described as a "hole." It was standard Plains palaver. Besides, getting mad wouldn't do him any good. He'd established that.

"Real involved plan."

"Worked, didn't it? No, don't put old Johnny down. Jovanne's one smart minge; she's the one doped out that it might be you when we ran across that crazy old mountain man who said he'd been seeing your cabin smoke all winter." *Well, so much for my brilliant concealment.* "She wouldn't let him be warlord if he didn't show some real red-devil class."

"Like she'd have some say," Tristan said cynically.

Tooth glared back at him, coming near high-siding the bike again. "Don't have you nay doubts, buddy boy. Jovanne is the Prez, she's the one. No question."

"Badheart seems to have plenty of questions."

"He's the warlord," Tooth insisted. "That's plenty for him."

"Sure."

Tooth turned his head forward and wouldn't speak to him again. That was fine. The wind smelled better that way.

A dance in firelight, steel and sweat and flying hair, beneath a black and shredded sky. Warlord John Badheart, stripped to the waist, long black hair unbound, was doing a form with two knives before the assembled Jokers.

The Joker named Zonker leaned close to Tristan, who sat with the others by the fire. "He's a real hardass. His own people kicked him out, and so did the Crazy Dogs."

Tristan grunted. The Crazy Dogs were an all-Indian North Plains MC. They had a bad and unpredictable reputation. It spoke eloquently that Badheart was too much for them.

He's good, Tristan thought. *Got to give him that. Even if he is using my knife.*

The fire waved its bright arms in the face of the night. The faces of the Jokers were pale balloons floating above the ground with no visible means of support as Badheart finished his moves, bowed, and withdrew.

Fuel was at a premium on the Plains, dry fuel more so. A dose of gas in a can of fairly dry dirt was a good way to dry grass and cow flops to the point they'd burn. A clan didn't generally have gas to burn, so to speak.

So the Jokers are trying to show class to the notorious Outlaw One, Tristan thought. *I'm so flattered.*

With the show over it was time for chow. At a nod from Jovanne the manacles were unlocked from around Tristan's wrists with a multiple click. He sighed, brought his hands around in front of him, and began massaging the wrists.

"Run and I'll let Badheart have you," said Jovanne, standing near him, but not so near a leg-sweep would take her down. So she didn't take things for granted; might be useful to know.

Of course, he'd probably never have a chance to use the information.

The Lakota was playing with Tristan's old Bowie knife. He caught Tristan's eye above the upturned flame-gilded blade and grinned.

"What's he going to do to me that the Catheads aren't?" Tristan asked.

"Let me show him," Badheart said at once. Depressingly predictable, that boy.

"You might be surprised," Jovanne said. "But think about it this way: Johnny's right here, right this instant. The Catheads—or whoever buys your skinny ass, and believe me it's all the same to us—are a couple days and a couple hundred miles away yet. Lot can happen between here and now and then and there."

At this point Tristan had a choice. He could play dumb, or he could play for mystique. "That's what I'm counting on," he said, with his most rakehell grin.

The Jokers laughed. They all knew he was whistling in the dark—or thought they knew it. But he was showing undeniable class. And maybe one or two of them felt just the slightest doubt, down deep.

"Better get him some food," rumbled the earthquake basso of Big Jupe. Big Jupe was a huge and dangerous-looking black man, a walking blunt instrument with a face that looked like you could pound nails with it, and looked like you had. He was the Joker healer. He had cleaned the piss and blood from Tristan's face with his own enormous hands, cleaned the cuts and treated the bruises with herb poultices. Jen Morningstar, herself a noted Healer, could not have been more gentle or proficient.

Jovanne nodded. A woman dipped up a plateful of rabbit and herb stew, brought it over to Tristan, knelt before him, and presented it to him. She had stringy blond hair hanging past her shoulders and a sad drawn beauty. She was Sooz the Singer, the MC's bard. She lacked the sparkle he generally associated with that role, but he'd heard her sing. Her voice was beautiful, pure and lonely as a rare, clear prairie night. She rode behind Red Dog, a short red-bearded rider with big shoulders and a quiet way to him. The way they looked and moved around each other didn't suggest they had anything going.

Her manner did not invite thanks, so he accepted the plate with a nod. She smiled faintly and went to sit on the other side of the fire from him.

"No spoon, huh? Afraid I'll take a hostage. Good thought." His smile mocked them.

Exasperated, Jovanne said, "Hambone."

A rider unfolded himself from beside the fire. He was a

gawky kid, and clean-shaven, which was rare. He came over and held out a spoon to Tristan. Good form was to plunge it right in. He took the spoon and made a show of grabbing up a clump of shirt grass to wipe it off before plunging it into his stew.

Something flashed in the firelight. He made himself *not flinch* as his big knife slammed halfway to the hilt in the turf beside his right buttock.

Suddenly Black Jack Masefield's Vindicator was in Jovanne's hands, aimed for the center of his forehead. "Make a move for it and I'll eighty-six our investment and your skull, all at the same time."

John Badheart was sauntering up with a smile on his face.

"Look sharp, Badheart, you dumb shit," said Jovanne. "What do you think you're doing, tossing a knife to a prisoner?"

The warlord's face went darker. He bent, caught the knife up, wiped it on the butt of his jeans, and walked away into the night.

Through all this Tristan sat perfectly still. Jovanne sighed and put the piece away. "Mister, you seem to have a way of stirring up trouble."

Tristan grinned at her through the steam rising off his stew. "I sure hate to inconvenience you all."

"He's a smartass," said a big kid whose patchy beard and incipient gut still didn't make him look a full-fledged warrior. "We oughta go ahead and let John work on him awhile."

"Shut up, Meat," said Little Teal, Big Jupe's squeeze. She was a tiny woman with skin that gleamed almost blue in the moonlight, and black hair cut in bangs that came to a point above her eyes. She sat next to the unspeaking bulk of the healer. "Let everybody eat."

"So how come I never heard of you Jokers?" Tristan asked, eating. His appetite surprised him. The stew was spicy, very good.

"You City types must not know much," Hambone said. "Everybody's heard of the Jokers."

"None of the bros ever mentioned you, in the clans that've moved through this area the last few years. And our clan never knew of any Jokers club."

"What do you mean, 'our clan'?" demanded Thin Lizzy, a

woman as tall as Jovanne and even thinner than Sooz. Like the Prez, she rode her own sled.

Tristan looked at her. "The Hardriders. I'm the last of the breed."

Her face twisted like a rag. "What kind of bullshit's that? The Hardriders are dead."

Hambone was blinking and looking generally blank. "You saying you're a bro?" he asked.

"He's not a bro!" Thin Lizzy said shrilly. "He's a City shit! Nothing else."

"I'm not *nothing* else," Tristan said levelly. "Else everybody wouldn't be in such a hurry to shell out good money for me."

"You caused some people some trouble," said the rider named Emilio, who wore a bandanna and a very neat Imperial-style beard.

"Nobody who didn't have it coming. Back-shooters and baby-rapers."

"How can you call yourself a brother, and then say that shit about Stormriders?" Thin Lizzy demanded. "You're a fucking fake."

"I'm a *real* Stormrider, in every sense of the word. Ever been Dancin' with Mr. D? Thought not. We—the Hardriders were hard-core razzers, no argument. But we took off City convoys, not kids and old coots. The people I put the sting on as a Striker were people no Hardrider would have broken bread with. People who'd try to rip you off at Rendezvous." *Like the Catheads,* he thought glumly.

Some of the Jokers, Thin Lizzy and Meat in particular, looked as if they wanted to at least stomp him some. Jovanne stood up.

"I think Johnny must have knocked a part loose in your head," she said. "Either you actually believe this crap or you think we will. Either way, it won't turn over. Sooz, why don't you tune up your flattop box and clue him in a little about what it means to be a Joker."

27

He came awake to the sound of a footstep behind him. "What's on your mind, Prez?" he asked softly.

He heard breath sharply expelled. "How'd you know it was me?" Jovanne asked.

He rolled over. He was hobbled, and his hands manacled in front of him for good measure. The Jokers let him sleep off by himself, though always watched, judging that he wouldn't try to light out overland taking little bitty steps. They were right.

"Sound you made walking. John Badheart's light on his toes, but he's not *that* light."

She hunkered down next to him. The overcast had almost unraveled; stars surrounded her. "Some of the sisters step pretty light too."

"I figured it could only be you wanting to talk or Badheart looking to cut my throat. Didn't take anything else seriously."

"Certain of the sisters seem pretty impressed by you. Don't take things for granted."

He sat on his elbows, drawing the manacle chain taut across his belly. "What was it you wanted to say? I was looking to catch some sleep. Got to keep my strength up for going on the block."

"You don't let up, do you?"

"Do you?"

She laughed, softly, shook her head. "I could almost believe you're StarBorn. One of the Folk."

"Everybody's StarBorn. You in the Lodge?"

"No."

She sat the rest of the way down. The wind blew a handful of seconds away. Off to the south, lightning played around the volcanic plume, visible as an ominous black mass blotting the stars.

"I'm not looking forward to hitting Taos," he said, pointing with his chin. "I mean, aside from the fact I'm due to be tortured to death."

She turned her face away. "You think I enjoy this?"

"Why not? I'm big, bad Outlaw One. Enemy to all the righteous bros and sisses."

"We're not from around here. You got that right. We heard about you, but you never burned our fingers any. It's just . . . catching you was a lucky roll. . . ."

She let her words taper into self-conscious silence, as if fearing she'd said too much.

"Yeah. You're pretty much in the dirt, right? You need to score big in a hurry, or you're done as a clan."

She glared at him. "What the fuck are you talking about?"

He lay back down. "You're way off your turf with forty-odd riders. Your panniers are flat; you have to snare bunnies to get by. You have no kids, no herds, no trucks or vans, not even your scramblers. Either you've had to leave them a long way behind you, or somebody took all that away from you. Either way you're in a world of hurt."

He laughed. "You'd be better off believing I *am* a Stormrider. Catheads would pay a whole lot more for Outlaw One if they thought he was actually the last of the Hardriders. There's an old prophecy that says a Hardrider will wash the Cats away for good. Or hadn't you heard that?"

"I heard." After giving him the stiletto of her eyes she was looking everywhere but at him again.

"Why'd you do it?" she asked the wind as much as him. "Why'd you fight the Folk?"

"So you believe me."

"I didn't say that."

He paused, and then shrugged and lay back down. "After the

first time I dragged the body of a five-year-old Digger girl out of the burning hovel she'd been thrown into after being raped, I didn't have too many problems with my line of work. Know what I mean?"

Her dark eyes swept across him, beyond him to the night. He thought he saw the shine of a tear. Wind might have brought it.

"I'm good for my people," she said in a low, fierce whisper. "I run this show, and I do it well. I've brought them through . . . through some heavy times, yeah. We're not all the way out. But I'm going to bring us out. Do you understand?"

"What about Badheart?" Tristan asked.

"He does his job. That's why I have him do it. He's difficult sometimes. But he's good. I can handle him."

Maybe, Tristan thought.

She chopped at the air with one hand. "This—this has nothing to do with you, okay? Some of the clans want to see the color of your insides. We happen to get you. We need what we can get for you. It's survival, see?"

He gave her the long eye, one eyebrow raised. "You want permission? Absolution? Fuck a bunch of that. You want understanding? All right. I understand."

Her lips opened, expectant.

"But it's still chickenshit. And it won't work, babe. You won't swim out of the rapids on my blood. I promise you this."

Elinor was there, in his dream. She was dressed the way she had been the last time he had seen her, dressed for her father's final party in her pale green gown. She was lovely and remote as snow-mantled peaks seen from Homeland in midwinter, her cheeks aglow like sunrise, hair shining with a silvery light of its own. Her eyes were bright as windows silvered by the sun.

He was lying before her, naked and bound, spread out for the torturer's knife. He tried to call to her, but no sound came from his mouth. She seemed to be talking to someone he could not see.

Then she looked down at him. And laughed.

He jackknifed up off the cold damp ground. Pain shot through his side.

Tooth was standing over him, curly hair a ragged black nimbus against the sky. "You was having a nightmare," he growled. "Kept us fucking all awake."

The vision blazed before him, bright as the sun at noon, huge as the sun at sunset on the open Plains. He crawled over lava that lacerated his hands and knees. When he reached a bloody hand toward the glow, its heat stung his palm.

He felt an imminence, a pressure, as if he were about to come. He knew that the vision was about to be made clear to him. To burst on his consciousness like a bomb.

It's a little too damn late, he thought, and then he was being kicked awake to hit the road to his destiny.

The day was almost clear. The clouds were high feathery wisps against a sky of washed-out blue. The Rockies were darker blue teeth along the western horizon. The country here swept wide between occasional mesas, tawny with unaccustomed sunlight. Homeland lay behind. The Jokers had forded the Arkansas, just commencing to swell with runoff, this morning. They were lining south for Taos and the gathering of the clans.

Tristan was back riding pillion with Tooth, who seemed to have gotten over being miffed at him for doubting Jovanne's sway over Johnny Badheart. "You know, she's never had a regular old man," the gap-toothed rider said over his shoulder. "Not for long anyway."

"That's funny. She seems like quite a lady."

Tooth laughed. "Oh, she is that, you can bet the last ounce in your stash. Thing is, ever' time she hitches up with a dude, pretty soon he gets to thinking he *ranks*, y'know? Crowdin' on her. Shit, some of these dudes get the notion they can hand *her* orders."

"She doesn't much care for that."

"Hoo! Might as well say a cat don't care for turpentine up his asshole. No, once an old man starts getting ideas about he helps run the Jokers, he's history. And once he tries tellin' her what to do . . . I tell you true, by the time that buck rides away, he's mighty grateful to have his man-tackle still swinging between his legs, 'stead of from her buckhorn bars."

He turned his face forward for a moment then, to negotiate

the soft, wide bottom of a dry wash. With a rebel yell Zonker went skating past, his dirty-blond hair flowing from the green bandanna tied around his head, feet off the pegs, legs straight out to the sides, veering madly and throwing up a bow wave of sand. He was showing off the wide-horned cow skull he'd found the other side of the Arkansas. He'd fastened it to his handlebars, and was trying to steer with it.

Tooth grinned, gave Zonker the high sign, then grabbed his own bars in time to keep his sled from tipping over. John Badheart came up with his engine blowing off like the volcano to the south to shriek at Zonker to quit fucking off and get back in line. Tooth switched the upraised thumb to a forefinger, then looked back over his shoulder again.

"That Jovanne," he said, "she never lets nothing get in her way."

"That's about to change," Tristan said.

Tooth's eyebrows writhed. One of them had a break in it, making it look like an interrupted caterpillar. "Why you say that?"

"I don't." Tristan nodded past him. "They do."

The crest of the ridge that rose in front of them had suddenly become lined with figures on bikes, black against the faded sky, a hundred or more strong. The sound of their engines gunning together rolled down the slope like distant thunder.

Even at this distance, the catamount skulls that topped their standards were unmistakable.

28

Drago, war-chief of the Cathead band, set back his head and laughed. It was a huge head, set on a big body with an extra-big belly. His laugh was bigger than all of him. His frizzy black hair was mostly a memory on top, though his beard was pure black—so pure that Tristan, twenty meters away, suspected it might have had a little help. His leather-and-studs outfit was also pure black, as were the outfits of four of the half-dozen riders who had ridden down to palaver with Jovanne, John Badheart, and their prize prisoner with escort. It was a new look for the Cats. Tristan didn't think it was any too practical for summer on the Plains, even if the sky was cloudy most of the time.

From the low-slung saddle of her brown and gold-trimmed bike Jovanne listened to him laugh with her arms crossed and a frown.

"So you plan to *sell* me your fine little captive." Drago's voice was big too. It boomed like the prairie wind. He shook his head. "My child, my poor dear child—"

"I'm not your goddamn child," Jovanne said. If the skin got any tauter over her cheekbones, Tristan thought, it would split wide open.

"—you just don't understand. Maybe the Most Effaced will enlighten you."

Aside from their dress, the Cathead riders were nothing out

of the Plains ordinary—two were skinny, two beefy, with lots of mead muscle around the middle. The two who had accompanied the Catheads, riding together on a stock Iron Mountain cruiser, were a different breed entirely.

"You propose a commercial transaction," said the man behind the cruiser's handlebars. "You do not yet appreciate that *trade* is an antiquated notion, unsuited for the spiritually evolved. It is anti-communitarian. We share what we have, and gladly. So should you share with us."

"*Fuck* that!" Badheart screamed. Jovanne held up a hand.

Her eyes didn't leave the man on the Iron Mountain bike. He was a small man, with sunken cheeks and eyes way back in his skull, which was totally shaven except for a red-dyed topknot that made him look like an overage Comanche scooter punk going for a trad look. He wore a yellow robe, with a white T-shirt beneath. Even by the flamboyant standards of the Plains, he was peculiar-looking.

"Who the fuck are you?" Jovanne asked.

The Cathead spear-carriers growled. Yellow-robe held up a hand, and they quieted down on cue. Tristan wondered how long it had taken them to learn that trick.

"Names have no importance," the robe said calmly. "Names weight us down. You may think of me as the Most Effaced."

"I don't want to think of you at all. Drago, what kind of bullshit is this? Are we doing business here or not?"

"Or not," said the person who had ridden down behind the Most Effaced, then dismounted to stand beside him. The speaker was a tall, tanned woman in an indigo robe. Her head and face—the only visible parts of her—were completely hairless. The way she moved hinted at athletic grace, but the robe gave nothing away. Her eyes were long and a striking sapphire blue.

"The Most Effaced comes to you with love," she said, "but he also comes to you with determination to call you to responsibility. Toward your fellow human, and toward your Earth. He will not easily be turned away."

"The Acolyte speaks well," the Most Effaced murmured, "but she also overspeaks herself. Sadly, she has much work ahead of her to complete the eradication of her ego."

Jovanne looked to Badheart, who had slumped onto his arms,

folded between the bars of his sled. He gave her back his stand-ard stone face. "Drago, just what the hell is your role in this traveling freak show anyway?"

"I am war-chief of course, Jovanne. The Most Effaced and his Acolyte are our spiritual advisors."

"Spiritual advisors?"

Drago laughed. "Things have changed for the Cathead Na-tion. As things must change across the Plains. We are harbin-gers of that change."

"Harbingers." Jovanne shook her head. "Times must be changing. Only yesterday I'd have bet my life you didn't know a word longer than two syllables except for 'motherfucker.' And the only reason you know *that* one—"

Belatedly Tristan had become aware that the other Cathead with a lordly biker gut had been staring at him fixedly, with an odd expression, as if whatever he'd had for breakfast had de-cided it wanted out. Now he pointed a trembling finger at Tris-tan, and rolling his eyes like a bull-calf being branded exclaimed, "*Him!* He's the one!" He sounded like a calf being branded too.

"I'm what one?" Tristan asked mildly. "I'm so many ones, it's hard to keep track of which one."

The man's china-blue eyes quit going every which way. They narrowed. His lower lip stuck out of his tangled beard. Tristan had the damnedest feeling he was about to burst into tears.

"What Chrome Dome means is that you are the City dog who did him down and put him in the dirt, so many years ago," Drago said. "Chrome Dome's head don't work so good since that day, but one thing it does still do is remember the face of the man who did *this* to him."

Chrome Dome turned his head. At the crest of his head, in the midst of unruly unwashed brown hair, was a bare spot. Not a bald spot. It had an angry-pink shine to it, and seemed sunken.

Tristan whistled. "You'll have to do better than that," he said. "I took so many scalps."

"We had you!" Chrome Dome screeched, tugging spastically at the thinning hair around the two-inch scalped patch. For a big man his voice had quite a shrill edge to it. "We had you cager bastards dead to rights. But you, you—" His anger bubbled up big then, and drowned his words in the form of spittle.

Tristan remained calm. "You were one of the bastards I downed when we busted that ambush up the Arkansas from here six years ago. That topknot of yours got me court-martialed, if that makes life any easier for you."

Chrome Dome uttered a gurgling scream and came lunging off his bike. Weapons had been left behind for this palaver, but Jovanne and John Badheart gunned the engines of their bikes, preparing to interpose themselves between the madman and their negotiable asset, and Tooth hunched over the bars, ready to bolt. But Drago was standing out in front of his little pack. As Chrome Dome came roaring past he stuck out a gauntleted arm and clotheslined him. Burly Chrome Dome dropped and began rolling back and forth in the weeds, sobbing uncontrollably.

Tristan gathered this little passion play had been acted out before. Drago was probably accustomed to bringing along his pet crazy-man as an extra bargaining lever. The Cats could be exceedingly clever. They could also be bone-crushingly stupid; no other Plains clan, to Tristan's wide knowledge, veered so alarmingly between those two extremes. Their arrogance—like their meanness—was a constant, though.

Tristan gazed at the weeping outlaw. "I thought I'd killed you last time," he said. "Next time I won't be so careless."

The two skinny Catheads came off their scoots and dragged Chrome Dome to his boots and then to his own bike. Drago watched this all as if it were powerfully absorbing, then turned back to the Joker party.

"You have till tomorrow's sun shows his full face," he announced. "At that time, you must decide."

"Decide what?" Jovanne asked.

"Whether you will voluntarily gift us with your prisoner, so we can help him adjust his karma, or whether we have to take him. And if we do that, we'll have to take you too."

"Do not misunderstand this pilgrim," the Most Effaced put in. "He does not threaten. If you fail to see the light, we will merely perform the joyous, loving duty of liberating you from the burden of identity."

He smiled. His teeth were brown and jumbled like the slats of a long-neglected fence. "Either way, you will enter our holy Fusion. Truly, my children, you cannot lose."

● ● ●

Out here the daylight lingered longer than it did in Homeland, where the mountains cut it abruptly off like a slamming shutter. This far out, Father Sun, grown fat and lazy, seemed to be slowing, settling down, trying to make himself comfortable among the peaks. In his red declining glow the Jokers slouched around their bikes, laagered on the ridge line across from where the Catheads had appeared, gathering brush for fires and setting up their tents in case the clouds gathering to the north decided to open up.

Jovanne stood on the crest of the ridge staring across the shallow valley. A muscle stood out in relief against the hollow of the cheek that Tristan, standing manacled nearby, could see. No Catheads were in sight, but the smoke of their campfires rose upwards into the mauve sky.

A shriek crossed the five hundred yards between the ridges like a bullet. Half a heartbeat later a comet of fire blazed over the opposite crest. It had a rider and a sled for a core.

"Father Sun, it's Dapper Dan!" somebody screamed. Pony, Dan's squeeze, who had hair so blond it was almost white, uttered a terrible cry, dropped an armload of semi-dry grass, and tried to rush over the ridge. Hambone wrapped her up in his gangly arms and hauled her moccasins kicking off the ground.

Impossibly, the burning bike stayed upright as it bounded down the slope. The rider's screams sounded like strips torn from a tapestry of all the voices in the world.

A rifle cracked, near enough that Tristan winced at the shock wave on his cheek. The burning rider jerked and slumped. The sled went down. Its tank blew.

Little Teal was lowering an Absaroka bolt-gun from her shoulder. Its butt was outlined in brass tacks, and it had a buckskin sleeve laced around the forearm of its stock with rawhide thongs. Without a word she turned and walked back down the reverse slope.

"So much for your scout," Tristan said.

29

"We can't just let them Pawnee us like this," Meat said, smacking a big fist into his palm.

"Pawnee us?" Hunkered by the fire, Emilio gave a melancholy laugh. "Hell, they're plain trying to take us off. Pawnee give you shit end of the stick, but at least they give you *something*." Like the others he wasn't sitting *too near* the fire. Everyone remembered the day's earlier flames, and how they'd eaten the flesh of their brother Dan.

Since the morning meeting with the Catheads John Badheart had been keeping to himself. Squatting now to one side, he raised hollow eyes to his clansmen.

"We have no choice," he said. "We must join them."

Jovanne had been sitting. Now she shot to her feet. "What the hell are you talking about?"

"Don't you see? They are at least a hundred, maybe twice that many. We are forty. But it isn't just numbers; that's white-eyes stuff."

He straightened. "The Cathead Nation's Power is great. This Fusion gives them Power, and no man can withstand it, any more than a man can stand against the Stalking Wind."

"A Stormrider can dodge the Stalking Wind," said Tristan. "Or didn't you know that?"

Badheart's dark handsome face turned a shade darker. "Be silent or I'll cut out your tongue!" He waved a hand at Tristan and

211

glared at the clansmen. "Is this what you fight for? This . . . this *creature*, who claims to be one of us, but who has stalked us and killed us for years at the whim of his City masters. You mean to fight for this?"

"It's not him," Little Teal said. Heads turned. She spoke almost as seldom as her man, Big Jupe, and like him, only to a purpose. "It's our freedom."

"Freedom?" Badheart laughed wildly. "What is that?" He spat into the fire. The saliva crackled, sputtered into steam, and was gone. "We are no more than that. What does it mean, the freedom to be consumed without a trace? We can become one with a great and irresistible Power, and make our names great."

"I hear tell the Fusion don't use names," said Zonker.

Badheart's eyes retreated far back in their sockets, and he turned a terrible look on Zonker. The blond-bearded Joker was not usually a confrontational type; his head sunk into his leather jacket.

"Look!" a voice cried from outside the circle. "Up in the sky!"

It was Pony, who had been sitting alone with her grief. She was pointing above the eastern horizon.

The High Free Folk lived their lives under Mother Sky's wide skirts, and they knew in their hearts where each of the stars she used for sequins was sewn.

There was a bright stranger in the constellation of the Bull. A new star that outshone Mother Earth's sister Venus at her brightest. The Jokers gasped, the debate and the Cathead menace that spawned it forgotten for a moment.

Something big was going to happen. It was a Sign.

Only Tristan knew truly what it meant. He stared for the space of five deep breaths at the shining guest, jaw slack. Then he dropped his head to his chest.

Jovanne had no eyes for wonder. "We're going to fight, John Badheart," she said. "With you or without you."

The Lakota's laugh cut like a whip. "Have you forgotten what happened the last time you led in battle? Do you no longer weep for the daughter you left dead on the Little Sioux? Who will lead what you have left of the Jokers out to fight if not me? Who?"

Tristan raised his head. His eyes burned like gas flames. The bomb had burst within him. He had seen at last the vision that had drawn him across half a lifetime.

Feeling as if he had the lightning in his veins, white-hot and crackling, he rose.

"I will."

With a snarl Badheart ripped Tristan's knife from its doeskin sheath. "It's time I shut that second anus of yours forever, white-eyes. Though you've got a power of screaming to do through it first."

He leapt forward, slashed for Tristan's face, rattler-quick.

The razor blade sparked against the chain, stretched tight between Tristan's upflung arms.

"Tell Father Sun good-bye, renegade," the last of the Hardriders said. "No way you see his face again."

He disengaged chain from blade, lashed out. The metal loop slashed across Badheart's face, laying open his right cheek.

John Badheart stepped back. He touched the fingertips of his left hand to his cheek with something like wonder, brought the reddened fingers to his mouth, licked them.

He smiled.

Like water downhill he flowed forward, cut for Tristan's eyes. Tristan danced back, barely bending away from the blade. Badheart grinned and plunged his knife for Tristan's belly.

Metal rang on metal as the manacles around Tristan's crossed wrists caught the blade. Tristan seized Badheart's knife-wrist. The Lakota was good; instantly he twisted the blade in his hand, to cut the hand that held his to the bone.

Instead steel ground on steel with a tooth-grating squeal. The manacle was in the way.

Tristan didn't have time to get too complacent. Badheart jabbed him in the face with his free hand. Tristan staggered back, blood starting from his own nose, warning Badheart away from following up his moment of advantage with a wild whistling sweep of his chain.

He's good, he thought, *but if I had a knife, I'd have him.*

As if in response a knife thunked into the turf at his feet. He looked down. It was a smaller knife than Badheart's, which was really his, eight inches of symmetrical leaf-shaped blade, double-edged. A fighting knife all the way. The hilt was carven bone, polished high by constant palm-friction.

His naturally dark face momentarily paler than Tristan's tanned one, John Badheart stared at Pony, who stood with one hand still on her empty Absaroka beadwork sheath.

"I'm your brother!" he exclaimed, barely able to speak from outrage. "Why do you do this?"

She faced him without flinching. "You want us to betray our Prez. And you want us to join the bastards who killed Dan!"

Badheart showed her all his teeth in a mad rictus. "You're dead!" he shrilled. "I'll roast your tits and make you eat them!"

"No," said Little Teal, cool and dry. "You end the night between the cold stone walls of Hell, I think."

With a wordless cry John Badheart launched himself at Tristan. While everyone else was talking, he'd been picking up Pony's knife. He easily deflected Badheart's long-arm cut, and gave his knife-arm a shallow slash into the bargain.

Badheart drew back and began to circle. Keeping mindful of the fire, the onlookers, and the bikes, Tristan began to turn to keep the Lakota in front of him. He was in a slight crouch, his left hand advanced in front of his knife-hand.

Badheart held his knife in approved Plains fashion, out in front of his sideways body like an old-days fencer. Had Tristan had both hands free he might have surprised him. As it was, he was working with both an advantage and a disadvantage at once.

The disadvantage was the chain, which gave about a foot and a half of play between his wrists. It would be hard to use his free hand to the fullest, grabbing for his enemy's knife-arm, or even absorbing a cut while his own blade scored on Badheart's body—a very effective trick that he was nonetheless wary of using; his foot-long Arkansas toothpick was a different breed of cat than the sharpened spoons of Dorm C. It could disable his arm at a hack, maybe even chop it off clean.

But there lay his advantage—because he could use the chain and the cuffs to block, rather than his own shrinking flesh. He could also use it to strike with, as he already had.

Badheart was perfectly aware of his foe's situation. The fight quickly settled into the sort of circling stalemate Tristan was familiar with from the Dorm. That happened when two opponents of roughly equal skill squared off. In such cases, the victory usually went to the fighter who had the courage to make the first hard move.

Tristan's left hand darted for Badheart's knife-hand. The chain snapped it up short.

Eyes gleaming with triumph, Badheart whipped his big knife up, a backhand cut across the eyes with the sharpened back-curve of the blade.

Tristan's right hand slashed across his body. Pony's knife laid the inside of Badheart's knife-wrist open to the bone.

Blood hosed over Tristan's face. The Arkansas toothpick dropped to the dirt.

John Badheart was already in motion. His left hand caught the chain on an upward sweep, pulled it high in the air over both their heads. Both Tristan's wrists followed.

Badheart kneed him in the groin. Reflex enabled Tristan to twist his hips sideways and block most of the blow. He still caught enough in the nuts to drive the air from him.

Before he could recover Badheart yanked the chain *down*, and then whipped a loop of sudden slack around the leaf-blade of Tristan's knife. A quick wrench torqued the weapon free.

He drove a punch into Tristan's solar plexus, rocked his head back with an uppercut as he doubled.

"White-eyes thinks he's *so* smart," he panted, as Tristan reeled back, struggling to breathe. "Now it's time . . . to die."

He snapped a front kick at Tristan. Tristan caught his fore-arms in the way, but the force of the blow threw him back. Badheart advanced, kicked with the other foot, was blocked, suddenly spun.

His heel smashed into Tristan's temple. White light flashed—

Tristan was on the ground, rolling desperately in a direction he hoped was away from his opponent. Badheart followed with skipping steps, thundering kicks into Tristan's ribs.

Tristan doubled abruptly, got a loop of chain around Badheart's ankle, jerked him off his feet.

Both men rolled in opposite directions, then picked their way to their feet. Fists before his face, forearms guarding his body, Tristan threw himself against Badheart's chest. The Lakota laughed hoarsely and got both hands on his throat.

Tristan looked him in the eye then, and smiled. He grabbed the warlord's neck with his own hands. He jumped in the air.

His right knee shot up and around and caught John Badheart in the short ribs.

Badheart's eyes shot wide. That hooking knee-kick was Empty's devastating trademark. Tristan had never seen it out on the Plains.

By the looks of him, neither had John Badheart. He gasped in agony, tried to jerk himself free. Tristan's hands held him like steel claws.

He snapped his forehead into Badheart's face, mashing the beautiful aquiline nose. A second head-butt bashed in all those perfect teeth.

John Badheart released Tristan's neck to grab his wrists, try to pry the clamping hands away. He was helpless as a child against Tristan's crazy strength.

"You burned my *house*—" Tristan gritted, and gave him another savage knee. "—you shot my *mule*—" Kick. "—and you *took my goddamned bear!*"

The warlord's ribs gave way before the pounding. Tristan heard them crack. He kicked again with redoubled fury, staring full into his enemy's fear-filled eyes.

A jagged rib-end speared into John's bad heart. It stopped. His eyelids fluttered, his body shook, pink foam bubbled from his lips, and that was it.

Tristan dropped him and turned to face the silent crowd. Jovanne was leaning against her sled with her arms crossed.

"All right," she said, "you made your point. You can have your goddamn bear."

He smiled at her. Then he held his arms up before his face. He pulled his fists apart to the chain's full extension. Then he pulled harder. The muscles stood out on his back like great wings. A vein pulsed on his forehead.

The chain broke.

He strode forward, seized the cow's skull lashed to Zonker's handlebars, tore it free. Then he caught up a tubular aluminum lodgepole, walked to the crest of the ridge, and drove it into the earth in plain view of the Catheads, if any were watching over the opposite ridge. He impaled the cow's skull upon it.

"Gas," he commanded. Wordlessly, somebody handed him a jerrican a quarter full of gasoline, kept handy to prime the campfire. He splashed the contents over the skull.

"Light," he said. A driftwood brand was brought. He held it high above his head.

"You doubted I was one of you," he said in a voice that rang so loud the listeners expected to hear its echo come back from the distant Rockies. "That doesn't matter now. What I was means nothing. Tonight I am truly born."

He pointed the brand toward the new star. "That is my star, the star which is my soul. Its fire has set the skull of the Bull alight. It is a sign—*my* sign. The vision that has pursued me all my life."

He whipped the firebrand down, up, around, whistling in a figure-eight until its tip glowed yellow. Then he touched it to the gasoline-drenched skull, which instantly exploded into flame.

"The Burning Skull!" he cried. "This is my Sign, this is my Power. With this torch will I set the whole wide Plains aflame!"

Tristan sat alone on the backslope of the hill, legs crossed, trying not to give way to the soul-deep exhaustion he felt.

He was still amazed that he'd had the strength to break that chain. It was almost as if confronting at last the vision that had tantalized him since he was eleven—the Burning Skull—had lent him superhuman strength.

But that was superstition, he knew. As it was superstitious to believe that the new star was mystically linked to him. He had studied astronomy in old Bayliss's Library. He knew full well that, ten or twenty thousand years ago, a star in Taurus had run out of hydrogen to feed upon and self-combusted in fury. Nothing magical about it.

It made for great theater, though. Maybe even life-saving theater. If you overlooked the hundred-fifty or so Catheads over 'cross the way . . .

A now-familiar footfall from behind. He didn't even reach for the Bolo, snugged back in its accustomed position beneath his left armpit. He turned.

She had her boots off and was skinning her jeans down slim-muscled legs.

"What the hell do you think you're doing?" he demanded.

She pulled one foot free of the jeans, kicked them off her other leg. "They're yours now. All of them. I've thought about

it a lot, and I've come to the conclusion that I can't stand the humiliation of being just another grunt rider. Can't take going independent either; I'm too used to this bunch. So I've come here
to offer you the only thing I have left to trade, so you'll agree to
let me stay on as your old lady."

She smiled at him. It was as though the expression was super-
imposed on the face of a drowning woman.

He shook his head. "No way," he said.

"What's the matter?" she demanded. "Am I ugly?" Her
Joker-colors vest had been discarded. She hooked fingers in the
neck of the black T she'd worn beneath it and pulled.

Her breasts were large without protruding far, full in a round
way. The nipples were pale and small.

"No," he said, "you're definitely not ugly."

"Look, I give great head," she said. Her eyes never left his
face as she bent to pull off her skimpy black panties. Her bush
was sparse, a trim vertical bar between firm thighs. "I take it in
the ass, I do other chicks. I'm hell on two wheels, honey. What's
the holdup?"

"Maybe another time. When you're doing this because you
want to."

Jovanne looked around as if searching. "What? Do you see
somebody I don't see, who's got a gun to my head? I'm here,
honey. Where Jovanne is is where Jovanne wants to be."

"No. Jovanne thinks she's on the spot. Jovanne thinks she's
losing it."

She went white. *"Who the fuck are you—"*

He held up a hand. She shut up. "I'm not going to do this to
you," he said. "I'm not going to help you do it to yourself.
You've earned your pride the only way, the hard way. Don't
throw it away."

She fell to her knees. The sobs that came rolling out of her in
waves like hot ash were the sobs of a little girl, lost and betrayed.

"They were mine. They were all I had." She raised a tear-
flooded face to him. "And now they're yours."

"No."

She collapsed to the turf. "You're jacking with me." She held
her face a moment, then looked at him, clear-eyed. "All right.
It's only fair. I was going to sell you to those cocksuckers to tor-

ture. Now you're taking your turn with me. I can take it as well as dish it up, honey."

She smoothed her short hair back from her face with her palms. "Go ahead. Hit me with your best shot."

Slowly he stood. "Okay," he said, drawing it out. "How about I make you . . . President for Life of the Jokers Motorcycle Clan?"

She winced as if he'd struck her. "Maybe I *can't* take it," she said, trying to laugh.

"I'm serious. I don't want your club. They mean everything to you, and you've earned the right to lead them.

"I have bigger plans. *Much* bigger. But if I'm going to get a chance to carry them out, we all have to survive past sunup tomorrow."

He bent over, started collecting her scattered clothing. "For now, you can regard me as Badheart's replacement as warlord of the Jokers. Once we're shut of this fix, assuming we make it, I'll go my way and you and the Jokers can go yours."

He held out a hand. After a moment she took it, let him help her to her feet.

"I don't believe you for a minute, you know," she said.

"Fine." He grinned his best devil's grin. "But right now you don't have any choice, do you, babe?"

He looked at the sky. His Star had rolled over the top and started down toward the mountains.

"Okay. It's time for your people to feed the fires up till they're taller than Big Jupe's hands stretched over his head.

"And by the way." He tossed Jovanne's clothes in her face. "Better put these back on, unless you think that silky-smooth pelt of yours is the best outfit to do hard riding in."

30

The Cathead Nation, claiming over a thousand lodges and planning to expand big-time, did not raffle off chieftainships of its major war-bands. When, sometime after midnight, the glow of Joker campfires hidden beyond the far ridge increased, Drago was instantly suspicious. When, an hour later, the scrambler-borne scouts he'd posted to watch the enemy camp cranked their bikes to stops in miniature dust-devils to report that the Jokers had pulled up stakes and fled northeast toward the Arkansas, he could not have been less surprised. He issued the orders he had long since formed in his mind.

He had under his command 153 riders, and half a dozen auxiliary vehicles, trucks and panel vans. No bunny-snaring for the mighty Cats. Nor did his people have only big, relatively slow cruisers to ride.

He sent out fifty riders on scramblers, in two groups of twenty-five. The Joker sleds left a distinctive trail, of course, and though naturally they kept their paths tightly interwoven to make it impossible to tell just how great—in this case, small—their numbers were, he already knew they were no more than forty strong. *His* scouts had not been intercepted, after all.

The scrambler parties were to follow the Jokers' trail, catch them up, and then, without making contact, work their way around and in front of them like pincers. Drago would follow with the trucks, his party mounted on their big war-bikes. When the scrambler-riders were in position, they would dig in as a blocking force, providing the anvil against which Drago's cruisers would presently arrive to crush the Jokers.

If there were a manual of Plains warfare, Drago's plan would have followed it by the numbers. Drago's one-percenters were veterans; they'd played this game before. It all worked flawlessly.

The Most Effaced was pleased.

When Drago's cavalcade rolled into sight the Jokers had gone to earth atop a flat little titty of a hill out in the flats. The Cathead flankers had dropped into a chest-deep dry wash that angled across the Joker line of retreat and that provided them natural breastworks to shoot from behind. Their eye for ground made Drago's heart swell in his giant chest. Their skill reflected well on his leadership.

The scouts reported their initial ambush had dropped several Jokers—they said ten, which led him to guess three; he knew how scouts were. It was an excellent start. They also reported that the Jokers were towing a large number of cruisers, which had slowed them considerably. That puzzled him. On the other hand, it was easier to count parked bikes from a distance than noses, and the scouts he'd had spying on the Joker camp earlier had followed the natural Plains thumb-rule of one man per cruiser. If anything, that could lead to underestimation, since women frequently rode pillion with their mates. But perhaps Joker riders had taken heavy attrition recently—an earlier ambush, a quick fever. It happened. Nothing to worry about with the situation so perfectly under control.

He put his trucks, containing provisions, the cruisers that belonged to his flanking parties, the extra scramblers, and a few random captives, behind the cutbank of a flat-bottomed arroyo, twenty-five yards across, about eight hundred yards southwest of the Jokers' hill. He ordered out fifty Cats on cruisers. Then he, the Most Effaced, and the Acolyte—lovely little wench, that, but of course her Power would give a man the worst kind of sickness if he laid hands on her, drat the luck—sat down to watch.

The fifty Catheads rode in a single wide rank straight for the Jokers' hill until, at five hundred yards, they began to take fire.

A couple of them went down. Plains marksmanship was pretty good.

The riders scattered, breaking up into squads of ten. They made darting attacks from different directions, suddenly charging, blazing away across their handlebars though they had virtually no chance of hitting the well-concealed Jokers. The Catheads had trucks to haul their ammunition around in, after all.

The Jokers *didn't*. That was the whole point. The embattled clan had to open serious fire on any probe that got too near; once one got to grappling range the rest would come swarming in, and the ancient outlaw rule of one-for-all-and-all-on-one would prevail. The Jokers had to take bad shots at the Catheads as they serpentined through the open, laying their bikes on one peg and then the other before hitting the dirt behind clumps of grass. In doing so they inexorably used up their small store of ammunition.

It was a tactic that called for a good deal of balls from the Cathead riders. No matter how well the Cats rode—and this was a handpicked band, with plenty of hair—the Joker sharpshooters were too good to miss all the time. A straight-ahead redline charge would have been simpler—but skilled, determined shooters could have dropped all fifty of them before they reached the Joker positions. It had happened before.

Like all Plains clans, the Cats were capable of the craziest kind of courage, though like all Plains clans their morale was volatile, and they came to pieces easily if they felt their Power was bad on any given day. Under the eye of their war-chief and the Most Effaced—not to mention that foxy Acolyte—carrying out a familiar well-tried plan against an enemy they knew they had hopelessly in the dirt, they felt altogether invincible.

Before the sun was halfway up the sky the clouds had closed in, in that black rapid way of Plains storms. When a raindrop struck Drago's cheek above his splendid beard, he rose and called for thirty of his remaining riders to mount up. The Jokers' fire had slackened to almost nothing. He wanted this finished before the skies opened. In the mind-bending fury of a full Plains thunderstorm his prey might well be able to slip away.

A beautiful parallel struck him. He laughed. "Why, it's just like the Hardriders' last stand!" he exclaimed. "How very appropriate."

He forked his cruiser—a vintage Carondelet, most prized of sleds, its every surface black and polished until it gleamed like obsidian. *Black Death* was its name. It was older than Drago, and more famous.

"Of course," he roared to his riders, "we are not City dogs, to cower in our ironclad cages. We deliver the deathblow with our own hard hands. *Catheads, ride!*"

The cavalcade thundered off toward the low hill. Behind them, a detail of twenty remained to keep an eye on the trucks.

Of course, nobody had any eyes left over for the vehicles, which weren't going very far. The stay-behinds lined the wall of the wash and watched with pulses accelerating as the survivors of the first fifty cruiser-mounted warriors rose up by ones and twos from the grass and joined the charge. It was like watching an avalanche gathering momentum.

The van in which the prisoners were kept was parked back by the far bank. An outlaw named Kipp, with gray in his long dark locks and droopy mustache, sat on a director's chair by the back door, a Cherokee Pump across his knee. He was taking the show in when he heard a sound like a big outlaw cruiser hitting 8000 RPMs real close.

He frowned. Impossibly, the snarl seemed to be coming from *behind* him.

He turned. The front wheel of a bike came spinning over the cutbank at him. It tore the skin from his face, and then the eight-hundred-pound combined weight of machine and man crushed him into the soft sand.

The giant black man rose up from behind the rampart of fallen bikes, flailing with the butt of his rifle. Sitting pillion behind the Most Effaced, some thirty yards away, the Acolyte flinched at the sound of the butt caving in the skull of a Cathead.

The Most Effaced patted her hand. "There, my child, be strong. There is no death. All who fall here are merely joining our great Fusion on another plane."

She smiled bravely, nodded her gratitude for his encouraging words.

"Take him!" Drago bellowed. "Take him, you cowards! He's just one goddamned man!"

The Catheads had their blood up. They had done all the shooting they cared to. They laid their bikes down and swarmed over him in a wave of black.

The rifle rose and fell. Catheads went reeling back with big blue dents in their heads and their faces streaming red. Knives flashed, chains hummed through the air. The rain was falling heavily now.

The Catheads fell back. The giant struggled to rise from a tangle of moaning bodies.

Drago cursed. "If you want the job done right," he said, "do it yourself."

He dismounted. A metal mace with a fist-sized spiked head was clamped to the frame of his Carondelet. He unclamped it, then stalked forward.

The huge black man, his body streaming from a hundred wounds, heaved himself clear of fallen enemies. His shoulders trembling with the effort of holding up his own bulk, his chest heaving, he raised his head to look full into the eyes of Drago looming over him.

"I do this for your own good, friend," the Cathead leader said. He brought the mace down on the black's forehead with all his might.

Holding the mace fastidiously out to the side to shake gore and brains from its head, Drago took stock of the situation. There were at least a dozen Joker sleds sprawled here, and several hundred spent cartridges were trodden into the earth. But he could find only six bodies that weren't clad in Cathead black.

He shrugged. There must be more Jokers hidden among the clumped boulders at the top of the hill than he would have guessed. He waved his mace at them.

"Hello!" he called. "You're out of ammunition. You're surrounded. You've put up a brave fight, we all admit that. But don't you think the time has come—"

A scarlet spray blew out the front of his throat. He swayed, righted himself. He stared down, appearing to gaze cross-eyed at his own lumpy potato of a nose.

He let go of the mace. It swung from a lanyard. He raised

heavily gloved hands to his throat. They wouldn't hold back the blood.

He dropped to his knees, and from there to his face. The mighty voice of Drago of the Cathead Nation was never heard again this side of the gates of Hell.

His riders turned. More than twenty bikes were thundering down upon them from behind. At their head rode a black-mustached man who held a burning cow skull aloft on a pole. Its gasoline-fed flames defied the rain.

Most of the Cats had dismounted when their master did. Caught afoot by a charge that they hadn't even been aware of until it was all but atop them, they scattered. A few who loitered had the chance to realize that their attackers were riding *their bikes*, the cruisers left behind by the flanking forces Drago had sent out in the morning's dark hours. They were ridden or gunned down before the realization did them any good—if it would have.

Those Cats who could fired up their bikes and boogied. The blocking force, still totally intact, watched in amazement as their comrades came streaming around both sides of the besieged hill in obvious flight.

The first fleeing riders burst over the bank of the arroyo. To the shouted queries of the blocking force they called the standard answer of routed forces throughout history:

"It's a trap! There's hundreds of 'em out there, riding bikes as big as buffalo and armed to the teeth!"

"Hundreds? Shit, you're crazy! There's a thousand if there's a one!"

"Save your topknots, boys! Ride while you still got wheels!"

The Catheads still outnumbered the surviving Jokers by better than three to one. They had no way of knowing that. An army that thinks it's defeated is defeated. That's how battles have always been lost or won.

The Cathead scouts jumped into the saddles of their scramblers and streamed off after their comrades as the skies opened for true.

The Burning Skull Fight was done.

EPILOGUE

The rainsquall passed quickly. Sky was showing through in patches when Tristan gathered the Joker survivors and their captives around him. Drago's choice of a vehicle park had not been ideal—even this far from the mountains, a gully-washer could live up to its name and sweep the whole caravan away on a sudden wall of water. It hadn't happened yet, though, and to the Plains-wise that meant it wasn't likely to, so it was as good a mustering-point as any.

Jovanne stood on his right hand, leaning all her weight on a handy lodgepole she was using as a staff. Her face was devoid of color. Exhaustion and shock had sucked all the strength from her. She wore a bandage wound around her head. A bullet had pierced her right ear.

To Tristan's left was Little Teal, her wedge-shaped bangs plastered to her forehead by sweat and rain. She had taken a break from tending the wounded to crouch here, stroking the tack-decorated butt of the rifle with which she had killed the man who murdered Big Jupe.

There were faces missing from the ranks of Jokers—plenty of them. Meat, gangly Hambone, Sooz the Singer, Twelve-Fingered Terry, Jackoo. Of the fifteen close comrades Jovanne had taken with her to draw the Catheads in pursuit, five still lived, and two of them were injured. Her eyes seemed focused on something miles away.

There were ten captured Catheads—and they were still

breathing anyway; the Jokers had been pretty enthusiastic there for a while, after the Cats broke. The prisoners had their arms bound behind them and were made to kneel in the dirt before Tristan.

"Who burned our scout?" he demanded.

The prisoners kept their heads bowed and didn't stir. Little Teal worked the bolt of her rifle, shouldered it, and blasted a round into the packed wet sand an inch in front of the right knee of the last man in line.

"Better tell," Jovanne suggested in a voice that was all the more dangerous for its quiet huskiness.

The man Little Teal had put the bullet near fell over and began weeping. The man next to him said, "Drago ordered it."

"Of course Drago ordered it," Tristan said. "Did he pour the gas himself? Did he light the match?" No reply. "He didn't. So, who did? Anybody here?"

The man looked right at his groveling comrades and left at the others. He moistened his lips. "No," he said. "Nobody here. They got away, or are dead. Who the hell knows?"

"Wrong answer. You hesitated too long. Now, I could bring your ex-captives out and ask them, but because you're such sag-nuts sacks of shit, I think I'll just have you all beaten to death."

He looked around at the Jokers. "Boys? Girls? Who wants a turn?"

They came clamoring forward. A few hung back, horrified. Jovanne was one of them.

"All right!" a blond-bearded Cathead shouted, struggling to his feet. "I did it. I was one. Tango, here, he was the other." He nodded his head at the man beside him.

"Is that true?" Tristan asked. The way the prisoners sidled away from the pair was all the answer he really needed.

"Yeah," said the man who was still on his knees. His dark hair was cropped short.

"So what happens now?" the blond-bearded Cat said. "We doused him, we lit him off, he screamed and died. So what?"

"So this." Tristan drew the Bolo and shot him through the forehead.

"There's a new law on the Plains," he said, "*my* law. Combat's one thing. Torture and murder are another. You boys crossed over the line."

The crop-headed man vomited into the sand. "What gives you the right to make laws?" he screamed, puke spilling over his underlip.

Tristan held up the Bolo. "This does." He shot the second man between the eyes.

The other captives had all flung themselves down in the wet sand. From the smell, the two deaders weren't the only ones to have their sphincters let go. "What about them?" Jovanne demanded.

Tristan sighed. "I don't know. They're still pretty dangerous; I'm not crazy about just letting them walk, though they'd think *walking* was almost as much punishment as their buddies got. Don't really want to punish them for riding with the colors either."

She leaned close to him on her staff. Her skin had a greenish tint, and sagged on the fine framework of her facial bones. "Did you *have* to kill them?" she asked quietly. Careful not to show him up.

"*Have to* doesn't enter into it. I did as I saw fit. What would you have done? It was your man they torched."

She looked at the ground. "I don't know."

It struck him then that her problem was she cared too much. He admired her for it—between that, her resourcefulness, and her physical courage, she put him in mind of his own mother, though Jovanne had no use for the StarLodge nor any mysticism that he could see. He could also see just why she was unsuited to be war-chief of her own band.

At least she knows it. He could name a dozen men, a score, who might be alive today if HDF brass had the same courage to face up to their limitations. That was her real strength.

"I wish we'd caught the Fusion missionaries," he said, as much to shift the gears of her mind as anything. He could see her working the question of what she would have done around in her head, beginning to brood on it. "I'd really like to talk to them."

In the final battle-ending charge of the Jokers, the Most Effaced had sucked a round and gone over. His Acolyte had dragged him onto the passenger seat behind her and lit out overland on the big bike in a display of rough-country riding that drew admiration from the very Jokers trying to mark her down.

She would probably not have made it had the Jokers not had more urgent things to shoot at—such as the Catheads, who still had them badly outnumbered and outgunned and could not be allowed the leisure to sort that little fact out. *Damn pity. I still don't know what the Cats saw in them. Or vice versa.*

He laughed at himself. *Still trying to carry out your last assignment for Black Jack, aren't you?* But that wasn't it, not all of it.

He had his own reasons for wanting to know how things went down on the Plains now. The beginning of his own agenda.

Jovanne searched his face with her dark, haggard eyes, obviously hungry to ask what he was thinking. *She wants to know if she gets to keep her club.*

A commotion hooked their attention. The Jokers had finally broken the heavy padlock that secured the Cathead prison-van and were helping the captives out. What they found was causing quite a stir.

"Who-*ee*," whistled Zonker. "Sister Moon, look who we got here!"

"Those Cathead sons of bitches!" somebody else exclaimed. "We oughta wash the rest of them away right now. They jacked up a *bard*."

Emilio approached Tristan. His right arm was in a sling. He'd been with Jovanne's group. A bullet had smashed his elbow.

"Okay, Mr. Big Boss Man," he said to Tristan, half-banteringly, half with respect, "you claim to be the last of the Hardriders. Well, here's just the man to tell you you *ain't*—"

Other Jokers were helping a man forward. A black man with a frizz of heavy-curled hair dusted with gray. He was medium height, pretty lean, though he had a hard little kettle paunch. He walked with the bandy-legged roll of the lifelong rider.

Wraparound silver shades obscured his eyes.

"Jammer!" Tristan exclaimed. "Holy Mother Sky, could that be you?"

"Ain't nobody else, unless somebody switched babies on my mama, in which case I got a lifelong case of confusion to clear up." He pulled off the shades and squinted at Tristan, hard. His eyes were gray-blue.

"Is that you, Tristan? I thought you were dead."

They lunged for each other, hugged each other tight. "I

thought the same of you, you son of a bitch!" said Tristan, voice muffled by the smaller man's shoulder.

Jovanne looked at Little Teal. "There's been a battle. I guess that means we have to put up with male bonding."

Jammer pushed Tristan away. "Hold on there, boy, you're about to choke the life out of me. You've done a power of growing since the last time I saw you, and a lot of it seems to have gone into those arms." He put his shades back on.

"How'd you get away?"

"Took a bullet in the hip—still pangs me when it's gonna rain, which unfortunately is most always. After that I played dead. Looked bad enough I guess the soldier boys didn't feel the need to make sure of me." He laughed softly. "After a while, I didn't have to put on much of an act. It almost wasn't one. What about you?"

Tristan sighed. "Old friend, that's a long story. I got captured. You can hear the rest of it later."

Jammer nodded. He turned away to face the Jokers. "Now did I hear one of you question whether this was Tristan Hardrider, son of Wyatt Hardrider, or not? I swear on my songs, this is the genuine article. The last of the Hardriders."

"No," Tristan said.

Everybody stared at him. Jammer tipped his shades down and peered over them at him. "Excuse me, boy?"

Tristan smiled. "I'm not giving you the lie, Jammer. It's just . . . it's not true any more. I'm not Tristan Hardrider any longer. I'm—call me Tristan Burningskull."

The Jokers gasped. Jammer smiled, slow. "So you lit off that cow skull over 'cross the way last night? Put a big wind up the Cat boys' butts, I'll tell you."

"That was me."

Jammer cocked an eyebrow. "Had a vision, did you, boy?"

"How did you know?"

"Bards know things like that. It's why we're bards. You didn't think we got this job 'cause of our singing voices, did you?"

Red Dog came limping forward, using a busted Cathead rifle with a makeshift tubular-steel stock as a crutch. His face was twisted up as if hands were trying to wring it from inside. He had taken a bullet through his right buttock—a clean wound, not too serious, but a bad one for a rider. That wasn't the real cause of his anguish. His ride-mate, Sooz, had died in his arms. Tristan had been keeping a careful sideways eye on him. He didn't like the way he kept eying the remaining Cathead prisoners, who had been herded over by the wash's cutbank.

"Is it true the Catheads kept you prisoner," Red Dog asked, every word sounding as if it were being torn from him with red-hot tongs, "knowing full well who you are?"

"Well, *I* sure told 'em often enough and loud enough that I was Jammer, the one and only Electric Skald, after they came riding up around my campfire after dark. I even invited them to break some bread with me, though all the chow I had wouldn't have gone too far. They said the old ways were gone, that what the Plains needed now were spreaders of the Truth, not bards. They busted up my axe and chucked my skinny butt into their four-wheeled *juzgao* until such time as they figured out what to do with me.

"Which brings me to the point of thanking all you kind people for pulling a bro out of a tight place. Old Jammer was a trifle worried there for a while, I don't mind saying."

Red Dog turned toward the prisoners, raising his hands, fingers curling into claws. "They all deserve to die. The fuckards. Let me do them."

"Hold on, there," Tristan said. "Wasn't them that made the decision to hold Jammer."

Red Dog spun. He gave Tristan a look of white-hot hate. "It's the Law of the Folk that any who hinder a bard shall die!" He flung his arm out, thrust a finger at Tristan's face like a spear. "You laid death on the others for violating *your* law. Law of the Plains is a lot older than your law!"

Mother Sky, this is getting a lot more complicated than I ever thought it could be. He found himself wishing that Red Dog would just go ahead and make a move for him, so he could let his Bolo straighten things out. He stopped that right away. That was not a way he cared to think.

He sucked in a breath. "I punished the men who put the torch to a bro. *Our* bro." *Not even* my *bro, remember? He was helping to drag me to something just as bad as he got.* "They did it with their own hands. They paid.

"Now, Jammer here is like an uncle to me. He rode with our

clan as often or not when I was a boy, held me on his knee, and helped my chubby little fingers learn the strings and fret-board of his axe. Now, if any bro or sister here has right to cry vengeance for the wrong done Jammer, it's me. Or Jammer. Jam, what say you?"

Jammer held up his hands. "These hooks are for sheddin' notes, not blood," he said. He swept a hand around to the north and east, where black turkey vultures were settling down around the mounded forms of Cathead dead, running off opportunistic gangs of crows with angry squawks and wingbeats. "My debt's paid out."

"Who ordered you thrown in stir?" Tristan asked.

"That fat bastard Drago."

Tristan nodded. "Drago ordered the wrong done. He paid with his head. Fifty or more of the Catheads have gone back to Mother Earth this day. That's enough for Jammer."

"It's not enough for Sooz!" Red Dog screamed.

"Do you think you're the only person on the Plains who ever lost a saddlemate? My whole family was washed away before my eyes." *And not just once,* he reflected.

He walked forward to tower over the red-bearded Joker. "If it's vengeance on the Cathead Nation you want, then have no fears, bro. After this day I doubt they'll let any man or woman who ever rode with the Jokers rest."

He made a fist, held it over his heart. "And I have a feeling *here* that any of the High Free Folk who have any interest in staying high and free are going to be across the line from the Cats and their new playmates. But you'll wait to claim your blood-price, Red Dog, until you face Catheads with iron in their hands and between their legs. You won't get it while they're helpless and hands-tied."

Red Dog gave him a final incandescent glare, then turned and stomped off as best a man on crutches can.

Jammer and Jovanne were watching him closely. *Okay, so it wasn't the best reasoning in the world. Didn't have to waste him, did I?*

It was Jovanne's turn to come gimping around until she faced him squarely. Despite the weariness that weighed her down like a cruiser strapped to her back, she made herself stand full upright.

"You pass out some mighty fine judgments, Tristan Whatever-your-name-is. I won't talk against them. But judging's what a President does. Do you remember that you gave your word?"

He frowned. "Because of what you did today, and what you lost, I'll forget you questioned my word," he said. Then, more easily: "I reckoned war-party rules still applied. Where there's a war-chief, his word is law until the sun sets on the last day of a raid or fight. Or do the Jokers follow different rules?"

Her shoulders slumped. "That's our law too." She paused. "So what do you say now?"

"I plan on making Rendezvous."

"Taos?"

He nodded. "Under slightly different circumstances than originally intended. I've got some things to do there."

"What about us?"

"You're the Prez, Jovanne. Now and always."

She gestured at the Jokers, gathered around and watching them as intently as a panther stalking its prey. Now it was as if her arm were all but too heavy to lift. "Do you really think they'll still follow me?"

"Yes. Maybe now more than ever."

She shook her head. "I really wish I could believe you."

Her right hand darted behind her back then. It came up with Black Jack Masefield's .40-caliber Vindicator. She thrust it, two-handed, almost into Tristan's face. Pale flame flashed from the muzzle twice.

Blinking, rubbing his cheek where the flash had singed and flying powder had printed his skin, Tristan turned.

Chrome Dome stood on the bank of the arroyo, his addled eyes staring out at the stain spreading over his T-shirt, dark against black. The Cherokee Pump slid off his shoulder, tipped down to vomit into the soft sand. He toppled on top of it.

Tristan turned back. Jovanne still had the Vindicator out and pointed at him. She tracked her eyes, left and right. Pointing with them.

Such Jokers as were armed had their pieces out and trained. On her.

"See?" she said. A tear rolled over the top and ran a shiny track through the grime caked on her cheek.

Gently he pushed the pistol aside. "It doesn't matter. They'll still follow you."

She put the handgun away. The Jokers lowered their pieces. "I thought you said you were going to be more careful with that puke next time," she said, and smiled.

He shrugged. "I screwed up. By the way, thanks."

"Don't thank me. I had to do it. That was a scattergun. He might have hit *me*."

Tristan grinned, started to walk away. Jammer touched Jovanne on the arm.

"Sister, please listen to an old man. Legends have started on a lot less than what went down today. Shoot, I've helped start a few myself. There's a plenty big part in this song for you."

He looked off to the south, at the cloud of black smoke from the erupting volcano. "If I wanted to pretend to see into the future—and Father Sun knows, if I really *could* do any such thing, I'd never be fool enough to let on—but if I *could* see into the future, I'd bet I'd see that the song is just beginning."

"Yeah. Well, I wish I knew what my part in it was."

Tristan stopped and turned. "Then come to Taos with me and find out."

He looked up at the sky. The clouds were rolling back, piling up over the Plains like a cliff about to fall on them.

"And if we ever want to get there—*let's ride!*"